Last Orders

by

Laura Strickland

A Buffalo Steampunk Adventure

Last Orders

Cover Art by *Diana Carlile*

The Wild Rose Press, Inc.
PO Box 708
Adams Basin, NY 14410-0708
Visit us at www.thewildrosepress.com

Publishing History
First Fantasy Rose Edition, 2018
Print ISBN 978-1-5092-2011-3
Digital ISBN 978-1-5092-2012-0

A Buffalo Steampunk Adventure
Published in the United States of America

Praise for Laura Strickland

Laura Strickland's novella *FORGED BY LOVE* won first place in the short historical category of the International Digital Awards.

~*~

"The world building is phenomenal."

~*Daysie W. at My Book Addiction and More*

~*~

"Laura Strickland creates a world that not only draws you in, but she incorporates it…seamlessly….the kind of book that keeps you awake well into the wee hours, and sighing with satisfaction when you've finished the very last page."

~*Nicole McCaffrey, author*

~*~

"As I read I became so involved with the story, I found it difficult to put down the book. …Definitely …an author to watch."

~*Dandelion at Long & Short Reviews*

Ginny glared harder at the tall, strapping hunk of man—police officer—who stood before her. She supposed being a police officer didn't exclude him from being a man, but at the moment she felt a little fuzzy about it. In any case, he was much too good-looking, well over six feet, with a good set of shoulders, reddish hair, and features that had been entirely too well carved. And those eyes—just look at those eyes: bright blue and snapping with rage.

She detested handsome men.

He had to be the most detestable she'd ever seen. And his voice! That Irish accent of his caressed his words the way his tongue might well caress a woman.

"I do not *wish* to be arrested. What blame fool would want to get arrested?"

"Then hand over your weapon. You can reclaim it tomorrow at the station."

How professional he was. How well he kept his anger under control. But Ginny could feel it, and she wondered what it would take to make him lose that control.

"I've had this steam cannon since I was fourteen years old."

"Well, you and it are going to have to spend the rest of the night apart. Dennis?" The officer jerked his head at the second cop—at least Ginny thought there were two and she wasn't just seeing double. The two of them closed in on her again, one from either side.

She raised the weapon, dimly aware it was a stupid thing to do.

Dedication

For my fabulous fans of this series,
in Buffalo and elsewhere,
with thanks for their enthusiasm and encouragement

Chapter One

Buffalo, the Niagara Frontier, September 1884

"It's happened again." Sergeant Brendan Fagan's superior, Police Captain Addelforce, delivered the news in a grim voice matched by his mournful expression. Addelforce of the Force, the men called him, though never to his face, him being well liked. A good steady captain, Brendan thought him, though not likely to blaze any trails.

Brendan liked blazing trails—one of his worst faults, so his ma said. She was one for playing it safe, though the old man had taken a chance or two in his day—like bringing the whole family here from Ireland when Brendan was only fourteen. Funny, that a woman who denounced risk-taking so heartily had agreed to follow the man clear to America.

Brendan had lived in Buffalo more than ten years and been a member of the police force for five. A rising star he was generally considered. He often managed to be in the middle of big things in the city and expected to make captain one day before too long. But he supposed no one would deem him a risk-taker from looking at him. Strong and steady he appeared—as hard to rock as a stone chair.

He donned his most stoic and impenetrable look as he stared into his captain's troubled face.

"That's ill news indeed, sir. Where did the murder take place this time?"

"One of those big houses up on Bidwell Parkway. The deceased"—Addelforce consulted a paper on his desk—"is a Mister Ronald Bell, an elderly man and quite wealthy. He lived alone and apparently kept a number of steam units employed as servants. His daughter, also a lady of some means, is making a lot of noise and demanding justice."

Brendan shifted on his feet but gave no other sign of discomfort. A police officer learned to keep his emotions close to his vest, but this wasn't news he wanted to hear.

The third unprovoked murder in as many weeks, and none of them solved, though in each case suspicion ran rife. The first murder had taken place on a street corner under cover of night. The victim, a prominent man of the city who had spoken out vociferously against the Automaton Rights Movement, had been walking home from one of the gentlemen's clubs. A passerby had seen him surrounded by a number of steam units and said they appeared to be talking politely.

At daybreak the man was found there, lying in a pool of his own blood.

The second killing had occurred at one of the small canneries down near the waterfront. At first it seemed much more straightforward, if far more grisly. The manageress, by all accounts a cur of a woman who made life hell for her automaton employees and everyone else she encountered, had been beaten, dismembered, and put through the canning process.

Everyone on the premises denied any knowledge of

how it had happened. Brendan had gone to interview witnesses and take reports. The steam units, all basic models, had told him the manageress must have suffered an accident—and no one had noticed.

Now an old man in a mansion.

"Sir, what was this Mr. Ronald Bell's manner of death?"

Addelforce leaned closer. The two men were alone in his office, but as Brendan knew, the walls of the stationhouse had ears.

"Beaten to death," Addelforce whispered. "The first of our men on the scene reported there being blood everywhere. He'd been pounded so hard some of his bones were pulverized."

"And the steam servants, sir? What had they to say?"

"Not much. None of them admits to seeing or hearing anything."

Brendan grunted.

"Now listen to me, Fagan. The situation is ugly and can only get uglier. The climate in this city since the steam units started getting ideas above their station is ripe for an explosion of some magnitude. We need to solve at least one of these murders as soon as possible."

"Above their station, sir?" Brendan knew he should hold his tongue, but he hated injustice of any kind.

"They're machines, for God's sake."

"Sir, with all due respect, you know they're more than that. You've worked with Pat Kelly and other members of the Irish Squad."

"The *Irish Squad*," Addelforce repeated with some disgust. "Whoever let those hybrid automatons start calling themselves by that grandiose name has a lot to answer for."

Brendan stiffened. "Actually, sir, that was me. And they are Irish—at least they were constructed from the corpses of Irishmen."

Two mad geniuses called Mason and Charles had constructed the units, mating frames of steel with the skin, eyes, and scalps taken from men—mostly Irish— murdered at the jail. Both had been attacked and severely beaten by their own inventions; Charles had since died, and Mason, so far as Brendan knew, was now safely locked away.

No one had been sure what to do with the hybrid units. Brendan, involved heavily in the nightmare, had suggested they join the force.

Addelforce looked surprised. "That's right. I'd forgotten."

"Sir, I wouldn't be standing here if they were just machines. They are in truth Irishmen."

"Or fancy themselves as such. I'll give you that. But they're made of steel, and they operate on coal like any other steam unit."

"Aye, sir." Brendan once more shut his feelings down. His job didn't require expressing his opinion. And if Addelforce wanted to be a pigheaded fool, well—that was his right.

Addelforce eyed him. "Fagan, you're a good cop. And you're Irish, I understand that. You're also human. Those hybrids have their place in the force; I won't claim they're not useful in the right circumstances. But given the latest rash of incidents and the demands the steamies are making, it would be unwise to attribute too much to them."

"Aye, sir."

"We need these murders solved—quickly, efficiently—and the miscreants brought to answer for their crimes, even if they're steam units—no, especially if they're steam units. That's why I've called you in. You're both quick and efficient."

Brendan quirked an eyebrow. "Thank you, sir."

"Take a fellow officer and get over to the scene on Bidwell. Go over the place from top to bottom and get me some answers."

"I will, sir."

"Results, Fagan—that's what we need. Results!"

"I'll do my best, sir."

Brendan left the captain's office and moved out into the busy main room of the precinct. That was the trouble with being good at your job—you got all the impossible cases. Aye, well, he'd never backed down from one and wouldn't start now, though Addelforce might not appreciate his methods. He always followed orders, but he wasn't above bending the rules.

The station looked crowded this morning. Many of the officers on duty were taking statements or scribbling at paperwork. The figure in the far corner, however, looked up when Brendan emerged from Addelforce's office and met his gaze with one of startlingly intense green.

Brendan smiled. "Morning, Pat. I'm that glad to see you on duty."

"Good morning, Brendan."

The big automaton got to his feet when Brendan paused beside his desk. A tall man at well over six feet, Brendan often towered above others. Pat Kelly matched him in height and breadth.

At first glance, you'd never know Kelly—an elite

member of the aforementioned Irish Squad—wasn't human. Only the faint clicking of his voice box gave him away. But in fact a coal fire burned in his thorax, and his only exhalations came in the form of steam.

Brendan, who owed Kelly his life, not only respected him but called him friend.

"We've an assignment, Pat. Will you come along with me?"

"The murder on Bidwell Parkway?"

No flies ever on Pat Kelly. "How'd you hear about that?"

"It is all over the city." Kelly studied Brendan somberly. "Are you quite certain you wish to take me, under the circumstances?"

"Under the circumstances, I think you're the perfect man to take. All the potential interviewees are steam units, as I understand."

"Captain Addelforce will not be pleased."

"Captain Addelforce was after telling me to take a man with me—he didn't say which one."

Pat Kelly emitted the soft grinding sound that denoted his version of laughter. "As you say, friend."

They went out into the bustling streets and set to walking with a will. Pat Kelly, as Brendan well knew, could walk all day and probably all night as well, and Brendan never minded hoofing it.

"How is Rose?" Brendan asked Kelly as they went. The big automaton had been married earlier this year to a human woman, no less. And that had been before the mass wedding at the park on Delaware the month before last, which had seen the marriage of numerous hybrid couples as well as another human and hybrid pair.

"Rose is blooming, as always. And your latest sexual exploit?"

Brendan rolled his eyes. Kelly enjoyed ribbing him about the women he saw, which weren't actually so many in number. But as a bachelor he did tend to walk on the wild side from time to time—strictly when off duty, of course.

"I happen to be between women right now," he confessed. The last one had been a mistake—clingy. Nothing on God's green earth worse than a clingy woman.

"Your exploits are legendary among members of the force."

"Are they so? The force needs more in the way of occupation."

"Plenty going on in the city at present. Emotions among the human citizens run high."

"And even higher, it might be argued, among the automaton population. What's the word on the street, Pat? Whom do they think is responsible for these murders?"

"The humans think the automatons are responsible. The automatons have not expressed an opinion."

Brendan shot him a look. "And what do you think?"

Pat contemplated it; Brendan could almost hear the whir of his artificial intelligence. "I think, friend, we are poised on the edge of a most dangerous situation."

Chapter Two

The big house on Bidwell Parkway stood eerily quiet. Apart from the single steamie that answered the door—a high-quality silver unit—nothing seemed to stir.

What a sin, Brendan thought, for one old man to have such a house to himself when people in this city went without a place to lay their heads. How could some have so much and some so little?

Brendan identified himself and Kelly, and the steamie ushered them in. "I would like to interview the staff," he told it, "and examine the scene of death. Are all members of staff still here?"

"Yes, Officer." The steamie had slight damage to its voice box and squeaked as it spoke. The sound grated on Brendan's nerves.

"How many of you are there?"

"Six, sir. We were greater in number before last week. Master Bell sent two of us to the yard then."

"To the yard?" Brendan echoed.

"The scrap man," Kelly explained, "where units are broken down and parts reused."

"I see." Brendan eyed Kelly askance. A motive? Kelly's expression, as always, remained bland. "Well, please call your fellow units so we may ask them some questions."

"Sir, we have already been questioned."

"I understand that. I would like to interview all of you again."

"Yes, Officer. Please come into the parlor, sirs."

The room, large and high-ceilinged, stood flooded with light. No question but this was the crime scene—the air still reeked of blood.

Indeed, walking farther into the room, Brendan saw that none of it had been cleaned up. The body may have been taken away to the morgue, but the blood—and other body fluids—lay pooled on the rug beside an armchair that showed great splashes of spatter.

"Who discovered the body?" he asked the unit.

"The maid, Chrissie, sir."

Brendan pulled out his notebook. "Chrissie, you say? Not you?"

"No, sir. Chrissie was the first in this room early this morning. She always comes before dawn to light the fire."

"A bit warm out for a fire, isn't it?"

"Master Bell insisted on it, sir. He frequently fell asleep here in his chair and felt chilly when he awakened."

"Ah, I see. And you—pardon me, but do you have a name?"

"Unit Two, sir."

"Unit Two?"

"We all have numbers, sir."

"What about Chrissie?"

"Chrissie, sir, is in fact Unit Five. She chose the name of Chrissie for herself. Master Bell did not use that appellation."

Brendan resisted the impulse to look at Kelly.

But the big automaton spoke. "What happened to

Unit One?"

"Sold for dismantling, Officer." Unit Two's sculpted silver face gave away nothing of its opinion. "That left me as head of the household servants."

"I would like to interview Chrissie, please."

"Very good, sir."

Unit Two trundled off, leaving Brendan and Kelly to scrutinize the scene.

"A mess," Brendan pronounced. And not just because of all the blood. Tracks showed clearly that steam units had rolled through the puddles, and more than once.

"It would appear he was sitting in his chair when he sustained the first blow," Kelly observed. "I would conjecture that caused this spatter on the back. From the amount of blood on the floor, however, I would say he died there."

"Asleep perhaps when the first blow took him down." Brendan could only hope so. It must have been horrifically violent.

Unit Two rolled back into the room, followed by another steamie, virtually identical.

"Sirs, this is Unit Five."

"Chrissie, is it?" Kelly asked kindly.

"Yes, sir."

"You were the first to find your master here, dead?"

"Yes, sir. It was not yet light when I came in to kindle the fire."

"What roused you so early?"

"My device, sir."

"What device?"

"I have a signal which brings me out of standby."

"I believe, Officer Fagan, she is speaking of an alarm," Kelly put in. "It is a new invention for saving power."

"Master Bell insisted we all be on standby overnight," Unit Two contributed. "He always complained we cost too much to run."

Not as much as a household of human servants on call virtually round the clock. All the wealth needed to keep this house, Brendan thought, and the bugger quibbled about a bit of coal.

"And," he asked Chrissie, "you found him in what position?"

"Face down on the floor, sir, there where you see the blood. At first I thought he had fallen. I went to him and saw the fluids, sir. I did not think it right for him to be leaking so heavily."

"I should think not." Fagan made notes.

Unit Two offered, "Master Bell did frequently leak, but usually only urine."

"And you lot looked after him, did you? The five of you?"

"We did, sir."

"Chrissie, is that what caused all the tracks through the blood? You checking on him?"

"I checked on him, sir, and then I summoned Unit Two, who summoned the others. We all attempted to revive him."

"I see." Brendan sighed. "And when you first entered the room you saw no weapon?"

"No, sir."

"He was battered. There must have been an implement." And right bloody it would be.

Unless the units had battered him to death with

11

their arms. Wouldn't be the first time—back in July those hybrid prostitutes had beaten their creator to death using only their arms, and in front of a thousand witnesses.

A malfunction, that had been ruled—and not one of them arrested.

Could this have been yet another such malfunction? Had these units pummeled the old man and then cleaned themselves up?

"And," he said, "was the front door locked all night long? Was there any other way someone could have got in?" And left again, presumably carrying the murder weapon.

The units assured him the door had been locked, as had the back entrance and the windows.

"And no one heard anything?"

"We were all on standby, sir, until Chrissie became operational this morning."

"And what time did you say that was?"

"Five," she answered.

"Very well. Please go and get the other units so we may interview them."

When the two rolled away, Brendan looked at Kelly. "What do you think?"

"I think we need more evidence in order to draw a conclusion."

"I agree. But the old man was no doubt abusive to his servants."

"No doubt."

"And the doors were locked."

There'd been a time a few years ago when no steamie in the city would dare raise a hand against its master. Much had changed, and now Brendan, as a policeman, must consider the impossible.

"Let us interview the others," Pat said, "before I give you my opinion."

****

Back out on the street, Brendan flexed his shoulders and drew a deep breath. The air in this city couldn't actually be called agreeable, containing as it did a reek of coal smoke, river water, and general unwashed humanity, but it beat that fug inside the house.

Lucky for the steam units left there, they had no sense of smell. Unlucky for them they'd never have the pleasure of scenting a pint—or a woman.

He glanced at Kelly. "What will happen to that lot with the old man gone?"

"Whoever inherits the property will also inherit them. They may be sold if they're not needed or, if sufficiently antiquated, sent to the scrap yard."

"Hardly seems fair, does it, after all those years of faithful service."

"Life is rarely fair, Friend, for an automaton. And to be honest, it happens to human servants also when a household is broken up." Kelly glanced back at the house. "Before that happens, it is possible someone may break in and liberate them."

Brendan raised his eyebrows. "You wouldn't be knowing anything about that, would you?"

Kelly hesitated, an action so unusual it made Brendan pause.

"Nothing certain," Kelly replied at last. "Only what I have heard through the grapevine, so to speak."

"Grapevine, is it?"

"A term I picked up through my reading. It may be

more correct to say something I picked up underground. There is now a powerful movement in this city."

"Of steamies, you mean." Now Brendan hesitated. "Militant steamies."

"Automatons standing up for what they believe is right."

Brendan took a moment to contemplate that incredible statement.

"Some fight for their rights and some for their existence. They are slaves. And though many humans have, in the past, experienced slavery, few know how it would feel to exist under the threat of being *turned off*."

"So." The idea—the very idea—that automatons of all grades admitted to possessing feelings and would fight to liberate themselves seemed so big even Brendan's quick wits quailed before assimilating it.

They walked a block or two in silence before he asked his companion, "Do you think these murders are part of this new movement you describe?"

"It is possible, Officer Fagan."

"And you think someone from this movement might 'liberate' those steamies back there?"

"Also possible," Pat admitted expressionlessly.

"Well, now, I'm thinking if there is such a movement, you—being a light among automatons and the Force both—might just be at the head of it."

Pat turned bland green eyes on him. "Brendan, I am a police officer. How could I do anything illegal?"

There was the question. He'd seen Pat bend the rules before—just as he sometimes did himself—if the cause warranted.

And what cause could be dearer to the automaton's nonexistent heart?

Chapter Three

"This is the location."

The man seated beside Ginny in the steamcab gestured out the window before opening his door and stepping out. Ginny followed more slowly, wondering again just why she was here. An inheritance, the lawyer back home had said—one from a woman Ginny had never known.

She climbed onto the sidewalk and stood beside Philip Ballister—yet another damned lawyer—though not too close. A woman who usually if not always followed her instincts, she listened when they spoke. And they'd been telling her since she met Ballister not to trust him.

Well, he was a lawyer, after all. Shifty-eyed and too damned good-looking.

She glanced back at the steamcab driver, who hung out his window, watching curiously. Much more the type of man with whom Ginny felt comfortable—ugly and honest.

Ginny had a decided weakness for ugly men. They could—and had—talked her into most anything. But you couldn't trust those slick, handsome fellows.

Ballister, who had a loose tongue, resumed talking, something he'd done virtually nonstop since she'd arrived in Buffalo and met up with him at his law offices. Buffalo—the Niagara Frontier, they called it—

was a rough and tumble place, for sure, and nothing wrong with that.

"You can see it's a fine, large site."

Large? Ginny's eyebrow twitched. Where she came from, a fine, large site involved the term *acres*. Clearly things here were different, and she refrained from saying anything.

Best to remain silent if one couldn't contribute intelligently, according to one of the adages her stepmother, Winona, was known to mention.

Remembering it made Ginny smile, which she hadn't done much since arriving in Buffalo. Still, it seemed an interesting city, and she meant to explore thoroughly during the brief time she was here.

"An important site," Ballister blathered on.

Ginny narrowed her eyes. All she saw was a corner bounded on two sides by streets, on the third by another building, and in back by an alley—cleared of all but a modest amount of rubble.

She waved a hand. "Sell it."

Philip Ballister turned his pale eyes on her. She could tell he now chose his words carefully. "That may not be so easy, Miss Landry."

"Why? You say it's a prime site, correct? It should be worth something on the market."

"Ah, yes. But your mother…" Ballister stopped speaking abruptly. When he'd first met her, he'd immediately offered his condolences on her mother's death. She'd lost no time in setting him straight.

"Let me make it clear, Mr. Ballister, I never knew my mother and feel no grief at her passing. No one could be more shocked than I at finding out she has left me this inheritance." Of which Ginny wanted no part—

it was a chore, and an inconvenient complication.

Ballister had seemed taken aback by her attitude and perhaps by her forthright manner of speaking. She wondered what sort of women inhabited this city, if they refused to own their emotions.

To Ginny, Candace Landry was just a name, one spoken infrequently. Her father and mother had parted ways when Ginny was a mere three months old. Her father had journeyed out west. Her mother, from what Ginny had been able to establish, had spent time in several Eastern cities before settling in Buffalo and practicing some hellish craft.

"Tell me about my mother, Mr. Ballister," she invited now, all too aware the cabbie still listened.

"Ah, well, Miss Landry. She was an extraordinary woman. Some say a genius. Others—others did not appreciate the manner in which she expressed that genius. As for the manner of her death…suffice it to say the city moved to tear down what was left of the Crystal Palace at once. But I'm not sure any buyer will touch the site with a bargepole despite its favorable location."

"That, Mr. Ballister, is not good news." She'd hoped to dispose of her mother's property as quickly as possible and get back to the Dakota territories where she belonged.

Ballister, being Ballister, pushed on. "There have been incidents since your mother's death, which unfortunately proved to be a sort of catalyst. Steam units as well as some more sophisticated automatons such as those your mother built—all grades, really— have joined forces in a movement for rights. This lot, where the Crystal Palace once stood, seems to attract them. They meet here occasionally and—er— encourage each other."

"The steam units do?" They didn't have many steam units in the wilderness. Nobody had the time or money for such luxuries. Ginny knew her father, a doctor out in the territories, abhorred them.

Maybe she should have asked him why.

"Yes, Miss Landry. Another reason potential buyers might shy away. They may fear repercussions, riots."

Oh, hell. In what kind of mess had she landed?

"Mr. Ballister, I need to sell all my late mother's properties as quickly as possible. I'm sure you will do your best for me."

"I will, Miss Landry." He sounded unhappy. "However, I would not like to see you undersell yourself. You can see this is a good area."

All things being relative. "Mr. Ballister, until a month ago I had no expectation of any inheritance from my—uh—mother…" Damn, it killed her to refer to Candace Landry as such. To Ginny, "mother" meant Winona, her father's second wife, a full-blooded Sioux. Winona had taught her all she needed to know about courage, compassion, and living in harmony with her world.

Yet she sensed little harmony here, only a wagonload of trouble.

She finished her statement. "So I would appreciate it if you'd just liquidate everything."

Ballister chewed his lips in consternation. His pale gaze wandered over her as if he couldn't help himself. Ginny didn't suppose he saw women like her often, wearing boots, a woolen shirt, and a buckskin jacket, her dark brown hair neatly braided and hanging down her back. His eyes probed the tiny steam cannon she wore strapped to her hip, and she saw him gather his forces with an effort.

"Your mother had other properties that may sell more readily, if you'd like to view them."

Must she? "Yes, your letter did state multiple properties."

"There's the dormitory on Hudson Street, where she housed her—er—experiments. And a house on Linwood kept for her own habitation, though very little used." Again he hesitated. "I thought you might like to stay there while you are in the city."

Ginny sighed. "Empty, is it?" Cold and barren, no doubt.

"It is still staffed with a full complement of steam servants. No one has been quite sure what to do with them. That will be your decision."

Steam servants again? This place seemed to be rife with them. "Very well. Please take me there."

Ballister nodded and climbed back into the cab. Ginny paused before following and leaned down to the front window, where the cabbie still watched her closely.

He had a broad and wondrously ugly face, a nose that had obviously been broken at some point in the past, and a bandit's smile. Just her type.

For his ears alone, she whispered, "What are you doing later, and when do you get off work? Maybe you would like to show me some of the taverns in this town."

His face lit. "I sure would. And I can ditch this cab any time you like."

She winked at him—a promise—and climbed into the back of the cab with Ballister who, of course, immediately resumed talking.

"Your mother, as I say, was a brilliant woman. Whether or not one agreed with her aims or admired what she accomplished, that fact cannot be denied."

"And Mr. Ballister, did you admire what she accomplished?"

Ballister barely hesitated this time. "Indeed. I have seen her hybrid steam units. They are amazing creations—one might almost call them works of art."

"These are the ones you say beat her to death."

"Well, yes."

"Within view of dozens of witnesses."

"Hundreds, actually."

"With no reprisals."

"That is a matter of some contention. Currently, automatons are not subject to the law. That may well change, but whether the laws would then be retroactive is another question."

"So Candace Landry's killers are now free and may remain so."

"They may, yes, particularly because they have shown no further signs of aggression. Most if not all of her Landry's Ladies—the appellation given to her mechanical prostitutes—have since married and are living peaceful...er...lives."

"Wait a minute." Ginny held up her hand. "You say she built mechanical prostitutes?"

"I do apologize. I thought you knew."

The pieces began fitting together in Ginny's mind. He'd said the Crystal Palace—once situated on the site they'd just left—had been open to the public. That fact had failed to penetrate till now.

"The men of this city agreed to visit mechanical...ladies of the night?"

"That's just it, Miss Landry. I've seen them, and it's very difficult to tell they aren't human."

She looked at him from the corner of her eye. "Seen them, or visited?"

He drew himself up. "Seen from a distance, I assure you. I did speak with one or two, given we are handling your mother's estate. Just so you understand, they all consider themselves liberated, following your mother's death. You could challenge that if you wish, since they are in truth part of your inheritance, and they are quite valuable."

"Really? Who would want to purchase a steam unit that beat its last owner to death?"

"There is that, miss. And given the current social unrest, I would have to discourage you from pursuing a claim of ownership."

"You say they've...married? But they're machines."

Now Philip Ballister sighed. "Indeed, Miss Landry. Indeed."

Chapter Four

"That's a right ugly house."

Ginny stood on the curb, staring up at the building Mr. Ballister said formed part of her inheritance. Tall and narrow, its boards painted dull gray, it huddled between its fellow buildings, a depressing row of them smashed so tightly together a cat could barely squeeze between their outer walls.

She'd been hoping for something better. Ballister said this was a fashionable street—if so, she would hate to see an unfashionable one. Apparently ugly houses didn't do for her what ugly men did.

She glanced at the cabbie, who stood just behind her with her luggage in his hands. Emerged from his cab, he proved to be short—no taller than Ginny—but marvelously muscular. She liked muscular almost as much as ugly. For her, the combination often proved irresistible.

He grinned at her and focused an appreciative glance on her fanny. She certainly didn't mind.

Later, she told him silently and followed Ballister up the walk. The door opened before they reached it; Ginny blinked in surprise.

A figure stood in the opening. All silver, it possessed vaguely human proportions—a head, a chest and abdomen, two arms, two legs. No features as such. Instead the facial area had been molded into an approximation of a face—two indents for eyes, a vague, jutting form for a nose, a suggestion of lips with a small grate between them from whence presumably a voice might emit.

Ah, yes, she'd seen a few of these on the train as she journeyed east. She certainly hadn't engaged with them. And this one most disquietingly wore a starched white apron as well as an absurd ruffled cap on its head.

"Welcome, Miss Landry." The words sounded clear, though the mechanical voice box whined a bit.

Apparently she'd been expected. Not sure how to respond, she said, "Thank you."

The unit swung wide the door, and they entered a high-ceilinged hallway that smelled pleasantly of lemon polish. The interior of the house appeared much nicer than the exterior—well kept and luxurious. Ginny relaxed a tick.

"You have four servants," Ballister announced even as three more units rolled in from the room beyond. "Why don't you introduce yourselves?"

The unit wearing the apron spoke again. "I am Millie. This is Floyd, Gus, and Frannie. We have been keeping your mother's home in readiness."

"Even though no one was here?"

"It is our assignment."

"I see." Ginny's stomach wobbled. It had been a long and not very pleasant day. For some reason, the presence of these units bothered her most of all.

Behind her the cabbie dropped her bags on the floor with a satisfying series of thumps.

"Well, now," Ballister said. "Since you've decided to stay here, I'll leave you to get some rest. We can meet again in the morning. Say eleven?"

"All right."

"I can show you the other properties then."

So he meant to leave her here alone with these machines.

"Come along," Ballister said to the cabbie, who glanced at Ginny.

She leaned into him. "After you drop him off, come back."

Ballister stopped abruptly. "Oh, Miss Landry, I almost forgot. Your key."

He produced it from his pocket and laid it in her hand. "Have a good night."

She fully intended to.

****

The house proved well appointed and comfortable, if only lightly used. Ginny allowed Millie to conduct her around in an abbreviated tour, during which the steam unit assiduously asked which of the four bedrooms she would like to use.

"Well," she asked in return, "where do the four of you sleep?"

Millie turned blank eyes on her. "Miss, we do not sleep. At off hours, we put ourselves on standby to conserve energy."

"I see." A lie, since Ginny truly didn't.

"Where should I have Floyd deposit your bags, miss?"

"Which room belonged to my mother?"

"This one, miss, to your left."

"Not that one, then. You choose any of the others. I do not care which."

Millie froze where she—it—stood. "Miss, I am not able to choose."

"Why not?"

The unit waved its hands in distress. "I am not equipped for *selection*. I am not...I am not equipped."

"Very well. I'll sleep in the yellow room. You do know which one is yellow?"

"Yes, miss, thank you, miss."

"All right. Let me freshen up."

"Dinner is ready whenever you wish to partake."

"Dinner? But how did you know exactly when I'd arrive?"

"Mr. Ballister sent word it would be sometime today. We prepared the meal over and over again."

And after that, Ginny could scarcely claim not to be hungry. "I will wash my hands and change my clothing, and come straight down."

"Yes, miss, thank you, miss."

The meal, taken in the narrow dining room in the presence of the four silent steam units, proved so unnerving Ginny could have chortled for joy when a knock sounded at the outer door.

"That will be my cab driver. Please let him in."

The unit called Floyd hurried off and returned with the squat and wondrously homely cabbie on his heels.

Ginny waved her fork at the newcomer. "Ah, welcome. I'm very glad to see you. Why don't you pull up a chair and dine?"

"Well, miss, I don't know."

"Best to get a lining in your stomach if we're bound for a tavern. I've heard about the taverns in this city. Have you already eaten?"

"No, miss, I didn't take time."

"Millie, please bring another table setting for my friend, Mr.—" She wagged her eyebrows at the cabbie in inquiry.

"Rexinger, but you can call me Fred."

"Bring a setting for Mr. Fred. As you can see, Fred, there is plenty of food."

"Don't mind if I do." He drew up a chair and pulled his cap from his head, revealing a shock of dirty blond hair. Ginny contemplated him through narrowed eyes. Could be cleaner, but beggars couldn't be choosers.

"So, Fred, how long have you lived in Buffalo?"

"My parents moved the family out from Philly when I was five."

"So most your life."

"Yes, miss."

"What's the best thing about this city?"

"Well, now, that's a tough one. Lots of good things. The beer, maybe."

She grinned. "Good to hear. What's the worst thing?"

Fred eyed the steam units. "Wouldn't like to say, in present company."

"I see."

"Say…" He waited for Millie to lay his place setting before leaning toward Ginny. "Is it true what that lawyer fellow said—your name is 'Landry'?"

"That's right."

"And you're related to that Dr. Landry lady?"

"She was my mother."

"Ah—my condolences on her death. A damn strange thing that was, though I wouldn't care to discuss that here, either."

"No."

"Some peculiar things been goin' on in this city

26

since your mother died. It has a lot of people lookin' over their shoulders."

"You'll have to tell me about it some other evening. For tonight, I want to forget about everything and have a good time."

"How good?" He eyed her speculatively.

"I guess that remains to be seen and depends, in part, on just how good that beer really is. Where do you mean to take me?"

"Well, now, Clancy's has some damn fine beer, but it's full of Irish."

"You don't like the Irish, Fred?"

"They're fine enough. But I've learned when they're around there's a higher chance a fight may break out."

"A fight might be refreshing." Ginny had a lot of pent-up emotions she needed to disperse.

"Refreshin'?" he echoed in surprise.

"Well, at least fun."

"Where did you say you're from, miss?"

"The western territories—Dakota. And you'd better call me Ginny." She returned his speculative stare. "Especially if we're going to become well acquainted."

Chapter Five

"There's a riot down at Clancy's. The duty captain says we need to get there quick."

Brendan's heart sank. Only an hour left of his shift and this had to happen. "What sort of riot?" he asked his fellow officer, Dennis, unhappily. "Not the steamies again?"

"No. Captain says there's reports of some woman shooting up the place with a steam cannon."

"What? And he's sending just the two of us?"

"It's an Irish bar. Nobody wants to go."

"Ah, hell. Where would a woman be getting a steam cannon? And what's become of the Irish Squad?" If one of those hybrid automatons took a steam blast, he'd be knocked out but would probably survive...unlike a human.

Dennis shrugged. "Apparently no one's on duty."

Brendan, never one to complain about his orders— not aloud anyway—stiffened his spine. "All right. You get the paddy wagon and catch up with me."

Clancy's, down on Elk Street, had a bad reputation. Brendan went there occasionally on his own time— though never at this late hour—and often enough on duty also. He tramped the several blocks from the station and heard the racket from a block away. Hoots, hollers, the unmistakable sound of several rapid steam blasts, and ensuing cheers.

"Jaysus, Mary, and Joseph," he muttered under his breath. He lived with the ever-present danger of taking a steam blast to the head that would end his life. This looked as good a chance as any.

Dennis pulled up in the paddy wagon just as Brendan put his hand to the door of the tavern. "Draw your weapon," he told his fellow officer, "and give me backup."

"Aye, Sergeant."

The noise inside Clancy's almost knocked him over backward when he went in, and he stared at the sight that met his eyes. The tavern, full to the gills and with every lamp lit, had been rearranged from its usual state of haphazard squalor, a few of the tables pushed aside, and an area cleared opposite the bar.

Brendan blinked. A long line of empties stood lined up on the chair rail halfway up the wall. Many more lay shattered and pulverized below, and the wall sported innumerable scorch marks. The place smelled like beer, piss, and steam.

A woman stood on the bar. How she'd got up there Brendan couldn't say, it being a high bar. But she made a most fantastical sight.

Skin-tight boots caressed calves and thighs well on display, since she'd hiked up her skirts. She wore a well-fitting tan jacket that didn't serve to cover her generous bosom, and she had one of the most glorious manes of hair he'd ever beheld—rich brown and streaming to her waist. Her stance of victorious and no doubt drunken confidence commanded every eye in the room, as did the tiny steam cannon in her hand.

Only one thing more frightening than a woman with a steam cannon, and that had to be a *drunken* woman with a steam cannon.

Dennis poked him from behind. "Let me see. Ah, hell!"

Dennis, like every other man in the tavern—and most of the patrons were men—stared at the figure on the bar with rapt attention. Brendan couldn't blame any of them. She was the most magnificent woman he'd ever seen.

But that was neither here nor there, and he was on duty.

"Line 'em up again," the woman cried in a husky voice.

"They're already lined up, miss!"

She shut one eye. "So they are. Stand back and let me at 'em."

"She hasn't missed yet." The man standing next to Brendan informed him, and then promptly did a double take before yelping, "Hold up! The coppers are here."

"To hell with 'em!" the woman cried and opened fire. The empties along the wall exploded in an even line, and the room blossomed with heat and steam.

Brendan, mouth ajar, watched in horrified amazement as the explosions continued—at least until the cannon needed to recharge.

"Wall's on fire!" somebody stated. One of the barmen ran forward and slapped out the flames with his cloth.

"Saints preserve us," Dennis breathed.

It would take more than saints. Brendan, gathering himself, marched forward and glared up at the woman. "Get down off that bar."

She focused on him—a bit blearily, but she focused. She seemed to contemplate his face, his hair, and his uniform before she sneered. "Says who?"

She accompanied the last word with a lean that allowed him a good view of her bodice, most of its buttons undone. *Sweet mother Mary, full of grace.*

"Buffalo police," he declared himself, proud to hear he sounded steady as a rock. "Cease and desist. And while you're about it, you can hand over the steam cannon."

The crowd booed. The woman looked around at them and waved her hand. "Go away, Officer. You're spoiling the entertainment."

"This is not entertainment. It's sheer stupidity. There are ordinances prohibiting the discharge of a steam cannon indoors."

"And aren't you the dull fellow to remind us of those ord-ord-ordinances?" She smiled the kind of smile the devil might. "How about if I blow out that wall? Then we won't be indoors, will we?"

"We will. At least," he allowed, "three-quarters. Miss, you're drunk and shouldn't have possession of a weapon. Hand it over, please."

"Isn't he polite?" She appealed to the bar at large, while Brendan's temper rose. He didn't lose it often but felt damned close now.

The other patrons hooted some more and stamped their feet.

Brendan called to his fellow officer. "Dennis, let's get her down."

Both of them tall men, each reached for one of the woman's arms, intending to swing her down from the bar. As soon as they touched her, though, she began to holler.

"Fred! Where are you, Fred?"

A fellow stepped forward. Squat and red-faced, he appeared at least as drunk as the woman. He balled up his fists. "Leave go of her now."

Ignoring him, Brendan grunted as he and Dennis swung their charge down, him all too aware she still had the now-recharged cannon in her hand.

He set her squarely on the floor, took a half step back, and held out his hand. "Give me the weapon."

"No one takes this cannon from me."

"Hand it over, miss, unless you wish to be arrested."

****

Ginny glared harder at the tall, strapping hunk of man—police officer—who stood before her. She supposed being a police officer didn't exclude him from being a man, but at the moment she felt a little fuzzy about it. In any case, he was much too good-looking, well over six feet, with a good set of shoulders, reddish hair, and features that had been entirely too well carved. And those eyes—just look at those eyes: bright blue and snapping with rage.

She detested handsome men.

He had to be the most detestable she'd ever seen. And his voice! That Irish accent of his caressed his words the way his tongue might well caress a woman.

"I do not *wish* to be arrested. What blame fool would want to get arrested?"

"Then hand over your weapon. You can reclaim it tomorrow at the station."

How professional he was. How well he kept his anger under control. But Ginny could feel it, and she wondered what it would take to make him lose that control.

"I've had this steam cannon since I was fourteen years old."

"Well, you and it are going to have to spend the rest of the night apart. Dennis?" The officer jerked his head at the second cop—at least Ginny thought there were two and she wasn't just seeing double. The two of them closed in on her again, one from either side.

She raised the weapon, dimly aware it was a stupid thing to do. The cannon had now fully charged; she could kill someone.

The detestable police officer moved too quickly for her, wrested the cannon away, and handed it to the second man. Yes, there were two of them.

Ginny saw red. While the tavern's patrons hooted some more, she drew back her arm and punched the detestable police officer as hard as she could, right in the face.

The blow—surely one of the best she'd ever delivered—barely rocked him back on his heels. The crowd gasped as one.

"Now she's done it," someone cried.

Oh, shit, she had!

Without a word, the cheek below his eye blooming red, the detestable police officer captured her wrists in fingers like iron. Before she could protest, he had her handcuffed and began to hustle her from the bar.

"Fred!" she called back over her shoulder, "don't forget me."

Looked like she wouldn't have the chance to spend the night in her ugly cabbie's arms after all.

Chapter Six

"I understand you're Candace Landry's daughter."

Ginny lifted her aching head from her hands and fought back the need to vomit. She had the grandmama of all hangovers, which she couldn't understand. Back home she could drink the local brew half the night with few ill effects. This Buffalo beer must be brewed in the bottom of a chamber pot.

And it didn't help that there stood Officer Detestable, looking bright, well-pressed, and not much the worse for the redoubtable night they'd shared. The only sign he showed was a large bruise on his left cheek, where her fist had connected.

That at least made her smile. She struggled to her feet. Two steps took her to the bars of the cell, beyond which he stood. The cell—one of few intended for women—lacked in space what it made up for in the abundance of prostitutes.

All of those, though, had now gone—released, every one.

Ginny looked into the officer's face. "What if I am Candace Landry's daughter? Does it make a difference?"

He inspected her slowly before he replied. His gaze moved from her hair, now in a tangle, all the way to her boots. "It may. Then again it may not. I've been informed you're from out of town. You may not have been aware of the ordinance prohibiting the discharge of firearms in public buildings."

Oh, that accent! So sweet it soothed the pain in her head. How could he sound so seductive and so authoritative at the same time?

"Wonderful. Give me the benefit of the doubt. So I'm free to go?"

"Not quite. There's the other charge."

"Other charge?"

"Assaulting a police officer."

Well, damn. She couldn't exactly deny that, could she, with the evidence right there on his face? Plus she recalled a lot of witnesses.

After an instant's consternation, she stepped closer to the bars. "Could I maybe persuade you to drop that?"

His gaze fell to her bodice which, with a circumspect movement, she shrugged further open. So that was the way of it, eh? She hated sleeping with handsome men. But she might be willing if it would get her out of this noisome cell.

A hint of ice invaded his blue eyes. "Trying to get bribery added to your sheet?"

"Me? Bribe you?" She widened her eyes. "I wouldn't dare. You're much too professional, aren't you?"

"I'd like to think so."

"Too proper. Too *dull*."

He looked annoyed. "Very good. So. I'll prepare the charges."

"Charges, plural?"

"There's drunk and disorderly as well as assaulting a police officer."

Damn, she'd really done it now.

He began to turn away. She reached through the bars and grabbed his sleeve. "Wait."

Did interest flare in his eyes? Not pausing to find out, she hurried on. "Will you do me a favor?"

"And what might that be?"

"Contact my lawyer. His name is Philip Ballister, and he practices here in the city."

"Sure and you're entitled to send a message."

"Oh, and Officer—I didn't catch your name last night."

"It's Sergeant. Sergeant Brendan Fagan."

****

Didn't catch your name last night, Officer—all nice and namby-pamby as you please. The woman was maddening. Of course she hadn't bothered asking his name before socking him in the face.

Aye, and what a punch it had been! No mere slip of a girl, that, despite her beauty.

She'd been a tiger in that tavern, and no mistake. Now this morning she looked at him all doe-eyed—large, beautiful brown eyes—and spoke as if butter wouldn't melt in her mouth.

Wanted out of the charges, she did…

And if he were a less ethical police officer—less ethical man—he might just contemplate making an entirely reprehensible deal with her. Tempting. She was very tempting.

He sat down at his desk and pushed aside a small mountain of paperwork. God, he hated paperwork. He scribbled a note, went out front, and called one of the lads usually hanging about.

"Take that to Mr. Philip Ballister. I think he's over on Huron Street."

A good lawyer, Ballister. Well known in this city. He had probably been Dr. Landry's attorney. Who would have thought Dr. Landry had a daughter at all? At the time of her death, they believed she had no relations, no one to inherit her property. Thus her creations, the hybrid automatons known as Landry's Ladies, had been set free.

He frowned as he returned to his desk. If the daughter—Virginia Landry, so the captain said she was—had come to the city because she'd inherited her late mother's estate, would she in fact now own those automatons?

Not good news for them, not at all. Most had married and now strove to take up lives around the city. And Buffalo could withstand no more unrest such as had accompanied Dr. Landry's brutal murder.

He'd better talk to Pat Kelly about this.

By rights, he shouldn't be on duty this morning. He'd come in special to swear out the charges. Quite apart from that, he'd like to hang around and see what happened when Virginia Landry's lawyer showed up. He'd have to search Kelly out later. Meanwhile, he'd better apply himself manfully to this paperwork.

Halfway through a report he paused, remembering what else Virginia Landry had said. She'd called him *proper. Polite. Dull.* His fingers contracted on his pen. Virginia Landry had no idea what he was like.

Suddenly, with shocking intensity, he wanted to show her.

****

The lawyer showed up twenty minutes later; the captain himself escorted him to the cells. Soon the two men returned to the captain's office and Addelforce called Brendan in.

"Sergeant Fagan, this is Miss Landry's lawyer. Mr. Ballister, Sergeant Brendan Fagan, the arresting officer."

Ballister put out his hand; Brendan had no choice but to shake it.

"Let's sit down," Ballister suggested, "and discuss this reasonably. I'm sure we can come to an understanding."

Brendan sat and said nothing.

"Last night's incident at Clancy's tavern was extremely unfortunate," Ballister began. "My client acted under the impetus of grief. I hope, Sergeant Fagan, you will allow for her level of distress. She perhaps handled her emotions badly, but I'm sure both you gentlemen will agree that in these circumstances a measure of mercy is warranted."

"Your client," said Captain Addelforce, "assaulted my officer. Plus she fired a steam cannon within the confines of a building—repeatedly."

"Which she did not realize to be an offense. You must understand, coming as she does from the western frontier…"

"Be that as it may"—Addelforce sounded severe—"no one of good sense would fire a steam cannon inside a wooden building. Fortunately the tavern didn't burn down."

"Fortunately. And I'm sure my client will be eager to compensate Mr. Clancy for any damages. She is a wealthy woman—a very wealthy woman."

Brendan huffed inwardly, though he gave no outward sign. He had no tolerance for those who abused the law under the protection of their wealth. And in his opinion Miss Virginia Landry needed taking down a peg.

"As for the potential charge of drunk and disorderly," Ballister said expansively, "I think we can write that off to the effects of grief. She drank away her sorrow—took a bit too much. Which of us has not done that at some point?"

Addelforce, looking sour, didn't comment.

"That leaves the assault charge," Ballister went on brightly. "And if Sergeant Fagan refuses to press that…"

Both men looked at Brendan.

"Why should I refuse to press the charge?" he asked steadily.

A slight flush came to Ballister's cheek. "For the sake of the aforementioned mercy?" he suggested. "I know your reputation in this city, Sergeant Fagan. You're a fine officer and a fair man—a light of the police force."

Was he, then?

"I know my client sincerely regrets what happened last night and is quite embarrassed. I know she would be grateful if you agree to drop the charges."

Brendan spoke at last. "We do not need any more loose cannons in this city, Mr. Ballister. And your client is—quite literally—a loose cannon."

"She isn't, though, Sergeant Fagan—not ordinarily. I assure you what happened at Clancy's was an aberration. She has been under great strain and let off some steam in a most ill-chosen way."

"My city, Mr. Ballister, is not the wild west."

"Obviously, Sergeant Fagan—and it is my city too." Ballister shifted uncomfortably in his seat. "The

39

situation is already difficult enough."

"And"—Brendan leaned forward—"your client's mother was responsible, in part, for the current unrest."

"Is that my client's fault, Sergeant? She never knew her mother and cannot be blamed for Dr. Landry's failings."

"Tell me, Mr. Ballister, what will happen to Dr. Landry's former creations if Miss Landry has inherited her mother's estate? Has she inherited?"

"She has, Sergeant Fagan." Ballister sighed. "And the fate of those automatons is yet to be decided." He quirked an eyebrow. "A reason to keep my client's good will, yes?"

Brendan rubbed at his face. "She socked me, Mr. Ballister."

"And deeply regrets it. Now, Sergeant Fagan, I'm sure you've been punched by drunks before, in the line of duty. Did you prosecute?"

"Usually not. But that was different."

"How so?"

"Your client knew exactly what she was doing."

"Can you say that for certain, Sergeant? Were you inside her head? She was quite intoxicated."

And what sort of woman, Brendan asked himself, came to a strange city on the occasion of her mother's death and promptly went out carousing? One who meant trouble, that was what.

He didn't suppose he'd want to be in her head.

He folded his arms across his chest and remained stubbornly silent.

Captain Addelforce cleared his throat. "Perhaps, Sergeant Fagan, this situation calls for both mercy and leniency."

Brendan fixed him with a stare.

"Sergeant Fagan." Ballister took it up. "I do not want to see my client in court."

He and Addelforce both watched Brendan carefully while the moments dragged out. Finally Brendan said, "I want an apology, and a sincere one."

Addelforce unclenched his hands, and Ballister blew out a breath. "An apology, of course. This is most decent of you."

Aye, he'd admit to being a decent fellow but definitely not *dull*.

Chapter Seven

"I have to do what?"

Ginny stood with her hands on her hips and regarded her attorney through the bars of her cell.

"Apologize. It's simple enough. You punched a police officer in the face, Virginia. He wanted to press charges."

"Then maybe he should."

"Virginia, given the ill feeling still existent toward your mother and given her…accomplishments in this city, I wouldn't count on finding mercy in court. Many, including some of the justices, blame her for the current unrest."

"Dammit." Ginny's head had started hurting again as soon as the police officer—Brendan Fagan—walked away. She felt dirty and unwell and—truth be told—just a little ashamed of herself. The last thing she wanted to do was apologize to the big, overly proper policeman.

"Look," Ballister asked her in a low voice, "do you want to get out of here?"

"Of course."

"Then I suggest you look him in the eye and apologize. And make it genuine. I think he deserves that."

"Hmph." Ginny dragged her hands through her hair and wished she could tidy herself. "Where must I make this grand apology? Here?"

"You'll be brought up to him."

Ballister strode off, and Ginny paced the tight confines of her cell, every step jarring her aching head. Facing the task ahead squarely, she asked herself, *Am I woman enough for this?*

Of course. He was just one big Irish policeman. She'd faced worse. But oh, how humiliating!

Minutes dragged by while she waited to be fetched, and she began to think Brendan Fagan had changed his mind. That made her stomach wobble alarmingly. She didn't need a court case.

At last an officer whom she'd never seen before appeared, unlocked her cell, and—she being the only one remaining inside—left it open.

"Please follow me."

She did, from the grubby area of the cells up some stairs and into a big room full of desks, where everyone stared at her. She must have come this way last night but didn't remember, which gave her pause.

Maybe she did need to apologize. Punching a policeman—that was a new one on her list of accomplishments. Wait till she told her Pappy.

A wave of what felt surprisingly like homesickness joined the other ill feelings in her gut as the officer ushered her into an inner office where stood Ballister, an older man in a captain's uniform, and Brendan Fagan.

Funny thing about Fagan—she'd been thinking about him more or less nonstop since his earlier visit, but now that she saw him again, he looked even more impressive. Or maybe it was the cramped room that made him appear so tall, so broad. Either way, he filled out that uniform far too well. His thick, reddish hair—neatly combed—swept back from a noble brow. On the whole, his face attained noble proportions that in some subtle way screamed *Irish*. But those blue eyes—yup, they definitely made an impression. A startling hue, quick and full of intelligence.

And, at the moment, fixed on Ginny. They'd found her the moment she stepped into the room, and they didn't waver.

She glanced at Ballister before stiffening her spine and somehow meeting that blue stare.

The older officer spoke. "Miss Landry, I am Captain Addelforce. I believe," he added wryly, "you've met Sergeant Fagan."

"We met earlier this morning."

"And," Fagan spoke in a voice like iron, "at the tavern last night."

How could his voice sound so hard and yet so soft at the same time? A man with an accent like that could persuade a woman into damn near anything.

Except her, of course. She wanted nothing to do with handsome men.

She cleared her throat. "Ah, yes."

The captain announced, "Sergeant Fagan has agreed to drop the charges against you in order to avoid any…er…ugliness. This is a significant concession on his part. But we discussed it and agreed that having you appear in court at this time would stir up unwanted ill feeling and could prove detrimental to the city."

"I see." Ginny held Fagan's gaze without wavering; in fact she couldn't look away. How could eyes be that blue?

Addelforce rattled on, "We are not in the habit of

arresting miscreants for just cause only to release them again. Sergeant Fagan is one of my best men."

"I'm sure he is."

"And I don't like asking him to bend the rules. In return for dropping charges, he has requested an apology."

Something appeared in Brendan Fagan's eyes—a hard light. Victory? Enjoyment? Did he relish the prospect of seeing her humbled? But an apology didn't mean she humbled herself. On the contrary; her father always said an apology demonstrated strength.

She drew a breath. "Sergeant Fagan, I honestly don't remember much of what happened in the tavern last night. I'm not sure why I punched you…"

"I attempted to remove your weapon, with which you were after shootin' up the place."

Ginny nodded.

Smoothly, Ballister inserted, "I will speak with the tavern owner; Miss Landry will of course make good on any damages."

Fagan snorted.

"Either way," Ginny went on doggedly, "I know I did punch you. I can see the evidence of that and feel the effects in my hand. I shouldn't have done that, Sergeant, and I am most sincerely sorry. Thank you for dropping the charges."

He grunted, a sound that denoted both acknowledgement and skepticism. The expression in his eyes had become guarded.

"Well, Sergeant?" Addelforce prodded.

Fagan gave Ginny a stern nod. "Very well so, Miss Landry. I accept your apology."

"But don't do it again?"

"I beg your pardon?"

"You were about to add, 'but don't do it again.' I could see you were."

He shifted on his feet. "Well, obviously don't do it again. That tavern was packed with people, and you might have burned it down."

"Yes, you're right." Ginny bet he was frequently right, or believed himself so.

"Are we finished here?" Ballister asked briskly. "I'm sure my client is anxious to get home."

Oh, she was. She wanted nothing more than to have the four steamies standing by in the house on Linwood to draw her a bath and make her a meal.

Fagan nodded and stepped back. Breaking eye contact with him felt like being slammed to the floor— a physical sensation.

"Brendan," said Addelforce, "why don't you take the rest of the day off? You're not scheduled for duty anyway."

"Yes, sir."

The word "sir" came out "sor." Ginny, her ears clinging to his accent, wondered how long he'd been away from Ireland. She also wondered what Sergeant Perfect did with his free time. Did he know what to do with it?

She could show him.

That thought shocked her. She had no business thinking about the man and, in truth, never wanted to see him again. But only imagine what he'd look like out of that uniform!

She turned to Ballister. "Can we leave?"

"Yes, Miss Landry, to be sure. Officers, thank you for your forbearance and professionalism. I know we can also trust in your discretion."

Ginny could feel Brendan Fagan's gaze between her shoulder blades as she left the room.

****

"Brendan, me darlin', will you be stayin' for supper?"

"I'd like that, Ma, so I would." The house on Haywood Street smelled of new-baked bread and tatty scones. Brendan inhaled deeply, and his mother pulled him into her arms.

Tall for a woman, Alanna Fagan had clear gray eyes—the blue eyes which marked most members of the family came from the Fagan side—and hair that, once fair, had turned to silver.

"It's been far too long since you stopped by," she declared and caught his face between her hands. "Why, what's this? Belted in the line of duty, were you?"

Alanna Fagan had a cluster of sons; only Brendan had pursued the vocation of policeman. All but the two youngest children—a boy and girl—had fledged from the nest. Alanna often proudly declared that all her grown children earned a good living.

They all sent money home, too. It augmented the income Brendan's father, Sean, brought in as a humble laborer and had allowed them to move to this comfortable house from the cramped flat where Brendan had been raised. Eleven children, all of them filled with energy, in three rooms. It had been enough to make a lad swear off breeding.

"A fight in a bar last night, Ma."

"Is it so? Well, I hope you arrested the brute who hit you."

"I did that." Brendan turned his thoughts sternly

away from Virginia Landry. "I have brought something for you." Reaching inside his jacket, he extracted a healthy portion of his pay. "Here."

"Bless you, Brendan." As always, tears came to her eyes.

"Is the old man to home?"

Her expression clouded. "He is not."

"Never tell me he's out to laboring."

Alanna turned away. "He will not listen to me. I tell him and tell him to give it up—by the mercy of the saints and our bairns we've enough to live on. Still he will go out."

Brendan grimaced. After a lifetime spent in hard labor, Sean's body had succumbed to various ills, the worst being severe arthritis. No one could persuade him to sit at home, though.

And they called the Irish lazy.

Bridget and Alan, the two youngest of the clan, came out to greet Brendan. Bridget, the family brain, consistently made the top of her class in school. Ma wanted her to stay in and make something of herself, though most of the others had left school early to work.

Alan, nearly fourteen, would probably quit his lessons soon and start earning.

Brendan greeted both of them heartily, and they all went into the kitchen, where he cadged a tatty scone cooling on the board. He devoured it while Bridie showed him her schoolwork.

"I'm so glad we're back in session," she confessed.

Alan made a face. "I am not."

Alanna, fussing around the room, said, "Brendan was always good in school—just like you, Bridie. What a brain he has, they said. I wish you could have finished, Brendan."

"Doesn't matter. I've a good job." Brendan eyed another scone. He wondered how long till supper.

"Except when you get punched in the face by some hooligan," Alanna declared. "How big was the sinner, to lay such a blow on you?"

"Not that big." Just the perfect size, actually, for kissing. He could almost feel Virginia Landry in his arms, those fine breasts of hers pressed against him, all of her gathered in—What the hell was wrong with him? Her mother had been a vile woman—he wanted no part of that.

Except he did.

"Well, he must have had a powerful arm, to leave a bruise like that."

"Ah—yes." A lot of strength in that slender body. He wondered what it would feel like beneath him.

He'd had his share of encounters with women— more than his share. Aye so, far more. He didn't always play it as safe as he might, and there had been some wild rides, the most notable being a few years back when he'd taken on Ruella Whedon. Ruella, who'd at that time worked as a cook at the jail and now worked for the McMahons on Virginia Street, had the heft and brawn of a man and didn't know the meaning of the word "gentle" when it came to lovemaking.

He'd collected some bruises then, and no mistake. But the experience—young and green as he'd been— was a challenge he just couldn't resist. They'd parted after about six months, under protest on her part and a desire for self-preservation on his.

The point was, Virginia Landry would no doubt be a wild ride but nothing he couldn't handle.

And here he sat in his ma's kitchen, of all places, getting all hot and bothered. Shameful, it was.

Alanna bent down and spoke in his ear. "When your da comes home, you try and talk him out of going out to work."

"I'll try, Ma. I always do try."

"Aye, son. I know how persuasive you can be."

Chapter Eight

"Millie, what's going on outside?"

The steamie trundled over to the big front parlor window through which Ginny could see a number of figures congregated on the sidewalk in front of her house. At first there'd been just two—she'd assumed they must be out on some errand. But they seemed to pass by much too frequently and were joined by more…and more.

Millie looked out. In her squeaking voice she said, "Servants, miss."

"Yes, I can see that. Why are they there?"

"I do not know, miss."

Ginny got to her feet from the comfortable wing chair that, with its twin, flanked the fireplace. Three days had passed since her night in jail. During that time, Philip Ballister had taken her everywhere around the city to inspect her mother's properties and view other enterprises in which she apparently had an interest— some of them questionable.

Ginny had told Ballister to sell them all. The problem was she'd grown fond of this house, especially the high-ceilinged parlor, which reeked of comfort. She almost wouldn't mind hanging on to the place.

Which made a good reason for getting rid of it. She had no time for comforts—or self-indulgence.

Still, being cradled here, with all four steamies

bustling around for the sole purpose of her comfort, made a potent seduction.

Now she walked to the window and took up a post next to Millie. Her eyes widened. No fewer than ten steamies marched back and forth in front of her house in a determined oblong, all of them silver, some newer-looking and some old and battered. Many carried signs: *Free us. Automaton rights. Down with oppression. Abolish steamie slavery.*

"My God," she breathed. "It's a protest. I'm being picketed—and only this house. Why?"

Traffic on the street slowed as vehicles passed the marchers and the occupants stared. Several of the neighbors, standing on their stoops, were also staring.

Millie made no reply.

Ginny glanced at her. "Millie?"

"Miss?"

"Do you know why I'm being picketed?"

"Yes, miss."

"Tell me."

"Your mother, miss, participated in experiments and activities which many among the automaton community considered oppressive."

"The automaton community?"

"Yes, miss."

"Here in Buffalo?"

"Yes, miss."

"Do you consider yourself part of that community?"

"I am in fact an automaton, miss."

"And do you and the rest of the automatons in this household want to participate in that?" Ginny waved a hand out the window. "Do you wish to be freed?"

"Miss, I cannot answer for my fellows."

"Please call them in here."

Ginny paced while she waited, still shooting incredulous looks out the front window as she did. The number of protesters continued to increase. She would have to do something about it.

Millie returned with the other three units in tow. Ginny waved her hand again. "Do you see this?"

"Yes, miss," Floyd replied. "It used to occur sometimes when Dr. Landry was alive. Not often."

"What did she do about it?"

"Called the police, miss."

"I'd prefer to avoid that if possible." She'd seen quite enough of the police for the time being. "Floyd, do you think you could go out and disperse them?"

"Yes, miss."

"But first I'd like to ask you, all of you—do you wish to be freed from my service? Because if you do, I'll let you go today. Right now. And I'll have Mr. Ballister draw something up granting you your independence."

None of the steamies reacted.

"Well?" Ginny looked at Frannie, the smallest— and shiniest—of the four. The newest? "Frannie?"

"Yes, miss."

"Yes, you wish to be freed, or yes, you hear me?"

"I hear you, miss. I do not wish to be freed."

"Are you certain?"

"Yes, miss. Where would I go? Where get my coal?"

"I'm sure others in this…this movement would assist you."

"Since being put in service I have never worked

anywhere else."

"I understand. But I must tell you this house will most likely be sold eventually. Quite possibly you will not be able to stay here then."

A barely perceptible tremor passed through the unit.

"What about the rest of you? Do you all wish to remain here?"

Floyd and Millie answered in the affirmative. Gus, who seemed to be the rough-steamie-about-the-house, merely nodded. Ginny had never heard him speak and didn't know if he could.

"Well, then, how about this? What if I draw up papers to free you but you keep on living here and working for me?" She certainly didn't want to lose them. "I can pay you a wage." Heaven knew her mother had left enough money, an obscene amount.

Floyd jerked, appearing to become distressed. "Miss, on what would I spend a wage?"

"I don't know. A supply of coal of your own, so you needn't be dependent on anyone?"

Floyd's voice box rattled alarmingly.

"Very well, you can work for your keep—silver polish and all the coal you can burn."

"Yes, miss. That would be acceptable, miss."

"Thank you, Floyd. Meanwhile, please go out and see if you can chase away those protestors."

Floyd jerked into motion. Ginny and the other steamies watched through the window as he emerged from the front door and rolled down the walk. The protesters clustered around him.

An odd scene, one that made Ginny wonder how steamies communicated among themselves. Did her servants chatter away when alone in this house? It boggled the mind.

She experienced a sudden flashback to Dakota—home—and the Sioux reservation where she'd sometimes accompanied her father in his official capacity of physician.

She remembered Pappy telling her one time, when she'd asked why most of the Sioux lived apart, "Well, kitten, there are folks think they're different from the rest of us—that they don't think and feel the same as we do."

Pappy had known better. He'd met his second wife, Winona, on the reservation. Winona had been the only mother Ginny ever knew.

Now she wondered if the same ridiculous prejudice affected these automatons. But they truly were different, weren't they?

Floyd's apparently peaceable conversation with the protesters continued several minutes before he broke away and returned to the house. The automatons resumed their slow loop on the sidewalk.

"Well?" Ginny asked Floyd when he entered the parlor.

"Miss, they refuse to disperse."

"Dammit. I really don't want to call in the police." Though, come to think of it, the Buffalo force must have many members. What were the odds Brendan Fagan would respond to the call?

Perhaps she should just ignore the protesters.

She returned to her wing chair, only to be brought out of it by a clatter some short while later. Two uniformed officers now approached the protesters outside her home.

Even as she watched, another drew up in a paddy wagon.

Her eyes narrowed. One of the neighbors must have called them—not too surprising, really, given the number of steamies now gathered.

The paddy wagon half blocked the street. Its driver got out and approached the protesters.

Ginny recognized him by the way he walked. *Oh, hell. Oh, damnation.*

She switched her gaze back to the first two officers—one tall and built like Fagan, the other shorter and decidedly rounder. The tall one spoke steadily to the gathered automatons, which at last began to leave.

The three police officers put their heads together and consulted. One glanced at the house.

Ginny's heart stopped and started up again with a kick. Why him?

The shorter, rounder officer climbed into the paddy wagon and drove it away. Brendan Fagan peeled from his companion and jogged up the walk.

Scenarios flitted through Ginny's head: *She let Millie answer the door; she answered the door herself and invited Fagan in; she dragged him upstairs with her to the yellow bedroom for a night of unbridled passion.*

That thought froze her where she stood—her, a woman who barely knew the meaning of the word "indecisive."

She remained poised in the center of the room until Floyd brought the sergeant in. No, maybe it hadn't been the size of Addelforce's office that made Brendan Fagan appear so imposing; he looked equally so now in her parlor doorway.

"Sergeant Fagan," Floyd announced.

"Thank you, Floyd."

Brendan Fagan pulled the uniform cap from his head, which did unexpected things to Ginny's pulse. His impossibly blue gaze inspected her swiftly from her hair downward, making her more aware of her body than she'd been in quite some time. He might as well have stripped her naked.

"Good afternoon, Miss Landry."

"Sergeant Fagan. I'm assuming one of my neighbors called you."

"So they did. It's not the first time we've seen protesters here. Unfortunate, but it's happening all over the city just now."

"I see you've made no arrests."

"My fellow officer persuaded them to leave." He smiled, to devastating effect. "I'd like you to meet him. Just wait there while I'm after calling him in."

She waited, not at all sure she could move anyway. She found herself hoping his fellow officer might be ugly and ordinary—something she could handle.

She was fated to disappointment. Fagan soon returned with a still-more strapping fellow at his side, also red-haired but with eyes of startling green.

"Miss Landry, this is Officer Patrick Kelly, a leading light of the Buffalo Police force and one whom I'm sure you'll encounter frequently if you remain in our city for any length of time."

"Officer Kelly." Ginny extended her hand.

Kelly's fingers engulfed it very gently. "Pleased to meet you, Miss Landry."

She heard something strange in his voice but failed to identify it. He too had a rich Irish brogue, and he too seemed almost too good looking.

"The same, Officer. Thank you for dispersing the protesters."

"They tend to listen to me," Kelly said. "Perhaps because they know I have a certain amount of sympathy for their cause."

"Oh? Are the police encouraged to take sides?"

"Not officially, no. We are required to remain objective to the best of our ability. But of course that is more easily said than done."

"Of course." What was it about his voice?

Brendan Fagan watched their exchange closely, and an odd smile curled his lips.

What did that mean, precisely? Ginny had the distinct impression she was missing something.

Kelly said, "I will do my best to assure I and other members of the Squad patrolling here keep the protesters clear of the area. Please enjoy your stay in Buffalo."

"Thank you, I will." Squad? Why did that jog her mind?

Kelly looked at Fagan. "I will now return to the station, Brendan."

"Fine, that. I'll join you in just a few."

Kelly went out. The curious smile remained on Fagan's face, and Ginny had a sudden desire to slap it off. Or kiss it off—yes, that.

"So, Miss Landry, what did you think of Officer Kelly?"

"He seems very accommodating, though I'm not sure why you felt it necessary to introduce him to me."

The smile turned into a grin. "Do you not?"

"No."

Fagan jerked his head toward the door. "That was the star of Buffalo's Irish Squad."

"Wait. They're…"

"Automatons, yes—very similar to the ones your mother created. Have you never seen one before?"

"Not up close, not one like that. I had no idea they were so realistic." No wonder Kelly had a connection with the protesters. He was, in fact, akin to them.

Fagan went on, "The units your mother created are still more sophisticated than Pat. You can perhaps see why they're poised to start a revolution."

"Well, I can, yes."

"Just thought you should be made aware of the situation."

"Thank you, Sergeant. I appreciate it."

He slapped the cap back on his head and turned to leave, only to swing back and scrape it off again. His gaze once more touched her in a way that swiftly rendered her breathless.

"Miss Landry…"

"Yes, Sergeant Fagan?"

"Would you be interested in having dinner with me sometime before you leave the city?"

"I…" Ginny's eyes went wide. All the words she might have said stuck in her throat.

Patiently, Sergeant Fagan waited, a force gathered and held.

"I—I'm very sorry, Sergeant Fagan, but I'm afraid I can't. You see, I make a habit of walking out only with ugly men."

Chapter Nine

"Makes a habit of walking out only with ugly men," Brendan Fagan repeated in a mutter as he stalked away from Virginia Landry's house and off down Linwood. "What in hell is that supposed to mean?" What kind of woman preferred an ugly man?

He didn't consider himself handsome; that would be conceited. But he knew he'd been blessed in several ways: with a good brain, a strong body, and a face that most women seemed to find pleasing. Why should Virginia Landry be any different?

Because she was. His mind told him so, and his heart acknowledged it as truth; he'd sensed that from the first he laid eyes on her. She possessed an indefinable *something* that had made him overstep his own good judgment and suggest they see each other socially.

Just as well she'd turned him down, then. He didn't need the complication.

But he needed to kiss her, and soon.

Better get that right out of his head. Life held enough hurdles without erecting more. And given the identity of her mother and the current mood in the city, she was a problem just waiting to happen.

Ah, but hadn't it been worth it all, just to introduce her to Pat Kelly? A sudden smile broke over his face. She'd had no idea Pat was an automaton. Didn't she have any idea what her mother was doing before she died, what an automaton, taken to the limits, could be?

Captain Addelforce called him into the office as soon as he reached the station.

"Sergeant, I'm sorry to say there's been two more."

"Beg pardon?"

"Two more murders. The calls just came in."

Brendan's heart sank. "Two, sir? Where?"

"One at a private residence over on Porter Avenue. A businessman grew concerned when his colleague failed to show up at their office. He went to the man's home, only to find his body and signs of an apparent struggle."

Brendan blew out a breath. "Intruder, do you think?"

Addelforce shook his head. "A damaged steam unit lay nearby. Looked like the man tried to fight it off. His other steam servants are missing."

"No one else in the home?"

"The man's wife is away visiting relations, according to the neighbors. The other case is even uglier. A pit on the lower east side."

"A fighting pit, you mean? Dogs?" Brendan hated those places.

"You ever heard of a man called Deke Cooper?"

"We've shut him down any number of times."

"Well, you won't be shutting him down again. Seems he's been running a new game—pitting steam units against one another. Details aren't too clear. I want you to get over there and take a full report."

"Aye, sir."

"Take someone with you, maybe a member of the Irish Squad if one's available."

"I was just on a call with Pat Kelly. I wouldn't mind taking him."

"Everybody wants Kelly, but I sent him on another call just before you got back. Choose someone else."

"Aye, sir."

"And for God's sake be careful. The last thing we need is more trouble."

"Has Cooper's body been collected?"

"At the morgue."

"Manner of death, sir?"

"Bludgeoned. That's all we know so far."

Brendan collected Terry Greely on his way back out. Greely, big and fair-haired, didn't tend to offer a lot in the way of conversation, unlike Pat. As they tramped their way to William Street, though, Brendan made the effort.

"So, Terry lad, how's the wife?"

Greely's new wife, Chastity—one of the hybrid units Virginia Landry's mother created—had once been forced to serve as a prostitute before all hell broke loose at the Crystal Palace. Terry and Chastity had numbered among the automatons joined in wedlock at the mass ceremony near Hoyt Lake the month before last. To Brendan's knowledge, the ceremony had been the first of its kind anywhere.

Terry's handsome face broke into a rare smile. "Mrs. Greely is doing most excellently, thank you, Sergeant Fagan. We are very happy together."

"Glad to hear it."

"I am no longer lonely in the house I bought."

Brendan gave Terry a sharp look. He'd never considered the notion of an automaton feeling lonely. He supposed he should be ashamed of that oversight.

"That's good."

"We are thinking of adopting a child."

Brendan's step faltered. "What?"

"We have learned there are many children in the city who are institutionalized for lack of willing adopters. Chastity's good friend Lily and her husband, Reynold Michaels, are looking into the adoption procedure. We thought we might follow."

"I see. Most admirable, Terry. But would—ah—such an adoption be permitted?"

"We are investigating that also. The situation for Reynold and Lily is a bit different, given that Reynold is human. But Chastity has discovered the plight of Negro orphans is particularly bad. We are hoping the authorities see fit to place one of them with us."

Hope. Just months ago most folk would have declared automatons incapable of it. "Well, I wish you luck."

"Thank you."

"Your wife is a right clever lady. I'm sure she'll come up with a way of achieving this."

"She is, Brendan. I believe her capable of most anything."

Like beating her creator, Candace Landry, to death. Chastity had been among the automatons who'd done just that. Would the authorities really hand an innocent child over to her?

And what would the child in question think? Of course, Brendan had seen the inside of those orphanages a time or two. He wouldn't leave a cat there if he could help it.

But cats were cats, and it didn't answer the question of what folk in this city would say if human children got adopted out to automaton parents. The good citizens might not want those wains, but all such considerations would go out the window in the face of ill feeling.

He changed the subject. "What do you know about Deke Cooper?"

"Only what I have been told. The last time James Kilter and some of our officers shut him down, he swore he'd get round the law. The next we heard, he was pitting automatons against one another."

"Let me ask you a question: What do you think of that?"

"Well, Brendan, it might be argued by those who are not automatons it is better than abusing living, feeling creatures." Terry looked at Brendan. "Only, being an automaton, I know we *are* living, feeling beings. It is remarkably like the situation with Chastity and the other Ladies. It was considered better to have them serve life sentences as prostitutes than to expose human women to that life."

And see how that ended up, Brendan thought. He wondered what Virginia Landry thought about her mother having been beaten to death by her own machines. Yet she kept a few of the things around her.

He should have warned her. He didn't want to answer one of these calls only to find her lying dead.

"What's going on in this city, Terry, eh?" he mused.

"Change, Brendan. Great and important change."

****

The scene at Deke Cooper's establishment proved ugly in the extreme. Little more than a large shanty ringed by smaller outbuildings, the place consisted of the pit surrounded by benches, a poor excuse for an office, and a tiny area fitted with a cot. It appeared, from the extensive amount of blood trail, Cooper had been pulled from that place into the pit itself, where he had died.

Disturbingly, a number of steamies in various conditions remained on the premises. That was the problem with these crimes—steam units couldn't be arrested, and no one seemed sure what else to do with them.

Could they be put on trial for murder? If found guilty, should they be decommissioned?

These units appeared battered, oft repaired, and scabbed together. All made from molded silver, none hybrid, many bore splashes of what could only be Cooper's blood.

"You interview half of them," Brendan told Terry, "and I'll take the other half."

The first unit Brendan interviewed had damage to its voice box and could barely speak. It denied all knowledge of Cooper's murder, even though its shins were splashed with blood.

The second, which looked like it had been put together from two separate units, admitted it had heard nothing because it and the other units had been on standby.

"We found Master Cooper in the pit when we came in to clean for tonight's session. We tried to move him, and there was a lot of blood."

"I see. Why would you need to clean?"

"We are ordered to do so."

"What's in the pit that needs cleaning?"

"Nuts. Bolts. Metal fragments. Spilled coal."

"He's been pitting you against each other, then?"

"Yes, Officer."

"Against your will?"

For the first time the unit failed to answer readily.

"Why do you—did you—fight for him if you don't want to?"

"We follow orders, Officer. We were created to follow orders."

Not until all the interviews had been conducted and Brendan rejoined Greely did they compare notes.

Terry reported, "None of them admitted to killing Master Cooper—even though all of them described him as cruel."

"That's the result I got, too, Terry."

"They say they discovered and attempted to revive him, thus acquiring the blood they show."

"And who's to say differently, eh?"

"Cooper had collected a stable of units for fighting. The others have absconded." Terry's eyes met Brendan's. "One unit also told me there are dogs in a kennel out back."

"Oh, hell. I suppose we'd better take a look."

They heard the dogs before they saw them—not barking but whimpering. The conditions inside proved so appalling Brendan took one look and decided Cooper had got precisely what he deserved—not that he could take that line, officially.

"We'll call in Jamie Kilter," he told Terry. "By God, some of these poor creatures are in dire shape."

Terry lowered his voice. "Brendan, one of the units confided to me that Cooper had been pitting some of the dogs against steamies. He did not like to say it, but confessed Cooper had been charging extra for those matches."

Brendan didn't know which was worse—Cooper or the patrons who came to watch. "Bloodthirsty bastards."

"Aye."

"Sometimes, Terry, I hate this job. But why did the unit want to keep it a secret?"

"I believe he was ashamed of following orders when it meant injuring a dog."

Well, Brendan thought, and they say steamies have no conscience.

Chapter Ten

"Miss Landry, I think I may have a buyer interested in one of your mother's investments."

Ballister had showed up at Ginny's door right after dinner, apologizing for arriving so late, but he explained it by saying time was of the essence.

"It's the charity hospital on Ellicott Street."

Ginny's nose wrinkled involuntarily. Ballister had taken her round to see that place, which she'd found to be bleak and, frankly, appalling.

"Unfortunately, the offer's on the table, and I need an answer right away."

"Why don't we discuss it in the parlor? Millie"— Ginny turned to the steamie—"will you please bring some tea?"

"Yes, miss."

Ginny led the way to the comfortable room. Outside the windows, the day had just begun to fade. She found herself looking for the wink of steamies pacing the sidewalk.

Ballister seated himself on the settee and spread a sheaf of papers on the low table that stood in front of it. "You did say to liquidate your mother's holdings as quickly as possible."

So she could get out of this city. "Yes. Who's the buyer?"

"Well, that's the thing." Ballister spread his fingers

across the papers. "It's what we need to discuss."

Ginny raised her eyebrows. "I can't imagine who'd want to assume my mother's interest in that place— don't know why she even held an interest."

"That's easily explained. Your mother was a doctor."

"So she housed patients there?"

"No. But that has always been one of the few hospitals that treat Buffalo's fallen women. Your mother volunteered her services there. We think it's where she first encountered the plight of the streetwalkers in the city. There's no proof, but it's also believed that's where she obtained the materials to build the batches of her Ladies."

"Materials?"

Ballister cleared his throat. "The cadavers."

Ginny's stomach dropped. "You mean to tell me she built them from actual women? Former streetwalkers?"

"Let's face it—she needed to obtain the skin, eyes, hair, and—er—other fittings somewhere. Obviously she chose only the most beautiful and then improved upon them, fixing teeth, scars, and so forth."

Now Ginny's stomach did a slow roll.

Ballister eyed her. "I see this has come as a shock. Have you ever met any of your mother's creations?"

"Met? No." Just Patrick Kelly. Had he, too, been built from a cadaver?

"I will have to see if I can arrange it. The effect must be experienced to be appreciated. I have to say, Dr. Landry was a genius."

"I did meet a member of the Irish Squad today. If they're like that…"

"They are, but still more advanced. Impressive, are they not?"

Ginny clenched her fingers together and nodded.

"Miss Landry, I understand how difficult this is for you."

"Difficult, disturbing, upsetting…you name it, Mr. Ballister. I say go ahead and sell my interest in that awful place."

He shuffled his papers and stared at them. "The buyer—or I should say buyers, for it's a consortium—is the Automaton Liberation League."

"What?"

His eyes, pale and very serious, lifted to meet hers.

At that moment, Millie rolled in with the tea tray. Not until she went out again did Ginny get to her feet and say, "I need something stronger than tea after all. Mr. Ballister, would you like a drink?"

"No, thank you, Miss Landry."

She stumbled to the side table and poured herself a tot of whiskey, which she tossed back like a lumberjack. She turned to face the lawyer. "Please explain."

"Your mother's death—her bludgeoning by her own hybrids—sparked a movement for automaton rights."

"Yes, you mentioned that."

"In the fire that took place at the Crystal Palace previous to your mother's murder, several of her hybrid units were destroyed. Their remains were claimed by the surviving Ladies and members of the Irish Squad, most of which have now formed marriage unions. Word is they have studied your mother's work and intend to begin building their own models."

Ginny gasped. "Can they do that?"

"It's not known for certain, but I would have to speculate they can. They are endowed with high levels of intelligence and are capable of both learning and adaptation."

"But why? Why would they do such a thing? If they want to be independent, why create others who'd have to exist in the same situation?"

"I think they consider doing so a mark of independence. They do not want anyone else—anyone human—resuming the process. Besides, they cannot have children."

"Oh, I see." At least Ginny thought she did. If these units couldn't bear children, building others would be their only chance to produce progeny. And doing so would feel far different from *having done* to them.

She recalled the look in Patrick Kelly's green eyes—bright, aware. Intelligent. A spasm wracked her body.

She poured a second drink.

"How many would they build? I mean, this gives them scope to increase their numbers many times."

"Not really. They are limited by time, expense, and opportunity. The main difficulty in producing hybrids is, as your mother as well as Mason and Charles—the two geniuses who conceived of the units which ultimately became the Irish Squad—discovered, is there's no easy access to large numbers of viable cadavers. Mason and Charles solved the problem by choosing their specimens and then having them killed to order. Your mother used the hospital and, being a doctor, may have had access to cadavers elsewhere. But only so many people die, and even fewer specimens, I imagine, are suitable to utilize."

Ginny wished Ballister would stop referring to Candace Landry as her mother. She chugged the second drink. "But Landry's Ladies and presumably the members of the Irish Squad were built to certain specifications. We don't know if the Automaton Liberation League will do the same. They might use inferior corpses—any corpses."

"That is true." Ballister leaned forward and lowered his voice. "I have heard a rumor they have built a child."

"What?"

"Children die in this city too, many of them orphans."

"But…a child would always stay…"

"A child, yes. Some of the couples who were married in July have also applied to adopt human orphans. So far, permission has not been granted, but it is still under debate."

"Would they, the powers that be, allow machines to adopt human children?"

Ballister shrugged uncomfortably. "Some of the children in question live in deplorable conditions. It might be argued they'd be better off in homes, even with automaton guardians. But as you may imagine, the idea isn't a popular one with the human contingent. The climate here right now is…shall we say, sensitive? Selling your interest in the hospital to the League and, in essence, giving them legal access to raw materials will not meet with much approval."

"And I'm already under scrutiny because of Candace Landry's actions." Ginny truly hated having to call the woman "mother." Her father's second wife held that title in her heart.

"Precisely."

"What a conundrum."

"Yes."

"Mr. Ballister, I want shed of this city." Away from the buildings, the people, and the tangle of problems. She wanted to return to the clean wind and the open spaces of the Dakota Territory. "But I'm not sure I want to contribute to the discord here."

Ballister spread his hands. "That is why I sought to present the bid. They've offered a fair price—not a great one. These are not wealthy...er...people. But fair. And quite frankly I do not see anyone else taking it off your hands."

"Is the interest I now hold a major one?"

"It is."

"Would I be better off just sitting on it so no one else can gain access?"

"That is something only you can decide."

"I need to think about it. Please stall them until I can give the matter and its ramifications full consideration."

"I will. As for the Crystal Palace—or rather the site where it stood—we have had no offers yet. In spite of it being a prime piece of real estate, I'm very much afraid the fog cast over the site by your mother's death is keeping buyers at bay."

"Yes, well, Mr. Ballister, keep trying." Ginny did want rid of that—unless the Automaton Liberation League stepped in there also.

Ballister gathered his papers together and rose. "I will be in touch soon."

"Thank you."

Floyd materialized and showed Ballister out. Ginny, left standing in the parlor, assembled the pieces of her situation.

A pariah—that was what Candace Landry had become, and Ginny too, by association. She could go home and let Ballister handle things here, but she had a vague sense that she should in some way make recompense for the woman's sins.

A ridiculous premise. She'd never known Candace Landry and had no responsibility for her actions.

She wished she could speak with her father. Michael Landry never seemed to have difficulty with moral decisions. Though far from conventional—and Ginny had no doubt inherited his unconventional streak—he nevertheless invariably cut to the heart of what was right and wrong. He'd offered his professional services on the reservation free of charge because he felt it right and because he could. His unconventionality never seemed to interfere with his conscience.

In this case, though, Ginny had no idea what might be the right course: offering the automatons of this city an opportunity to fulfill their objectives or curtailing actions that might ultimately prove dangerous to the human community.

She needed another drink—but not here. Suddenly she wanted nothing so much as to escape this house.

A boozer—that was the ticket.

Chapter Eleven

"Well, if it ain't Brendan Fagan."

Brendan froze as the familiar Cockney accent sliced through the noise in the crowded tavern. He turned and his heart sank even as he pasted a big smile on his face. He'd come into the bar following a lead— one of the barmen here roomed next door to the cannery where the unpleasant manageress had been murdered, and he wondered if the fellow might have seen anything relevant.

He certainly didn't expect to bump into an old lover. Such an occurrence seldom proved comfortable—especially a former lover such as this.

"Ruella, it's been an age. How are you?"

Standing by the bar and half blocking it, Ruella Whedon eyed him up and down. Back in the days when she still worked as cook at the jail downtown, she'd wooed him with the best scones he'd ever tasted. Scones, however good, shouldn't be enough to lure a man into a woman's bed, and truthfully they hadn't. Looking at her now, Brendan couldn't really imagine what had attracted him, other than his innate sense of daring.

Ruella possessed a good heart, but going to bed with her had been a bit like an exercise in survival. Almost as tall as Brendan and built like a wrestler, she could break a man's back if she chose. In a fistfight, she gave as good as she got. In fact, it wasn't safe to tangle with her in or out of the bedroom.

"I'm fine and dandy," she said now, continuing to examine him closely with her slightly protuberant eyes. Brendan remembered that look and to what it had all too often proved a preamble.

She'd better not be getting any ideas.

"Come and have a drink," she bellowed. "You're not on duty, are you?"

He wasn't, not officially. He wore his street clothes and had come in here on his own time, hoping to nail down some of the questions that plagued him. Such as why were witnesses being so cagey about who—or what—they'd seen going in and out of these murder scenes?

He shook his head, and Ruella threw a beefy arm around his neck. "Come and sit down, lad."

"No place to sit."

"I got a table over there. Get yourself a drink. You still like the black ale?"

"Aye."

Ruella signaled the barman with a raised eyebrow—not the fellow Brendan wanted to question— and two ales materialized with impressive speed. Ruella thrust one into Brendan's hand and dragged him off to a scarred table up against the wall.

"So," she asked when his fanny met the seat of the chair, "what brings you to this charming place?" The East London accent, bright as the clatter of tin, prompted a lot of memories for Brendan, many of them less than welcome.

Breaking up with Ruella hadn't been easy; persuading her things between them had run their course had taken every drop of blarney Brendan possessed.

"Well," he said, hoping to distract her from any amorous thoughts, "it's about these murders."

"Grisly, ain't they?" She tipped her glass at him. "See, that's the trouble with you, Brendan Fagan. You're never really off duty even when you're off duty. That's why it didn't work between us."

"Right." That and his well-honed sense of survival. Still, he was glad he'd had his wild ride with this woman—something likely to comfort him in his old age.

"You look good." She eyed him again, apparently not about to be distracted by the murders. "Real good."

"So do you," Brendan declared. In truth she looked the same as ever—face like a particularly comely bulldog, brown hair caught in two bunches over her ears. He took a large gulp of ale. "You still working for the McMahons?"

Her face lit. "I am. Did you hear Mrs. Clara had a sprog?"

"I did."

"Good as gold is little Graine, and adored by everyone in the house."

"I'm happy for them."

"As am I. They deserve it, do the McMahons. Good people." She leaned back in her chair. "I'm thinking of following their lead, actually."

Brendan's mouth fell open. "Eh?"

"It's a fine thing, innit, giving rise to the next generation? Despite how dangerous this city is, sometimes."

Brendan's blood ran cold. He hoped she hadn't

come here searching out a likely father for her proposed child.

"Tell me, Brendan Fagan, who do you think's behind these murders? You're a canny lad. You and I, we've seen both sides of these automatons. There's those like Dax at the McMahons—not a nasty patch on 'im. And there's those like Charles and Mason tried to create…killing machines. You remember that night?"

She widened bulging eyes, and Brendan nodded. Ruella had been there with him the night when, strapped to a cold table, he'd very nearly been killed by the two madmen who created the first hybrids.

"You have to remember Charles and Mason might have created their automatons to be killing machines, but the units didn't stay that way. They're now upright and·valuable members of the Irish Squad."

"True."

"As for who's behind these murders…"

"Automatons beating their masters to death. Can you warrant it?"

Brendan shook his head. "I wouldn't have thought it possible if I hadn't been there at the Crystal Palace when Landry's Ladies beat Candace Landry to death."

"I didn't see it, me. I was otherwise occupied." Ruella glanced toward the bar.

"All I know is something about these murders just smells wrong. That's why I'm here, actually. I need to talk to one of the barmen."

"Oh? Which one?" Ruella cocked her head, which made her look even more like an intelligent dog.

"Name's Jeremy Black. He lives next to one of the murder scenes."

"Oh." An incredible expression crossed Ruella's

face, part coyness and part what looked like mal-de-mer. "Because the other barman over there—Bart—he's my beau."

"You don't say?" Brendan looked to the bar and caught a glimpse of a massive figure with black hair, a wide moustache, and biceps at least as bulging as Ruella's.

Well, there was the puzzle of a potential father for Ruella's offspring solved, though Brendan's mind boggled at what sort of infant such parents might produce.

Brawny, to say the least.

"A couple, are the two of you? Is it serious?"

"Serious as typhoid!" Ruella confirmed with satisfaction. She thrust out a meaty hand. "Just take a gander at this." A diamond sparkled on her finger.

"By God, Ruella, congratulations! I'm that happy for you." And he was, deeply and sincerely. "How'd you meet?"

"In a wrestling match. The fool thought he could take me." Ruella grinned broadly.

Ah, well, Brendan could have told him better.

"I hope you're not too disappointed, lad—me being off the market and all. What we had together was good, but all that's in the past, you understand."

"Agreed."

"And take heart. Someday you'll have a love of your own."

"Will I, then?"

"You just need to loosen up some. I always thought that, back when we were seeing each other. A bit too devoted to his duty, is Brendan Fagan—near famous for it."

Brendan bristled. Coming on the heels of what Virginia Landry had said about him—what had she called him, Officer Proper?—he didn't need to hear this. Sourly he said, "It takes a great deal of hard work to advance in the force. Not many men make sergeant by my age."

"That's true, lad, and it's proud of you I am. A light of the Buffalo Police force, so everyone says. But I'd hate to see your youth pass you by and nothing to show for it but a sergeant's stripes." Ruella's bulgy eyes met his. "Take a chance from time to time, Brendan. Have some fun."

A vision of Virginia Landry once more appeared in Brendan's mind. Aye, it would be fun to set her straight about him. Show her of just what he was made. Shock her a wee bit. Kiss her senseless.

"Well, now, I wonder what that look in your baby blues means? Come along, I'll introduce you to my Bart."

"I'd like that." Brendan tossed back the rest of his drink and followed her to the bar, where the black-haired barman greeted her with a gap-toothed smile.

"Ruella, my lovely."

"Hello, Bart. Look who I met. This is Brendan Fagan, police sergeant in the force."

"I've heard of you, Officer Fagan." Bart thrust an enormous hand over the bar, and Brendan shook it. "A rising star in this city, aren't you?"

And when had that become his reputation around the city?

"And," Ruella said proudly, "he's a former lover of mine." Everyone at the bar, unable to keep from overhearing, stared. Brendan waited for Bart's fist to crash into his face.

But the fellow just nodded.

"Bart and I got no secrets from one another," Ruella declared. "It's the only way to begin a marriage, innit?"

It was. Brendan tucked it away for future reference. "Congratulations," he told Bart sincerely. "You've won a woman in a thousand."

"Ain't that the truth? I'm the luckiest man alive, and no mistake."

"I wish you every happiness. When's the blessed day to be?"

Bart's smile grew still wider. "My birthday, the day before Halloween. Hope you'll do us the honor of attending—in an unofficial capacity, of course."

"I'd be honored."

"He's off duty now," Ruella put in, "but still looking to talk to Jeremy there about them murders going on round the city. Always working, this one."

"Go talk to the officer, Jeremy," Bart instructed his fellow barman. "I'll cover for you."

The amiable Jeremy complied, and they moved to the corner of the bar. Forthcoming as the barman was, it turned out he'd seen and heard nothing the night of the murder and was of the opinion that the automatons working at the cannery had been a mild-mannered lot, usually on the receiving end of their mistress's temper.

"Hard to imagine them lifting a hand to her," Jeremy concluded before returning to his post.

So it might be, Brendan reflected, eyeing Ruella and Bart, who shared a kiss across the bar. On the other hand, the most damned unexpected things did happen all the time.

Chapter Twelve

"Well, Miss Landry. Do you spend all your time in taverns?"

Ginny blinked as the warm Irish accent blossomed somewhere above her head. She knew that voice. At least her body seemed to; it lit and heated instantly, achieving an effortless state of half-arousal.

Looking up, she encountered just what she expected—a pair of intensely blue eyes in a handsome face.

"Sergeant Fagan." Reaching out a bit unsteadily, Ginny seized both his arms at the biceps and felt a big, sloppy smile spread across her face. "So we meet again. Have you come to arrest me?" She leaned closer. "Surely there's something I might do to duck whatever charge you mean to level at me?"

"I've just come off duty. And you're drunk."

"Off duty? How very un-un-usual." Ginny backed off a step, though she didn't let go of him. A swift inspection showed her he wore a rough-woven white shirt open at the neck and a pair of plain brown trousers. "Damn! You're even handsomer out of the uniform." Again she leaned close. "As if that were possible."

He steadied her, one hand at each shoulder. "That's not necessarily a good thing, is it? Not the way I understand it."

"No, not good, Sergeant Fagan. If only you were homely." She widened her eyes at him. "I wouldn't mind some male company tonight."

He lifted his brows. "A dangerous proposition, Miss Landry. 'Tis not wise, looking for male company in such a place as this."

"I can handle myself." She sized him up with a glance. "In any case, you're here now to protect me, aren't you, Sergeant Fagan?"

He gave a rueful smile. "Since I'm not on duty, you'd better call me 'Brendan.'"

"Brendan." She tried it out on her tongue.

"You do know this is one of the roughest taverns in the city?"

"Better hope there's no trouble, then, especially since I don't dare pull my c-cannon. Never know when some big, proper policeman will turn up and start throwing regulations around. Who's your friend?"

Brendan Fagan turned to the man who hovered at his shoulder. "A colleague I just bumped into, Mitch Glenning."

Glenning, nearly half a head shorter than Fagan, had sandy brown hair and an ordinary face. Ginny leaned into him. "Hmm, now, you're more like it. You're not an automaton, are you?"

"No, ma'am." Glenning grinned.

"Good, because I hear they're singularly ill-equipped." Ginny abandoned Fagan and looped her arm through Mitch's. "Let's get a drink."

"I'd love to, ma'am, I surely would. But I'm married."

"If you're married, what are you doing out in a boozer with this rapscallion?" It took her three attempts to pronounce the final word.

"My wife's expecting our first baby, ma'am, due any day. And she's awful crabby. She told me to get out of the house. I bumped into Brendan, and he kindly bought me a drink."

"Isn't that...nice. Is Sergeant Brendan often so kindly?"

"He has his moments. But ma'am, if I start drinking with another woman, Betsy will have the flesh off my bones."

"But how will Betsy know, eh? Just one drink. Oh, that's right—Officer Morality here might feel compelled to tell her."

Strong fingers seized the back of her jacket; she was lifted effortlessly away from Glenning and set down again. "Leave the man be. And"—those blue eyes again, right in her face—"you've got me all wrong. I'm off duty, understand?"

"I'm not sure I do. I got the distinct impression you're never off duty."

"Wrong again. That being said, I think you've had quite enough to drink, Miss Landry. Why don't you let me see you home?"

"Landry?" Glenning yelped. "Is she the one—?"

Ginny told him sorrowfully, "My mother was a terrible, terrible woman. But you see, I never knew her. Can I be blamed?"

"No, I guess not." Glenning shot a glance toward the door as if he'd developed a sudden desire to escape.

Ginny cried, "Let me buy you a drink. What will you have, Mitch? And you, Brendan?"

The two officers exchanged speaking looks.

"Maybe just one," Glenning said.

"And then, Miss Landry, I'll be after seeing you home."

"Will you, Officer Brendan? Even if I do not wish to go?"

"Mitch, go grab a table if you can find one. We'll get the drinks."

Ginny leaned up, chest to chest with Brendan Fagan, and peered into his face. "Do you like giving orders? She licked her lips. "Want to give me some?"

"I'd love to, but I'll have to get that cannon off you first."

"Why don't you try?"

A curious look came into his eyes. "Because you're tipsy. And dangerous."

At the bar he ordered three ales and scanned the room in an effort to locate Glenning. "Come on, then."

Ginny obeyed—she didn't quite know why—pausing only to eye several ugly men along the way. One of them leered back at her, but Fagan grunted and the fellow, sizing him up, turned away.

Glenning had found a small table in the corner. Fagan set the glasses down and pushed Ginny into a chair. "Sit. Drink that slowly."

"Sure that's a good idea, Brendan? She's already pretty sloshed."

"Good ale never hurt anybody." Fagan took a long draught of his own before looking at Ginny steadily. "Now, tell me what you're doing here."

"I already did. I have decisions to make, and my house was too lonely."

"So you came to the worst boozer you could find?"

"The liveliest. Seemed most likely I'd find companionship here."

"Jesus," Glenning said.

"Miss Landry, you are going to get into serious trouble if you keep this up. You choose the wrong fellow for 'companionship,' and you just might wind up in an alley somewhere."

"You think I can't take care of myself?"

Fagan's gaze inspected her once again, slowly. "I'm sure you can, under ideal circumstances. This is far from ideal. Finish that drink and I'll see you safe home."

"Good idea." Glenning took a big gulp of ale. "I have a feeling in my bones trouble's brewing. I'd better get back to Betsy."

"You sure about that, lad?"

Glenning rolled his eyes. "If she goes into labor while I'm away, I'll never hear the end of it."

"I suppose not."

Glenning flicked a glance at Ginny. "You need help?"

"Definitely not."

Glenning drained his glass and got to his feet. "Nice meeting you, Miss Landry."

"You too. Good luck with your new baby."

Glenning nodded and went out. The atmosphere at the table changed. Ginny raised her eyes to Fagan's.

"So you think you can handle me, do you?"

"Aye."

"A confident man. I like that."

"Too bad I'm not ugly, as well."

"An awful pity."

He knocked back more ale. "Perhaps you could contrive to overlook my physical appearance."

"Well, now, that would be difficult, Officer

Brendan. Very, very difficult."

"What is it you have against handsome men?"

"Can't trust 'em. With a homely man, now—what you see is what you get. Warts, scars, broken teeth and all."

"Ah."

"A man with a face like yours could be hiding anything." She sipped some ale and licked the foam from her lips. "A face and a body like yours...pure deception."

"I see."

"Plus I've always thought ugly men to be just a little more manly."

She could see, by the way his gaze kindled, he didn't like that. "You saying I'm not manly?"

"No, not that. I could never say that, Officer Brendan. That's not true of you." He had to be one of the most masculine men she'd ever met; it came off him in waves and prompted all sorts of sinful thoughts in her mind.

"I'm not sure what to make of you, Miss Landry."

"Don't call me that. Especially not here—the name has evil connotations."

"So it does. Virginia, then."

"Not that, either." She wrinkled her nose. "My mother gave me that name—one of the few things she ever gave me besides life. But it's woefully inappropriate. Can I confide in you, Officer Brendan?"

"If you must."

"I must. I truly feel I must. The name Virginia is so...virginal. And I haven't been that since I was sixteen."

Did he look shocked? Hard to tell; he had a good

poker face.

"Well, now, your secret's safe with me. Finish your drink, and we'll get you home."

"So soon?"

"I want to get you away out of here without any trouble."

"We haven't finished our discussion. Will you call me 'Ginny'?"

"Would you like me to?"

"I really think you should."

"Ginny," he said, and the way it sounded on his tongue—all warm and honeyed—made the heat flare inside her.

They stared into one another's eyes. "You sure you can handle me, Officer Brendan?"

"Utterly sure."

"Let's find out." She hooked a hand behind his neck and drew his mouth down to hers.

Chapter Thirteen

Holy mother of God.

The words stuttered through Brendan's mind as he fell into a pit of fire, darkness, and flaring heat. He considered himself by and large a practical man, his wild streak well disciplined. But now desire tore through him, so hot it instantaneously threatened to dissolve his control.

He'd kissed a lot of women but never one like Ginny Landry. Her soft lips molded to his, wooed, and seduced them apart. Her tongue, a daring thing, speared into him; her flavor, potent as whiskey, went straight to his head.

Dangerous? She was far beyond that.

And he didn't care. She'd come looking for a man, so she said. Sure and she'd found one.

His heart pounded in his ears as they strained together across the grubby table. When his brain went on sabbatical for lack of air, she finally let him go. Not far—just so she could look into his eyes.

"Oh. My. God."

Did the words, spoken aloud this time, come from her or from him? Her, he thought. He gazed into her eyes—deep brown and dancing with light. Mischief and desire enough to start him breathing again.

"Let's get out of here," he told her.

"Yes."

They arose from the table as one. She gravitated to him the way iron flew to a magnet, coming hard up against his side and wrapping one arm around his waist. Her head at his shoulder, he guided her out into the night.

"Now, then, let's try that again." He backed her up against the building, just as any tramp might a doxy, eager to explore this thing between them. Deep, unplumbed, erotic—he'd never felt anything like it.

Much better without the table between. She pushed right up against him, snaked her arms around his neck, and rubbed hard.

A woman who knew what she wanted was Ginny Landry. She wanted him—despite the fact that he wasn't ugly.

He dove into her, searched the hot depths of her mouth, and set his hands to roving. Strength lay beneath her dress, lurked in her slender back, and flexed in her buttocks. Strength and softness—a beguiling combination. He bet she'd be a tiger between the sheets.

"There, now." He ended the kiss with reluctance. "Still think I'm not up to handling you?"

"Um." Her mouth reached for his again. He held her off.

"Not so fast." With an effort, he resisted. "You're drunk."

"I *was* drunk. Not anymore."

"Eh?"

"Whatever this is between us has sobered me." She licked her lips again, and he felt it all the way down his body. "What is this between us?"

"Lust?"

"I've felt lust before. Not like this."

She was right. This was unexpected, unwelcome. Undeniable.

A boisterous group exited the tavern, nearly jostling them aside.

"Come on," he said.

They ran, her hand in his, off into the dark. As the noise and brightness faded away behind them, wildness gripped his heart. The dual pounding of their feet echoed, and she kept up with him till they reached a street corner, where she paused, laughing.

"What?" he asked.

"This is fun."

She moved once more into his arms. This time he buried his hands in her hair while he kissed her. It came loose in his fingers and streamed down her back.

"Gorgeous. You're gorgeous," he gasped.

"So, unfortunately, are you."

"It's dark here. Maybe you can overlook it."

"Take me home. I'll leave the light off in my room."

"You sure?" He tried to fight back the waves of heat and think clearly. "That's a thing that can't be undone."

"I'd like to undo you. Right out of those clothes."

Out of his mind, no doubt.

She ran her hands down his body, over his stomach, and lower to cup him through his trousers. "Can't deny you're ready."

"I won't deny it. And you?"

Only a few buttons on her bodice separated him from warm flesh. He conquered them with shaking fingers and thrust his hand inside. He could feel her heart hammering through her breast as she pebbled against his palm.

Her breath hitched. "Hurry or I'm going to climb you right here on the street."

"That wouldn't do. It wouldn't do at all."

They ran again, still hand in hand. Good thing he knew the city so well, because all his logic and control had flown away. On some level, his sense of direction still operated.

He hoped they didn't meet a policeman. How embarrassing would that be, she with her bodice flapping open and him so hard he could barely run.

They turned onto Linwood Avenue and stumbled to an immediate halt. Ginny Landry swore. "My house!"

Brendan took in the scene with professional eyes. A crowd of onlookers. The police he'd hoped to duck. A fire wagon and several lost-looking steamies on the sidewalk.

Ginny drew her fingers from his and flew forward. He followed, assessing the damage.

Not as bad as it might be. The flames had been extinguished, and only a lazy plume of smoke arose from the rear of the house. Looked like a lucky escape.

But Ginny might have been inside.

Heart thumping, he joined her where she'd engaged the police officers, both of whom looked at him, startled.

"Brendan."

"Harry, Stan. What goes on here?"

"Arson," Harry announced grimly. "Neighbors called it in pretty quick. There's not a lot of damage."

"Is everyone all right?" Ginny touched one of the

steam units on the arm. "Millie? No one hurt?"

Hurt? Or damaged? Brendan wondered.

"We are all right, miss. Gus was singed while attempting to put out the fire."

"Gus?" Ginny called. "Where are you?"

A blackened unit trundled forward; Brendan almost thought Ginny would embrace it. It made no reply to her as she fussed over its damaged finish.

He stepped forward. "That will wipe right off, sure." He demonstrated using the sleeve of his shirt. "See?"

"That's good. How valiant you were, Gus! How courageous."

One of the firemen approached. "All the damage was confined to the rear entryway. Some smoke in the kitchen, but that's it."

"Thank you," Ginny told him. "Thank you all."

She certainly seemed sober now—every bit of it. Almost like a different woman.

"Miss Landry, we're just about finished here," Harry told her. "Just let me take a statement from you as to your whereabouts." He glanced a bit doubtfully at Brendan. "Then we'll be on our way."

"Very well. Will you come in?"

Brendan laid a hand on her arm and addressed one of the firemen. "You sure it's safe inside?"

"It is now."

Ginny led the police officers in through the front door, and Brendan followed, trailed by all four steamies. The interior of the house smelled heavily of smoke.

A close call and no mistake. What if Ginny Landry hadn't decided to go out on the town?

The steamies bustled about, the one Ginny had called Millie trundling off to the kitchen. The officers finished their business, nodded at Brendan, and left.

"Oh, hell," Ginny said. She turned troubled and very sober eyes on Brendan. "Somebody wants me out of here."

"It would seem so."

"And that makes me feel stubborn, all the more determined to stay."

Why didn't that surprise him? "Well, now, there's no sense taking foolish chances."

"I'm in a pickle. I need to make some decisions about my mother's property before I leave the city. That's why I went out tonight. I needed time to think and figure out what to do before I'm away for good."

Away for good. A sick feeling settled in Brendan's gut.

"Want to tell me? I've a decent head on my shoulders. Maybe I can help."

She began to pace the room. "I've had an offer for my mother's interest in a hospital down on Ellicott Street. From the Automaton Liberation League."

"I see."

"On one hand, I don't want to keep anything my mother touched. Except maybe this house. Why'd they have to hit the house?"

"Because it was easy. And threatening. We'll get to the bottom of it."

"You think so?"

"I do."

"I could have lost my steamies. They're so—so innocent. So well meaning. They don't deserve to be harmed on my account."

"On your mother's account," he corrected softly. "Very little of this is to do with you."

"Yet if I fail to make the right decisions, the city will go up like a tinderbox."

"Well, you don't have to make any decisions at this very minute." He went to her, caught her shoulders between his hands, and halted her pacing. "Listen, if you're afraid to stay here tonight, you're welcome to come back to mine."

"Afraid? Me?" A smile crooked one corner of her mouth.

"Perhaps I misspoke."

"Your place, eh?" Heat flooded her gaze. "Tempting."

"Well, then."

"Officer Brendan, I'd still like nothing better than to get you out of those clothes and then lick you—slowly—up one side and down the other. It's going to happen. But I'm afraid it won't be tonight."

Brendan struggled to hide his disappointment. "Why?"

"How can I leave the steamies here alone?"

He ran his fingers up her spine. "Let me stay here then." Rarely did he ask; rarely did he need to.

"Not too discreet, is it? Everyone's seen you here." Damn.

"I'll feel uneasy leaving you here on your own."

"Not to worry. I have my steam cannon."

"Thank God."

She pressed close against him for the third time that night, tipped up her face, and engaged his eyes. "If we say our goodbyes, that means I get to kiss you good night." Her lips, warm and alive, claimed his. The last shreds of his sanity flew away. How long the kiss lasted he never later knew. It seemed like forever. And not long enough.

"When?" he asked her raggedly—all he could manage.

"Soon. It better be soon."

"Fine, that. I'll find a potato sack."

She looked askance.

"To wear over me face."

Chapter Fourteen

"This is Lily Michaels. Lily, this is the lady of whom I spoke to you—Dr. Landry's daughter."

Ginny shuddered inwardly. How she hated that label! She gazed, fascinated, at the woman who stood before her, who looked like precisely that—a woman.

Indeed, no signs indicated she might instead be a hybrid automaton. Almost too beautiful, she had a wealth of golden hair and stood a few inches beneath Ginny's height. A complexion of ivory and roses, ice-blue eyes, and a form both well-curved and slender in all the right places completed the picture.

Lily offered her hand. Her skin felt cool and dry, not unpleasant.

"Mrs. Michaels," Ginny said. "It is 'Mrs.,' isn't it? Mr. Ballister did say…" Ginny's gaze moved to the man who hovered at Lily's back. Big, broad, and in his mid-twenties, he had brown hair and worried brown eyes.

Lily turned. "Yes, Miss Landry. This is my husband, Rey." She smiled charmingly. "I do love that word—'husband.' "

The man placed his hand on Lily's shoulder and said, "I didn't like the idea of Lily coming to meet you on her own. I wouldn't like her upset." He had a deep, gravelly voice. Ginny wondered if he'd be a nasty customer in a brawl.

"Nor would I," she said as graciously as possible. "Mrs. Michaels, I'm grateful you agreed to see me. I hoped we might have an opportunity to become acquainted."

"All right, but I'm staying," Michaels said.

"Of course. You're very welcome to stay."

Michaels relaxed marginally, and Ginny's curiosity flared. What made a man fall in love with an automaton? She saw how beautiful Lily was, but it took much more, surely, than that.

"I reserved you a table here in the corner," Ballister said, leading them farther into the tearoom where he'd arranged the meeting. "Miss Landry, would you like me to join your discussion? If not, I do have other business."

"No, Mr. Ballister, that's fine." She glanced around the tearoom; no one seemed to pay the least bit of attention to them. "Thank you."

Ballister smiled, nodded, and took off. Ginny indicated their table. "Shall we sit?"

They did so, Lily moving with grace that outshone her plain ivory cotton dress. The waitress came to their table, and Ginny ordered tea for three before she caught herself.

"I'm sorry," she said as soon as the waitress walked away. "Mrs. Michaels, can you drink tea?"

"No, nor eat any food. Fortunately, Rey eats enough for two. Do you not, my love?"

Michaels gave her a look of pure adoration.

Ginny cleared her throat. "I wanted to meet one of my mother's…well, her creations."

"You were curious." Lily stated it calmly.

"Well, yes, I can't deny I was. But I'm also

attempting to make decisions about the disposal of her estate. She seemed to have her fingers into many things."

"Like an octopus," Michaels grumbled.

"Yes. I hoped you might be able to help me clarify a few things in my mind."

"Me?" Lily spread fragile-looking hands. "I'm just an ordinary automaton going about her life."

The statement set Ginny back on her heels, robbing her of speech.

"I am very sorry for the loss of your mother," Lily went on. "No matter what she was to me, she was your mother."

"Would you mind telling me your opinion of her?" Ginny asked, wondering if a hybrid automaton was actually capable of forming an opinion.

A slight shudder shook Lily's body. For an instant her face and eyes went blank. Michaels put his arm around her. Very carefully she said, "Dr. Landry, as you have noted, was my creator. As such, I must be grateful to her. Had she not fashioned me, I would not be here and would never have met Rey."

Ginny looked at Michaels again, a question. He returned a defiant glare.

Ginny drew a breath. "I don't blame you for feeling hostile. Mr. Ballister told me some of what happened—not all. Please know I am not my mother. I never knew her. My father and she parted ways when I was very young. I went with him when he moved out west."

"Why?" Lily's innocent gaze robbed the question of any nosiness.

"Why did he choose to move away? I think it was

in an effort to distance himself from her. But he always wished for adventure. I've a measure of that urge inside me also."

"I meant why did they part ways? Why would she allow herself to be parted from her child?"

"I know only what my father told me. He says he realized almost immediately they shouldn't have married. She never wanted to be a mother. From what I can gather, she was obsessed with the notion of virginity and detested the sex act."

Mr. and Mrs. Michaels exchanged a look. "Well, then," Michaels huffed.

Lily folded her hands on the table. "Miss Landry…"

"Call me Ginny, please."

"Ginny, I am the only surviving member of Landry's Ladies who did not participate in your mother's murder. Perhaps that is why Mr. Ballister chose to introduce you to me. It might be uncomfortable for everyone involved, introducing a woman to her mother's killer."

"You…did not participate? May I ask why?"

"I was in a coffin at the time. The coffin was in a grave. Rey buried me in order to protect me."

"I see," Ginny lied. Things became muddier the more she spoke with Lily Michaels. It was impossible to fathom this warm, charming woman wasn't in fact a woman.

She decided her mother truly had been a genius—if one conspicuously lacking in heart.

"Ginny, before coming to Buffalo, were you aware of the manner of your mother's death?"

"Yes, Mr. Ballister informed me in his first letter."

But it felt far different being here, seeing one of her creations and imagining it.

Michaels spoke huskily. "I was there that night and saw it all. You have to understand, Miss Landry, the Ladies acted in their own defense. Dr. Landry threatened to shut them all off. That's like death to them."

"Mr. Michaels, I'm not here to accuse or blame anyone. I have problems to solve and, quite frankly, don't know how to go about it."

Michaels scowled. "Then you're not here looking for revenge?"

"Absolutely not."

The waitress arrived with a tray bearing three cups, a teapot, and a plate of dainties. Michaels chafed visibly till she left, when he spoke again.

"Because you see, Miss Landry, when this Mr. Ballister asked us to meet you, we thought maybe you'd come to stake your claim."

"Claim, Mr. Michaels?"

His worried brown eyes met hers directly. "After Dr. Landry died, the Ladies all believed—hoped—they were free. We didn't know she had an heir. Now that you've turned up, does that mean they have an owner again?"

Ginny felt like she'd been punched in the gut. She eyed the couple before her—so visibly bonded it made her ache—and tried to imagine how it must feel fearing the person...being...you loved most in the world might be declared property. Desperately, she sought for a way to reassure them.

"I'm no expert on the finer points of the law, and Mr. Ballister has proposed nothing definite about repossession of the hybrid units."

"Yet you've inherited everything that belonged to your mother."

"Yes. But I assure you I want no part of owning anyone. Mr. Michaels, news travels slowly to the Dakota Territories. My father and I were appalled when we learned what Candace Landry had been doing here in Buffalo, even though he knew she'd had an interest in such research back before they parted ways. He says she was obsessed with what she called feminine purity and had spoken about alternatives to prostitution. But my father had no idea of the extent to which her research had progressed. And I had no idea till Mr. Ballister told me that she'd actually constructed hybrid prostitutes."

She met Lily's pale blue gaze. "I understand she forced you and the other units into that service."

"Yes." Lily toyed with the cup in front of her. "It was not supposed to matter to us, you see. We were not supposed to mind, because we had no feelings. But we were also created to learn and adapt. The truth is we learned to mind being touched by strangers and being expected to perform lewd acts."

"Don't talk about it," Michaels growled. He both looked and sounded like a guard dog, but Ginny didn't blame him. Something about Lily made her, too, feel protective.

"Of course you minded," she said. "No one could meet you and expect you not to mind. I'm so sorry."

"It is not your fault." Lily lifted her chin. "And I always say it was worth it because that is how I met Rey."

Ginny exchanged a speaking glance with Michaels.

"I understand. How many of you—former Landry's Ladies—are there?"

"Twenty-three of us remain. There were originally ten built, then a second batch of ten, and a third."

Building so many units, Ginny thought, would require a lot of corpses.

"Some were destroyed in the fire at the Crystal Palace. A couple were out of service before that—one had been shut down for disobedience. I have a good life now. I am married, and Rey has a fine job. I read a great deal. Rey and I are attempting to adopt a child."

"I heard something about that, yes."

Rey spoke. "There's a lot of feeling against it. Folks think it's not right for machines to be in charge of raising human children. But half the big houses in this city have steam servants as nannies who bring up the kids. So what's the difference? Anyway, I've seen the way children live in these orphanages. Almost anything would be better."

"Do you think your attempt to adopt will be blocked?"

Rey flicked a glance at Lily. "I think we have a chance, if only because I'm human. I'll probably have to end up applying to adopt in my name with Lily listed as steam nanny. It's not right, but..."

"I don't mind," Lily said. "Rey took me to see the orphanage. There was this one little girl in particular. Miss Ginny, she weeps every night for her dead mama. She needs a mama and we need a child. It is only right."

Ginny's throat closed. "I hope you succeed. If there's anything I can do..."

Michaels gulped some tea and said, "To be frank, we thought adopting was our biggest problem, till you turned up. Now, Miss Landry, you could scuttle the whole thing—our adoption and our marriage—if Lily's declared your property."

"I don't want that." Ginny reached across the table and covered Lily's hand with hers. "As I've told you, I'm only here to tie up Candace Landry's business. I have no interest in…in disrupting anyone. I promise I will do my best, through Mr. Ballister, to have you legally declared free."

Once more Lily's pale gaze met hers. "Truly?"

"I do so promise."

"And what of the others, Miss Ginny? After the night Dr. Landry got killed, most of the Ladies and members of the Irish Squad paired up. They'd like to adopt too, but it'll never be allowed, not with feeling so against steamies as it is right now. Perhaps if you declared them free, as well…"

"Of course. Mr. Ballister described to me something of your struggle for liberation." She lowered her voice. "In fact the Automaton Liberation League has made me an offer for my mother's interest in the charity hospital on Ellicott Street." She looked at Lily with sympathy. "I understand that's where you"—she waved a hand helplessly—"came from."

"Really?" Lily brightened. "I've always wanted to learn more about the woman who first possessed my skin, eyes, and hair."

"Girl," Rey corrected. "She was just a beautiful girl."

"I would like to know her name."

"I should have access to the hospital records. I could look through them and see if I can make sense of anything. Of course, there may be no list of the women my mother chose to...that is, we may not be able to identify her."

"I understand. I would appreciate any information you can find, Miss Ginny."

"I'll do that as soon as I can. And as I say, I will speak with Mr. Ballister about having you declared legally independent. Give me your address. If I discover any relevant information, I'll drop it by."

Michaels pulled a paper and pen from his pocket and printed out the address with laborious care.

"We just moved," Lily said, "and have a lovely new flat with plenty of room for a child."

"It's in what's beginning to be known as 'steamie town' to the human residents of the city," Michaels said. "Some of the Irish Squad bought there, and now others have gravitated to the area also."

"Are there many automatons living on their own?" Ginny thought of her own four units refusing to leave the security of her house on Linwood.

Michaels folded his arms. "Mostly just hybrids, for now, but they're bringing more and more regular steam units along with them. They've been forced to buy some—those living in the worst circumstances—and have then liberated them. Others run away from their owners. They go into the underground or come to us. That's all I'm going to say."

"Ah. And, Mr. and Mrs. Michaels, may I ask your opinions as to what I should do about selling my interests in the hospital to the Automaton Liberation League? If I do sell to them, do you think it will cause a protest and even more ill feeling among the human population? The last thing I wish to do is add to the discord in the city."

Lily leaned toward her across the table. "You must follow your conscience. It is a special capacity possessed by humans. All my reading has told me so. The outcomes of many crises rely on the rule of conscience."

"Yes, indeed." Ginny hadn't spent much time following her conscience, even though her father—in his own generous and loving way—was a slave to his. *Anything at any time* had more or less been her means of operation. "Thank you, Mrs. Michaels, for being so generous and kind as to meet with me. I value your opinions, and I'll take up no more of your time."

Lily was right; she, not they, needed to make these decisions.

Rey Michaels stood up, drawing Lily with him. She wound her arm around his waist. Ginny rose also.

"You won't forget?" Lily asked. "To…liberate me?"

"I'll speak with Mr. Ballister about it just as soon as I can."

"Thank you."

"No, thank you again for meeting with me." Ginny once more offered her hand. To her surprise, Lily left her husband's side and stepped forward to embrace Ginny. She smelled sweet, and Ginny could feel the heat in her thorax.

"Do not—as they say—be a stranger," Lily bade.

"I won't."

They gathered themselves once more to start away, and on an impulse, Ginny begged Rey Michaels, in a whisper, "Take care of her."

Fierce brown eyes met hers. "You can bet your life on it."

Chapter Fifteen

"Another murder—the owner of one of the steam laundries this time." Captain Addelforce tossed Brendan a look. "Word is the man was a real tyrant to his workers, most of which were steam units. Seems he used to hire humans exclusively but realized he could run the steam units round the clock and be as abusive to them as he chose."

"A real prince, eh?" Brendan knew he wasn't expected to give his opinion of individuals with whom he came into contact, especially victims. But he hadn't slept well the last few nights—ever since running into Ginny Landry at that tavern, in fact—and the last thing he needed was another grisly murder scene. "Who reported it?"

"One of the human workers. Came running in here like a madwoman." Addelforce flipped open the notebook that lay on his scarred desk. "Name of Ida Flude. Says when she got to work her employer, Mort Gressling, was lying across one of the steam presses with all the steam units gathered around him. He'd been..."

"Pressed?"

Addelforce shuddered. "The body's being collected now. I want you to take someone down there and assess the scene. Interview the steamies, see if you can get them to talk."

Brendan wanted to ask, "Why me?" But a good cop never allowed himself to so much as think that question.

Addelforce must have read his mind. "You're my best man, Sergeant. I need you on this."

"Yes, sir."

"I've just been in touch with Commissioner Messenberg. He's had people besieging his office, demanding we put the automatons down. He thinks there's going to be a riot if we don't get to the bottom of these murders."

"Yes, sir. Any news, sir, about the arson at Miss Landry's home?"

"Someone claims to have seen a steam unit sneaking round back of the house. But since Miss Landry employs four steam units, it may have been one of hers. I've sent a man over to ask them further questions."

And why couldn't he have got that assignment rather than the flattened corpse?

He nodded. "Any of the Irish Squad on duty, sir? I'd like to take one with me. Sometimes the steamies open up better to them."

"Check the roster. I think Dempsey's on."

"Will do."

He found Kevin Dempsey sweeping out the jail yard. A big man, like all Mason and Charles' victims, he had sandy hair and mild brown eyes.

"Murder scene, Kevin," he said briefly. "Will you come?"

"Anything for a fellow Irishman."

****

"Now that is an ugly scene and no mistake."

Dempsey spoke judiciously, and Brendan lifted his eyebrows at the staggering understatement. They'd arrived just as the coroner prepared to lift Gressling from the place where he'd died.

"Never seen anything like it, myself," said Ben Rail, the coroner. "To tell you the truth, Captain Addelforce said he'd be sending someone over. I waited so you could see."

Brendan blew out a breath. The pressing machine, monstrous in size, had been cranked open to reveal the body of a middle-aged man with graying hair. He might once have been overweight. Impossible to tell for sure, now.

"Cause of death?" he asked, feeling foolish for asking.

"I'll need to determine the exact cause at my laboratory. You can see his sides burst when the machine clamped down on him. He's also burned, but I doubt that killed him. All a matter of timing. If the machine came down fast, I'm sure his lungs ruptured. If it came down slowly…who knows?"

"Jaysus, Mary, and Joseph," Brendan whispered.

Rail had the nerve to look amused. "You can see many of his organs have been pushed out the sides." He pointed. "That's his liver, what's left of it." He clasped Brendan on the shoulder. "You have a strong stomach, Sergeant. I don't think many men could look at that and not lose their breakfast."

"Lucky for me I had no breakfast. Where's the woman who reported the murder?" He pulled out his notebook and consulted the page. "Ida Flude?"

"Here, Officer." The woman, tinged decidedly green, scrambled up from the floor and came over.

"Kevin, would you mind speaking to the steam units? See if you can find out what they saw."

"I will, sor."

Brendan drew Ida Flude aside, away from the pressing table, where Rail and his helper had begun the removal.

"I understand, Miss Flude…"

"It's Mrs., though I'm a widow. If I weren't, I wouldn't have spent the last eight years here."

"Mrs. Flude, I understand you found the body."

"Well, yes. When I got here this morning." Her eyes flicked wildly. "But I wasn't the first, was I?"

"I beg your pardon?"

"I mean the steamies must have found him first, right?"

"Do they usually arrive ahead of you?"

"You don't understand. They live here. Day and night. They have nowhere else to go. If Mr. Gressling had the orders, he made them work all night."

"I see." Brendan thought furiously. "But you were the first human to arrive today."

"Yes."

"And no one was working?"

"Well, that's just it. The first thing I noticed was the quiet. That hardly ever happens here, with all the machines running. No," she corrected herself, "the first thing I noticed was the smell." Mrs. Flude wrinkled her nose. "I'd never smelled nothing like it. You can still catch a whiff now."

"Aye, I can smell…something."

She leaned closer. "Like seared pork. Bacon."

Brendan's empty stomach turned over. He loved bacon. *Had* loved bacon.

"Was the presser cold when you came in?"

"You think I went close enough to tell? Went anywhere near that…that? It smelled hot in here, but it always smells hot in here."

"Well, what did you see?"

"At first I just seen the steamies standing all in a circle, like, around…around the presser. They were in the way. I couldn't see him. Then I came in a few steps, called out to one of them, 'Hey, what's going on here?' And I saw…him."

"No question he was already dead when you came in?"

Mrs. Flude choked.

"Sorry, ma'am. I have to ask."

"He was…was like that. Some of my fellow workers…humans…came, and I made them stay outside."

"Good work."

"I asked some of the steamies what happened. *What happened?* None of them said anything."

Brendan stole a look at Kevin Dempsey, speaking steadily to one of the units.

Mrs. Flude lowered her voice. "Do you think they killed him?"

"No way to say, ma'am."

"The thing is, I know them all. There's not a bit of harm in any of them. And he treated them so badly." Mrs. Flude's eyes filled with tears.

"Did he, ma'am? How so?"

"Look at me—crying. But not for him. He was one mean son of a bitch, if you'll excuse my language."

"Was he abusive to the units?"

"He was abusive to all of us. Tell me, Officer, do

you see so much as a stick of furniture in this place? A stool where a woman might sit down for one blessed minute? Sixteen hours a day I worked here—rain, shine, sick or well. And not an instant's rest.

"But Mr. Gressling had a special hatred for the steamies. Never left them alone and nothing they did was ever good enough. He denied them maintenance and then complained they were too slow. If they got injured—everyone got injured here—he battered them for it. I know they don't feel pain, but…"

Brendan glanced at Kevin again. "Mrs. Flude, did they mind? The steamies, I mean."

She gave him a thoughtful look. It was no ordinary question, and he guessed she tried to decide how much to say. "Well they're stoical, aren't they? Never say much. I think that's what made it so awful. But yes, I think they did…mind. They're not as unfeeling as people like to say."

"Do you think they—or any among them—had the ability to turn on their owner?"

"I would have said no." Again she lowered her voice. "But then there was them Ladies that turned on that doctor woman, wasn't there? I'd have said ours were all gentle. But something very nasty happened here last night."

The coroner and his assistant had wrapped Mr. Gressling in a tarpaulin and shuffled him out the door. Brendan glanced at the gory presser and told Mrs. Flude, "Why don't you go home and get some rest?"

"But, Officer, what will happen here? Will this place stay open?"

"Not today."

"What am I to do for work?" She pressed a shaky

hand to her mouth. "I'll never make the rent."

With real sympathy, Brendan said, "I'm sure I don't know. Try not to worry. Maybe someone will take this place over."

She nodded and went out. Brendan crossed over to Kevin.

"Officer, did you learn anything?"

"Many things, Sergeant Fagan. I have written it all down."

"Are the units willing to talk to you?"

"Some of them are. Some seem to have partially shut down. Those say nothing at all. I still have a few to interview." Kevin paused. "Several of them are severely damaged. They have had no repairs yet were expected to perform their jobs."

"Yes, that's what Mrs. Flude said."

"One told me his hand got flattened in that selfsame presser. The deceased called him clumsy and left it there until all the joints were burned out."

"An unpleasant man and no mistake. Do you think one of them killed him?"

"They say not. They say they ran out of work and he put them on standby. When their timers restarted them this morning, they found him like that."

"Do you believe them?"

"Yes. They are not capable of lying."

Brendan, not so sure about that, said nothing.

"When they found him," Kevin went on, "they did not know what to do. They gathered and waited for instructions."

"Found him? Surely they knew he was dead?"

"That is uncertain. Sergeant Fagan, these are very basic models, most of them, and in poor condition.

They lack a higher unit's ability to discriminate."

"Would you like my assistance interviewing the others?"

"I believe they will speak more freely to me."

"Then I'll just wait for you, shall I?" Brendan glanced at the presser and away again. "Terrible stink in here, though."

Kevin smiled. "Fortunately for me, Sergeant Fagan, I have no sense of smell."

Chapter Sixteen

"Only three more streets," Ginny muttered to herself as the tram rumbled slowly to a halt, belching steam. Then she could get off and walk the rest of the way to the house on Linwood. It felt like a long ride home from her meeting at Phil Ballister's office, where she'd gone to request he draw up plans to dissolve her interests and ownership in the surviving Landry's Ladies. To free them all.

She hated the tram, which lurched and swayed, threatening to make her lose the contents of her stomach. To Ginny it seemed to epitomize the things to which she objected about life in the city—dirt, noise, and overcrowding by rank humanity.

Well, humanity and steam units. A number of the latter rode along with Ginny and the human passengers, most looking like they were out on errands for their owners. One stood in the aisle next to Ginny, who shared her bench seat with a large woman holding a sleeping baby.

It would have been faster had she taken a steamcab home. But she detested those even more than the trams. Darting everywhere far too quickly, cutting off pedestrians and other vehicles, she considered them a menace.

She should have hired a horse-drawn cab but hadn't seen one, and the tram had stopped right there outside Ballister's office.

Her thoughts broke off as the tram, still stopped at the corner, suddenly rocked violently. Several people in the car exclaimed, and the baby next to Ginny woke up.

"What was that?" Ginny asked the woman.

"I don't know. The—"

The car rocked a second time, far more aggressively. The steam unit next to Ginny, a large silver model, swayed and banged into her seat. Someone screamed, and the baby in the woman's arms began to wail.

A man near the front of the car got to his feet and pushed up toward the driver. "What's happening, driver?" he asked. "The tram should have left the stop by now."

Before the driver could reply, people all around Ginny began to exclaim, "Look, look! Oh, my God, look!"

She leaned across the large woman and peered out the window. Now, at late afternoon, the descending sun glinted off something silver. Here, there…there again…all around the tram car.

She felt a bump, hard, on the outside of the car, and it swayed again, mightily.

"They're trying to push us over! They're going to kill us all!"

Ginny leaned into her neighbor's lap and pressed her face to the window. She saw steam units, a veritable chain of them, each one beside another, shoulder to shoulder, surrounding the tram. She stared into the molded silver face of the one right outside her window. It had its arms extended, braced against the tram, its very expressionlessness terrifying.

She heard the tram driver exclaim. Seated about halfway down the aisle, she couldn't see him very well, but he sounded alarmed, and fear gripped her throat. If the steam units pushed the tram over, people—and an awful lot of metal—would go flying. With the big steam unit beside her, she could be mangled or crushed.

She glanced at it as the tram rocked again. The steamie steadied itself, using the bar that ran up from the floor beside her seat, and gave no outward sign of alarm.

The tram shuddered, and the floor beneath Ginny's feet began to rise. The car seemed to teeter on the far wheels before crashing back down onto the street with a force that rattled her teeth.

The passengers screamed. Ginny's neighbor cried, "Oh, my baby!"

"Cuddle him against you like this." Ginny wrapped her arms around the woman, holding the wailing infant close.

The tram tipped the other way, and everything inside shifted. Ginny's neighbor was thrown against the window with Ginny on top of her. The large steam unit, perhaps pressed by others, came pushing in. She was going to die, crushed here, no breath in her lungs.

That thought exploded into her mind before the left-side wheels crashed back down into contact with the street. A terrible roaring filled her ears; it took her a moment to realize it came from outside. The attackers pounded on the skin of the tram and cried out in dozens of mechanical voices.

The woman seated just ahead of Ginny began weeping hysterically. The tram rocked again.

This time she felt cool metal fingers catch and

steady her even as her neighboring unit pressed against her.

"I beg your pardon," it clicked in a deep voice.

"Can you make them stop?"

The tram crashed back down, and she heard a dual whoosh as the mechanical doors opened. Her heart leaped into her throat.

The silver units would come in. They would…

She had only a poor view of what happened next. A glint of silver—arms?—and the driver was hauled from his seat, down the steps, and out the door.

Everyone screamed.

The baby next to Ginny wailed at deafening volume. Its mother had turned milk white. "We're all going to die."

Were they? Damn it all. She hadn't even slept with Brendan Fagan.

As if her thoughts had conjured him, she saw a flash of blue outside her window. Not him—it couldn't be him—but the police had arrived. In fact, it appeared a full-fledged riot had erupted in the street outside.

What if Ginny's neighboring unit, as well as the others onboard, decided to join in? What if every steam unit in the city did? The human population would not stand a chance.

Yet her metal neighbor continued to steady her gently as the tram rocked once more, less violently this time.

"They're moving. They're moving away," the baby's mother gasped.

"Thank God."

It took a good ten minutes for the police to clear the units away from the tram. All that time—which seemed much longer—the interior of the car continued to heat up. The woman in front of Ginny had stopped weeping and slumped forward. Ginny wondered if she had fainted.

Eventually a police officer appeared at the rear door, which still stood open, and shouted, "I'd like everyone to exit. In an orderly fashion, please."

"Is it safe?" a man boomed. "Are those vicious mechanicals gone?"

Vicious mechanicals? Ginny wondered what her silver guardian thought of that. Did it think? She had no time to decide; a stampede began.

Everyone wanted off the tram at once. They exited both fore and aft—or attempted to. The aisles, already full of standing passengers, mostly steamies—immediately clogged, and the screaming resumed.

"Off! I want off," Ginny's neighbor wept, tears running down her face.

"I can't move," Ginny told her.

The steam unit beside them turned its head. For an instant the molded metal depressions that served as its eyes met Ginny's gaze. It stiffened its back and held off the pressing crowd.

"Go," it told them.

She squeezed past, so close she felt the heat from its boiler, knowing it could kill her if it chose. Instead it helped, waiting till her seatmate also pushed past to move. She led the woman with the baby the few short steps to the rear door and down into the street.

The scene outside did not look much better than that inside the car. People milled everywhere, passengers and onlookers alike. Here and there a silver steam unit had been pushed over. Water ran from them like blood. Police made a strong presence. Ginny stumbled away, her arm around her neighbor.

"All right? Is the baby all right?"

"I don't know. I think so. He's still hollering."

So he was. "Do you need help getting home?"

"No—it's just up there—my mother's house. I was on my way... Oh, I've never been so scared."

Neither had Ginny. Her heart still pounded, and her legs threatened to give way beneath her.

She looked around, trying to spot the steam unit that had maintained its station beside her. She wanted to thank it but couldn't catch a glimpse of it anywhere.

When she turned back, the woman with the baby had gone, swallowed up by the crowd as if she'd never existed.

Ginny stumbled back from the thick of the crowd and up a walkway, where she sank onto the stoop of a stranger's home. She put her head in her hands.

That was no better, for now she could hear everything. A stream of competing conversations, the shouts of the police, and a persistent pounding. No, that was inside her head.

"Miss? Are you injured?"

She looked up into the face of a police officer—not Brendan Fagan. What were the odds he'd find her here? Suddenly she wanted him to, so much it frightened her.

She wanted him.

"Miss, do you need an ambulance? They're on the way."

"No. No, I'm...all right."

"Will you give a statement? You were on the tram?"

"Yes. I didn't see much."

"Name?"

"Virginia Landry."

Did he do a double take? Hard to tell. He scribbled in his notebook rapidly.

"I was on my way home. The tram had stopped at the corner. It—it just started rocking. They came from nowhere…"

"Yes, miss. Give me your address. Someone may want to speak with you later."

She rattled it off. "Officer, there was a steam unit on the tram—it protected us, me and my seatmate, who had a little baby. They're not all bad."

She thought of her steamies back home, earnest and concerned for her comfort.

The officer's expression did not change. "You sure you're not hurt? Do you require assistance getting home?"

"No, I…just need a minute."

He went away. Ginny lowered her face back into her hands, wishing the rest of the world would follow him.

Chapter Seventeen

"Miss Landry? Ginny?"

Brendan's heart had seized in his chest when he caught sight of the familiar figure crouched on the stoop of the house on the corner. Hunkered down tight, she seemed to have curled in upon herself. The demeanor—so at variance with what he knew of Ginny Landry—frightened him.

She'd been on that tram which had very nearly gone over in a rush of fire and steam. She might well be hurt.

He'd battled his way over as soon as he caught sight of her, and posed his query in a voice that barely sounded like his own.

She looked up at him. Dark eyes burned in a chalky face. Half her hair had tumbled down, and her expression stopped his breath again.

Dropping to his knee beside her, he asked, "Are you hurt?"

"No, I—just shaken."

"Are you quite sure?" He put his arm around her. Not strict protocol, but at the moment he didn't care. She'd almost been in the middle of a riot. When human pedestrians on the street had started beating off the chain of steamies bent on tipping the tram, it had very nearly spiraled out of control.

She leaned into him. It felt so blessedly right that

for an instant he couldn't focus on anything else.

"Funny."

"What's funny?" he asked; he couldn't imagine.

"I was just sitting here wishing for you."

"Were you, now?"

"Yes. And you c-came." Tears filled her eyes. She blinked them back. Shaken but still not the sort to weep, this one. "How did you find me in all this?"

"Chance. Luck. Fate."

Her gaze met his, and heat kindled impossibly. Not here, not now, he told himself.

"Hold up a bit. I'll get someone to see you home."

"I can go on my own. Just getting some strength back into my legs. I'm sure everyone's needed here."

"I am not after letting you walk on your own, not given who you are."

"You think they'd attack me?"

"God knows what could happen. Those units may have dispersed, but we're not sure how far they've gone. We're still trying to take statements. Can you hold tight?"

"Will you be able to see me home if I wait?"

Damn it. He wanted to but didn't know if he could manage it. "I'm not sure."

The door behind them opened. A steam unit stood there, along with a woman.

The woman said, "Miss, would you like to come in? I saw what happened…"

Brendan helped Ginny up. "That would be most kind, ma'am. I will call for her as soon as I can."

"Come inside, my dear. Roxie, prepare some tea."

The door closed. Brendan sucked in a breath. Off the street, at least, and out of the chaos. Would she recover her usual spunk?

Hoping so, he turned away and plunged back into the mess.

****

Hours later, or so it seemed, Brendan returned to the house on the corner and rang the bell. His shift had expired sometime in the midst of the insanity. Night had fallen, and he expected Ginny to have given up on him and left her temporary shelter. But when the steam unit ushered him into the woman's parlor, he saw her ensconced in a chair, looking somewhat restored.

She sprang to her feet and set her tea cup aside when she saw him.

"Officer," said the woman who kept her company in the parlor, "is everything resolved outside? We had another policeman come and take our statements earlier, but Miss Landry here wished to wait for you."

Brendan looked at Ginny. "I'm that glad you did."

She cleared her throat. "I waited as—as you asked."

And when had Ginny Landry ever been so obedient? He had a sudden vision of her lying beneath him, obeying his every request, and despite his weariness he rose to the notion.

"I'll see you home now, if you wish."

"Oh, yes. Mrs. Howell, thank you so much for your hospitality. I can't tell you how grateful I am."

"I'm only glad I could help. Such a terrifying spectacle. Officer, I hope you and your colleagues have everything in hand."

"Yes, ma'am."

Ginny moved to Brendan's side and caught his arm, pressing tight against him. They went out into the

September evening.

Evidence of the near riot still lay all around. Puddles of water, shards of metal, a residual police presence. Brendan turned Ginny away from it all and up the nearest side street.

"I'm that relieved you waited for me."

"Are you?"

"Oh, yes. I'll have you home in two shakes. It's not far."

"I know."

He measured his steps to hers and caught her when she stumbled. She must be even more exhausted than he.

"That woman was very kind. Imagine taking in a stranger."

"People can be kind," he agreed.

"There was a steam unit beside us on the tram. It was kind too. I wish I knew what happened to it." Her voice roughened. "Oh, Brendan, I was so scared. And I pride myself on not scaring easily."

"I know that."

"How? How do you know?"

They stopped walking. Brendan couldn't explain that he seemed to know her even though he barely knew her. "I just do. Come on. Your place is up here."

A light shone from the parlor window, and a steam unit opened the door as they approached, the one Ginny called Millie.

"Miss?"

"Oh, Millie, there's been an…incident. Sergeant Fagan saw me home."

"Dinner awaits you, miss. Will you dine?"

"I'm not sure…" She turned to Brendan. "Are you

hungry?"

"I am, a bit. Don't remember if I ate since breakfast."

"Then that would be wonderful, Millie. We'll dine."

Millie bustled off, and Ginny turned to face Brendan. "That is, if you can stay. I didn't think…you must have duties."

"Fact is, I'm off duty now."

"Good." She moved into his arms and laid her cheek against his chest. His heart began to thud. "I need…"

So did he but doubted it would happen this night.

"Ginny, I near fell down where I stood when I saw you there. Why were you on that tram?"

"Coming back from Mr. Ballister's office. Listen, I want to go upstairs and change. These clothes are filthy."

"Go on, then."

"Wait for me in the parlor. You will?"

"Sure."

"Promise?"

"Ginny, I'm not going anywhere."

He realized, as he went into the parlor, just how much he meant that. He didn't want to leave this woman.

Ever.

Alarming—this had never before happened to him. A consistent love-'em-and-leave-'em sort of fellow, he'd managed to keep himself remarkably unencumbered—except that first time with Ruella, and he'd even wiggled out of that with no hard feelings in the end.

Ginny returned to the parlor wearing a yellow blouse and a brown skirt, her hair all loose on her shoulders. "Millie says dinner's ready to be served, if you'll step in."

He followed her to the dining room, a narrow but pleasant chamber with a high ceiling. Casually elegant, it made him acknowledge the distance between them. She came from money, he from struggling immigrants.

Yet the way she looked at him made nothing of that. Nor did her smile when she said, "I'm so glad you're here. But I should have given you a chance to wash up first. Floyd, please see Sergeant Fagan to the water closet."

He came back a few minutes later with hands and face scrubbed, hair wetted down, and having shed his uniform jacket.

"Thank you, Miss Landry. That's better."

"Ginny. You're supposed to call me Ginny."

"Aye."

She inspected him minutely from across the table as one of the steam units began ladling soup. "So can you tell me what happened back there?"

"Not sure." He went for his glass and hesitated when he saw it held only water.

"Floyd, please bring Sergeant Fagan whiskey, if there's any left. Me too."

One of the units hurried off. "Thank you," Brendan said with real gratitude.

"You're off duty. And you need it; we both do."

"Aye. As for just what happened back there and why—it seems like an act of pure aggression."

"Planned or spontaneous?"

"Must have been planned for so many units to be in

the same place at the same time. I spoke with Pat Kelly, who's more or less orchestrating the Automaton Liberation movement. He says he had nothing to do with this, and I believe him. This was a rogue action."

"Troubling."

"I should say so. If this sort of violence happens again, the city may spin out of control."

She stirred her soup but didn't sip any. "If there are riots, you could get hurt."

Their gazes met across the table. "As you very nearly did," he returned.

"Brendan, it was so awful." She laid her spoon aside. "The woman next to me had a little baby. He screamed and screamed."

"Aye."

"And in the aisle right next to us was that big steam unit I told you about. I thought he was going to fall on us. But he ended up helping us instead."

"Are you sure you're not hurt?"

"A few bruises, that's all."

"Do you need to see a doctor?"

"I'm the daughter of a doctor. I know what to do for bruises."

They fell silent. Brendan concentrated on eating his soup.

Eventually Ginny said, "I've never been in the middle of anything like that. When I was very small there were sometimes troubles on the reservation. But nothing so…personal."

"Indians, you mean?" he asked with interest. Oh, the life she'd led!

"Yes. My father married a Sioux woman. My stepmother's been very good to me."

"Only imagine." Brendan laid down his spoon. One of the steamies whisked his bowl away and replaced it with a platter overflowing with food. "You have good staff."

"Yes I do." Ginny smiled at the nearest unit. "I value them highly."

"I always wanted to get my ma a steamie to help with the backbreaking labor of keeping a big family. Now that I might be able to afford it, there's less need. All but two of us are moved out on our own. Och, but"—he shook his head—"that woman worked hard. My da, too."

"They taught you to work hard. I admire that."

Did she mean she admired him? Or did she just make conversation while she pushed her food around on her plate, not tasting a morsel?

"Look, Ginny, you're exhausted. I should leave."

"I wish you wouldn't. I really wish…"

He waited for her to finish the thought, but she gestured at the steam units and let it trail away.

"Eat something," he advised the way his ma might.

"I don't think I can."

"You'll be sorry if you don't. You've had a shock." He desisted as she lifted the glass of whiskey Floyd had brought and drank deep.

"This is what I need."

Brendan frowned.

"Don't look at me that way, Sergeant. I'm s-safe in my own home." She hesitated over that word, perhaps wondering if she really was.

Brendan applied himself to finishing his meal. The steamie offered dessert, which he refused, and Ginny towed him off to the parlor, where she once more moved into his arms.

"Stay the night."

Everything within him flared—protectiveness and desire in equal measures. "I cannot. Better not."

"Please."

"You're tired, and I…"

She kissed him, not the kiss of a woman teetering on the edge of exhaustion. This kiss contained dominance and pleading all wrapped up in dizzying passion. He could taste the whiskey on her tongue, and a whole lot of woman.

"Ginny, I…"

"Stop talking. Can't you come up with a better use for those lips?"

"Several." Enough to last a whole night. "But I don't suppose you're thinking too clearly right now. And I don't have my potato sack with me."

"Oh. There may be one in the kitchen. Or I think— I really do think I'm growing accustomed to your distressingly extreme handsomeness. I truly believe I could overlook it for one night."

The last three words came accompanied by kisses feathered over his lips.

Oh, hell.

"There's a bed waiting upstairs. And I don't think I've ever been more ready for a man."

"You should really rest tonight. You should—"

"I don't want to be alone tonight." She shivered. "Brendan, I don't."

Fecking hell. What to do now? Here she stood, warm and willing in his arms, so willing it felt as if she might just crawl up him. He threaded his hands through her hair, drew her head back, and kissed her—really kissed her, the kind of kiss that made no secret of his desire. When it ended he said, "It's probably a mistake. A travesty. A terrible blunder." He knew that going in.

"I don't care."

"You should."

"Maybe. Maybe not. Are you so regimented you've never followed an impulse?"

"Ah, now, don't start all that again." He'd show her regimented. Did she think he couldn't throw caution to the wind and make her plead?

She smiled, and mischief flooded her eyes. Just as if she could read his mind, she whispered, "Show me."

Carrying her up the stairs, he never hesitated.

Chapter Eighteen

"Take off your shirt." Ginny barely recognized her own voice. She sounded drunk even though she'd had only half a whiskey. Could a woman get drunk on a man?

Brendan had deposited her on her bed and now stood gazing down at her. He smiled crookedly. "I can do that, sure."

He pulled his shirt from his uniform trousers and unbuttoned it.

All the breath left Ginny's body. She groaned, "Oh, sweet lord. Sweet leaping Jesus dancing on a tree stump!"

He laughed, tossed away the shirt billowing like a sail, and sketched a rough bow. "Glad you like what you see."

"Like?" A broad chest well-sprinkled with reddish hair. A well-muscled stomach leading the eye down to…

Mercy, she might not survive if he shed his trousers. Might not want to survive. Dying here and now seemed a good bet.

His hands moved to his belt. "I'm still not sure this is a good idea."

"Hush."

"Not that I don't want it. I want it fine." He gestured to himself. "I expect you can see that. But I don't think…"

"Hush, for God's sake."

"Ginny." He put one knee on the bed. She reached out like a woman going down for the third time, snagged his belt, and pulled him closer.

"Are you going to make me beg?"

The smile in his impossibly blue eyes deepened. "Now, that might be interesting. Would you?"

"Maybe."

"The strong and independent Virginia Landry on her knees. Just imagine."

"Oh, I am imagining."

"As am I."

"You're not a cruel man."

"I am not."

Her lips curled. "Maybe before the night ends you'll be on your knees to me."

"Maybe I will, at that."

"Meanwhile, I'm about to explode here without you."

"Now, that would be a dirty shame."

She tugged him still closer; he knelt on the bed. She unfastened the belt and the buttons beneath—a challenge, given the bulge straining them from within. The trousers came open.

"My God."

"That's what I like, a woman who prays in bed. What else do you do, Ginny?"

Anything he asked. But she couldn't tell him that. "Why don't you try and find out?"

"Not so fast."

Her gaze met his again—hanging, pleading, demanding.

"What about your clothing?" he challenged.

"Take it off."

Oh, how she wanted to feel those hands of his on her—broad hands, strong hands. Everywhere. The very thought made her shiver.

He raised an eyebrow. "You giving me orders?"

"Yes. No. Do you want me to?" she asked hopefully.

He laughed again and reached for the buttons on her blouse. One undone. Two. Three. Ginny forgot to breathe.

Please. This time she didn't say it aloud. He probably already had a big enough head, handsome as he was.

He parted the wings of her blouse. She wore nothing beneath but skin. He half knelt there, devouring her with his eyes while heat stole through her from the roots outward.

She unfastened her own skirt, shucked it and the bloomers beneath, all while she watched him watching her. She wanted so desperately to be naked for him, she couldn't think.

"By God, lass, you're beautiful. Every inch of you."

"You going to do something about it?"

"So long as you're sure…"

"Say that again and I'll scream this house down."

This time the smile turned wicked. He kicked his trousers off and came all the way onto the bed, all six-feet-plus of him. Their mouths met, clung, and meshed with a hunger that very nearly tumbled Ginny over the edge.

She moaned, the only available form of

communication. He understood and positioned himself between her thighs. Hot, so hot. She wanted to devour him, wanted him to devour her.

But this time, this first time, they couldn't wait. Their bodies fused as their mouths had, hungrily, blindly, wordlessly. Pure bliss flooded Ginny from her fingertips to her toes, accompanied by searing heat. Stabbed through with aching pleasure, she was burning up and loved it.

She climaxed quickly, strongly, shatteringly, and didn't at first realize he'd withdrawn before finding his own release. They held each other, breathing deeply of one another's scents, Ginny's heart hammering out of her chest.

"Why didn't you stay inside me?"

"Do you want my bairn?"

Maybe. The unspoken answer shocked her. She wanted everything about this man. Each drop of him.

"Anyway"—he kissed one corner of her mouth— "that was just for starters."

"Good."

"I did not even get to taste these lovely buds on your breasts. I'm meaning to spend a powerful length of time over them."

"Yes?"

"As well as this gorgeous neck of yours." He pressed an open-mouthed kiss just beneath her jaw. Ginny's pulse accelerated alarmingly.

She might not survive this night. Thanks be to heaven.

"Promises, promises, Sergeant Fagan."

He laughed low and husky before he lifted his head and their gazes met. "You will learn about me, Ginny. I always make good on my promises."

"Prove it."

He laughed again, and Ginny's arousal spiked, fierce. "Aye, but first—I need a towel or somewhat, to clear away the evidence."

"Just a moment." Very deliberately, she ran a finger over her own abdomen, where he'd released himself, and placed it in her mouth. Her eyes widened. "Delicious."

His gaze kindled. "Ginny, by God…"

"Here, use this." She fished for and found her bloomers. "Don't take too long."

****

"I love the way your hair smells." Brendan's face had come to rest among those fragrant tresses after the last time they made love. Now Ginny lay cuddled close against him, with his head on her pillow. He'd never done this with a woman before. Never.

Usually he got straight up, put on his clothes, and got out of there before things became complicated. Now, though, he couldn't think about that, only about touching her, kissing her, tasting her.

What a wild woman she was when aroused. She'd been all over him from stem to stern and not ashamed of how she enjoyed it, either.

A woman in a thousand.

"Umm?" Half asleep, she stirred. He should let her rest but didn't know if he could.

He told her, "And you taste good too, some places more than others."

"As do you. I've never had Irish before."

That set him to wondering about the men she had been with. He didn't like the idea. He'd never been possessive about women, but now he heard himself growl, "A variety, was it?"

"You know it was. I never tried to hide that."

He frowned. The room had gone dark, the candle guttered long ago. He spread his fingers across her breast and played with the nipple.

"God," she whispered. "God, it seems I'm not done praying." She kissed him hard and fierce. "All you have to do is touch me and I want to explode. No, all you have to do is look at me."

Good enough. The past was the past. Now was now.

"Not tired of me yet?" he half teased.

"Not hardly. I haven't yet seen you on your knees."

"That's only because the candle went out. It happened a while back." He ran his fingers down to the damp curls between her legs. "Remember?"

"That's eternally seared on my memory."

He hoped so.

"Not but"—her voice hitched as he slid one finger inside her—"I wouldn't like to experience it again."

"Imagine that." He kissed his way down her body, and she opened for him with a frank eagerness that had him enflamed. A lot of women didn't permit this. It happened to be his personal favorite.

Sated as she was, it took a measure of time for her to quicken—he had a wondrous long while to indulge himself, relishing the scent and flavor of her before she convulsed around his tongue. He could have let her rest then, but she made it clear she wanted him inside her, so he slid into her silken heat. Mouths joined, they swallowed one another's gasps.

"I think," she said raggedly then, "I think I may be

getting over my prejudice against handsome men."

"Cured you, have I?"

"I seem to be on the mend. No doubt I'll need a few more treatments."

"You think so, do you?"

"At least once a night for the next week." She stretched her body against his like a cat.

"And what after that, lass?"

"After that, I'll probably be able to get back to Dakota."

Brendan froze.

She shifted a little. "I can't wait to get shed of this city."

Did she truly mean to walk away as if this meant nothing? As if they meant nothing? Fecking hell.

"Uh," he stammered, "Buffalo's not so bad. Good place to bring up a family." And what had him thinking such a thing? He'd never done that before, either.

"You must be joshing. With all the unrest? Those murders and what happened today? There could scarcely be a worse place."

"Aye, I can see how your experience today—yesterday—would make you say that. But by and large…"

"I'm no city girl. I'm used to wide open spaces. I'm anxious to see my father and stepmother, and all my friends."

Brendan swallowed what felt like a knot of pain. "Do you have a special fella out there?" Of course she would. A woman this beautiful and passionate would have those rustic westerners all over her. Frontiersmen, probably. With rifles.

But she answered, "No. I tend not to take these

things seriously."

Ah, God! Fine that—now she had him praying.

This was no doubt the punishment his ma had oft predicted for what she commonly called his philandering. Not that any of the women with whom he consorted ever complained. Of course, that was probably what Ginny thought about him—that he was fine with a casual physical relationship. No strings.

For the next week. Until she left for good.

What man in his right mind wouldn't jump at that? Him. *Him!*

There had to be some way he could get her to stay.

He cleared his throat. "Aye, but surely you'll settle one day."

"Why? Because I'm a woman? Brendan, 'settling' implies—well, settling. Accepting what you can get because you can't get better. I won't do that."

"And nor should you." But was he second best? He liked that idea even less than the thought of all the other men.

He stirred in the bed. "Where's me uniform jacket?"

"Downstairs, I think." She stretched luxuriantly. "You're not leaving already, are you?"

"I need to work, come morning."

"Damn."

He kissed her, something for her to remember.

"Umm," she purred appreciatively. "You'll come back later tonight, won't you?"

He said nothing. He shouldn't. He really shouldn't.

"Brendan?"

He wanted her to beg again. Not proud of it, but there it was. "What, lass?"

"You'll come back? Please?"

"Well, since you ask so nicely." Feck, he was lost.

"What time does your shift end?"

"Six o'clock."

"Come straight away. Come for dinner. You'll spend the night?"

He fought a war with himself and quickly lost. "I will."

She scrambled up and whispered in his ear, "I only hope I can last till then."

Chapter Nineteen

"Fagan? In here."

Brendan stumbled obediently into Addelforce's office in response to the summons. Two days had passed since he'd first made love to Ginny Landry. Two days and as many nights steeped in pleasure so intense he never seemed to completely lose the effects. He'd thought about keeping away from her but couldn't, even though he knew she probably only used him to occupy her time until she could kick the dust of Buffalo from her heels.

He moved through his days thinking only of her, trying to come up with ways to convince her to stay. So far he'd thought of nothing viable save an offer of marriage, and he wasn't that desperate.

Yet.

"Yes, sir?" He had to pull himself together and start thinking straight. Addelforce likely wanted to know what he'd found out about the tram incident. Witnesses insisted a single steam unit had provoked it all. None would admit to knowing to whom that unit belonged or from what local business it might have come. All agreed it had incited the other units already present to attack the tram as soon as it halted at that stop.

The gathered units who had participated in tipping the tram denied anyone had summoned them. All claimed to have been in the vicinity for legitimate purposes, even though most had assignments elsewhere.

Jesus, why couldn't he think?

"Sergeant Fagan, I've been hearing rumors about you."

The last words Brendan expected from his captain's mouth.

Mouth. He'd spent at least an hour last night exploring the inside of Ginny's, a sweet cavern of heat, sharing searing kisses, and as a consequence now knew it as well as his own.

"Rumors, sir?"

"Now, I don't like hearing gossip about my officers. I don't appreciate that at all."

"No, sir." His half-blasted mind darted wildly. "What rumors might these be, sir?"

"That you've been spending your nights with Candace Landry's daughter."

Damnation. That hadn't taken long.

"Yes, sir."

"Yes what, sir?"

Brendan stiffened his spine. "Yes, Captain Addelforce, it's true."

Addelforce stared, his mouth gaping. "Sergeant Fagan, I'm flabbergasted. Of course I understand you're a young man. But if you need to…er…exercise your urges, I would expect you to be more discreet."

"I feel I have been discreet, sir. Were the young woman in question not a figure of some infamy, I doubt the matter would have come to your ears."

"But Sergeant Fagan, she *is* a figure of some infamy. Becoming involved with such a woman displays poor judgment, very poor judgment indeed. I expected better of you."

"Aye, sir. It's only that good judgment rather goes out the window when—when…" He relived the sensation of Ginny's tongue sliding through the hair on his chest and heading downward. He lacked words.

Addelforce sighed. "I understand. But Brendan, this is unacceptable. I advise you to break it off. At once."

"Sir—?"

"I do not want to hear it, Officer. You know very well this job is more than a job. Sacrifices must be made."

"But—"

"Sergeant Fagan, an association with this woman—a personal association—could be construed as a bias in this conflict amidst which we find ourselves. Her mother…"

"Sir, she can't help who her mother was."

"Sergeant Fagan, this association is not good for your career. I cannot put it any more plainly than that. You've worked very hard, son, and are on the fast path to advancement. Don't muck it up for a woman."

"No, sir."

"I wouldn't like to resort to disciplinary action."

"Disciplinary?" That made him mad. "For what?"

"Compromising an investigation."

"Take me off the investigation then."

"And what of the evidence you've already handed in? If the automatons get themselves a good lawyer…" Addelforce grimaced. "I hear they've already approached Theodore Collwys. He may take the case."

"Yes, sir." Brendan had made the acquaintance of Mr. Collwys. A fair man, he just might.

"So are we finished here, Sergeant?"

"Sir, I'd like to know who reported me."

"And what purpose would that serve?"

"None, but…"

"None, correct. Be off about your duties."

"Sir, I…"

"Sergeant Fagan, you've never been insubordinate. Do not start now. You're much too smart for that—especially considering it's just a woman. One woman in a sea of thousands. You can find another. Given my wife Alice's opinion of your appearance, you should have no difficulty."

That struck Brendan silent.

"There's been a dispute at Crawford's on the waterfront. Go investigate."

"Yes, sir."

"Dismissed."

Brendan marched back out of Addelforce's office, seething. Whose eyes turned toward him in the big room? Did anyone watch for his reaction? If he found out who'd squealed on him, he'd…

Ruin his career for sure.

His career. Mere days ago it had been the most important thing in the world to him—the only thing.

Maybe Addelforce was right.

****

Ginny sat with her chin in her hand, staring out the front window of her house, chewing on her lip and trying not to panic.

What had she said to Brendan Fagan that might have driven him off? For the last hour—ever since the arrival of his missive canceling tonight's tryst—she'd been busy recalling all the stupid things she'd ever said to him, one by one.

Those utterances now seemed manifold, but one kept clamoring for her attention as the worst.

I've never had Irish before.

Most men of her experience didn't like being compared to other men. And they didn't appreciate the mention of other men during the sex act.

But that had been on their first night together. And Brendan Fagan didn't seem insecure. He shouldn't be, with a face like that and a body like that. *Oh, God, his body.* But his excuse for not meeting her tonight as planned seemed just that—an excuse. And it tore her up inside.

She thought they'd been having fun, enjoying each other to the fullest. She didn't quite understand why his absence bothered her so much now. After all, they'd have to part company soon anyway, when she went home. A matter of days.

But what if she never saw him again? Never touched or tasted him again? A drench of black depression washed over her at the thought. She'd spent her life being determinedly positive, seizing her joys and her opportunities. But never seeing Brendan Fagan again…

Couldn't be helped. It was just the way things went.

Maybe he was wise to break it off now.

Given he had broken it off, and work hadn't merely got in the way of tonight's assignation. Maybe they'd get together tomorrow instead. Earlier than usual. Before evening, so she could see him in daylight. All of him.

"Oh, God."

She got to her feet and began to pace restlessly. She couldn't stand it, she couldn't.

Maybe she should get out of the house, go to a tavern and seek other company.

She discovered somewhat to her surprise she didn't relish that prospect. She wanted Brendan or nothing.

She'd already been on her knees to him, as he had to her, during their lovemaking. She remembered how the light burned in his eyes when she took him in her mouth, how he buried his fingers in her hair and flexed that strong, beautiful body.

Maybe if she went to him and begged...

A fantasy unwound in her mind: she'd go to the police station, find him there all tall and official in his uniform. Disregarding everyone else in the place, she'd sink to her knees in front of him, unfasten his trousers, and...

Sweet lord, she had to get hold of herself, but she didn't quite know how. She'd never dreamed of wanting a man this much.

Even Hank.

That thought knocked her back on her heels. She'd desired Hank, true. He was the one who'd taught her the ins and outs of lovemaking, showed her it could cause a woman's body to tremble, burn, and sing. She'd trusted him with her body and her heart at the mere age of seventeen.

A fatal mistake.

Things had come much too easily for Hank, as to most handsome devils. He'd had no trouble casting Ginny off before moving to the next conquest.

Was that what Brendan Fagan had done?

Damn him.

She never chased men, especially good-looking men. She made a point of that. She wouldn't start now.

Would she?

But she wanted to find him, stare into those impossibly blue eyes of his, and demand honesty. If he wanted to break things off, then do it. Don't lie and blame his job.

Where would she find him at this hour?

She stuck her head into the hall and summoned Floyd. "Call me a steamcab, please, will you? I need to go out."

****

She really did hate steamcabs. She discovered why all over again as she threaded her way through the city at breakneck speed, tossed against one wall and then the other, bouncing off the smudged glass. The interior of the cab stank of perspiration and coal, and the motion turned Ginny's stomach.

"Don't wait for me," she instructed the driver when she got out at the police station. Taking a deep breath, she barreled in.

"I'm looking for Brendan Fagan," she told the desk sergeant. "Is he on duty?"

"Not tonight."

Liar.

The sergeant gave her a sharp look, and she wondered if she'd spoken the word out loud. "Where can I find him?"

The sergeant raised his eyebrows. "Is this official business?"

"Yes. He's investigating the arson at my house. My name's Virginia Landry, and I have new information." If he could lie, so could she.

"Wait just a moment, miss."

The sergeant disappeared into the big room beyond. Ginny walked to the doorway and saw him make straight for Captain Addelforce's office.

Damn.

Stepping into the room, she instantly became the center of all attention. She asked the man at the nearest desk, "Is Patrick Kelly working?"

"Yes, miss. He's out on a case."

Addelforce emerged from his office and gestured Ginny in. Stiff-backed, she went.

"Miss Landry," Addelforce said before she could speak, "I hear you're looking for Sergeant Fagan."

"I am."

"I'm afraid you won't be seeing him again."

Ginny stared. "I beg your pardon?"

"I'm taking him off your case."

"What? Why?"

"I believe it prudent. I've also advised him not to see you again on an—er—unofficial basis."

Ginny flushed. "I don't understand."

"I'm sure you do. I could only counsel him against any association, personal or otherwise, between the two of you. I'm sure you appreciate the sensitivity of our present situation and the unrest in the city at this time. Your association with Sergeant Fagan is a conflict of interest."

"I don't see that."

"The Force does. I'm certain that if you are…er…fond of Sergeant Fagan, you will not wish to do anything to harm his career."

"Of course not. But why should…"

"He is one of my best officers, a light of the

department, with a bright future ahead of him. I expect you would no more want to harm him than touch off an event in Buffalo that could affect hundreds detrimentally."

"Why should what we do privately affect anyone?"

"Because you are who you are—Candace Landry's daughter—and along with her properties have inherited a measure of her reputation."

"That's not fair."

"I didn't say it was fair, Miss Landry."

"Damn it—"

Addelforce's expression hardened. "Miss, I don't appreciate cursing in my office, especially from ladies."

"I'm sorry, but…"

"Go home, Miss Landry. It's not safe for you to be out on the streets after dark. Would you like an escort?"

"No. Yes." Her mind bounded forward. "I would appreciate that."

"Very wise." Addelforce smiled benevolently as if he thought he'd convinced her of his point of view. Damn fool.

He summoned a younger officer, called Gardner, to see her back to Linwood. As soon as they went outside she said to the officer, "Do you happen to know where Sergeant Fagan lives?"

"Uh—" The man hesitated and rolled his eyes at her. "Yes, miss."

"Tell me."

"I can't, miss."

"You most certainly can."

"I don't think Captain Addelforce would approve," Gardner said.

"Officer Gardner, have you ever been in love?"

"Yes, miss."

"Then I'm sure you understand my need to see Sergeant Fagan." She was massaging the truth, but she felt sufficiently desperate now to warrant it.

"Yes, miss. Only Brendan, he usually doesn't settle on one woman."

"Is that so?"

"Maybe I shouldn't have said it."

"It's all right." It went with the territory, when it came to handsome men. "Officer Gardner, in the past he may have known plenty of women." She looked him in the eye. "None like me. Understand?"

Gardner gulped. "Yes, miss."

"He'll be very grateful if you give me his address."

"I don't doubt it."

"And even more grateful if you keep mum about it."

"Oh, heck, miss. You're putting me in a bad spot."

"Think of it this way, Officer. He may not be home at this hour. He may be visiting friends or at his parents' house. Then what harm will you have done?"

"I suppose that's true. He goes to his parents' a lot, so he does."

Ginny's heart sank, but she pressed, "So you might as well tell me."

He gave her a number on Tracy Street. "It's in the rear. But please don't say I told."

"My dear Officer Gardner, I wouldn't dream of it."

Chapter Twenty

"Ginny? For God's sake, what are you doing here?"

Brendan Fagan answered the door wearing a soft, off-white shirt and his uniform trousers. When he saw her, his eyes widened.

"What do you think?" she retorted. Planting her hand in the center of his chest, she pushed him back into the room, followed, and shut the door. Toeing up to him, she stared into his face fiercely. "You lied to me."

Acknowledgement flooded his eyes. "Aye, lass. I am that sorry. I was following orders." The sincere regret in his voice should have mollified her; it didn't.

"Oh, do not try and put the blame on *orders*. Do not! You might have been honest with me rather than sending a message saying you were working."

"I was working; I got off not long since."

"You said you had to work tonight and couldn't see me."

He held up his hands. "Very well so; you are right. I rarely do lie to women. I made an exception with you."

"Why?"

"Come and sit down."

"I'm too angry to sit. Angry and...and frustrated. I was looking forward to our time together. You disappointed me."

"I am sorry."

"I trusted you. And I never trust good-looking men."

His eyes met hers. What did she see there? An emotion she couldn't quite identify.

"I didn't suppose it mattered a great deal anyway," he began.

"Not matter a great deal?"

"Since we would have only a few more days together before you left to go home."

That knocked all the wind out of Ginny's sails.

"Break it off now or a few days from now." He shrugged. "What's the difference?"

She gasped, feeling curiously as if he'd struck her across the face, and backpedaled. "You might have been honest about it."

"Aye, I might. I should."

"Besides, Brendan, we would have had a few more days. A few more nights. I needed that." Furiously, she added, "I need this!"

Without further words, she threw herself into his arms. Her mouth found his in a kiss as demanding as it was deliciously intimate. When she came up for air, she looked into his eyes and uttered the words she'd never imagined speaking. "I need you."

"Oh, God, lass." He swallowed convulsively. "Don't say that. It's as good as my career."

"Why? I don't understand why."

"Conflict of interest."

"That's what that ass Addelforce said."

"You've been to see Addelforce?"

"I went to the station looking for you."

"You shouldn't have done that, lass. I don't doubt

it's made matters worse."

"Explain."

"Someone reported I've been spending my nights with you. 'Tis difficult to claim I can remain objective if you and I are…involved."

"Well, but…"

"Addelforce wanted to take me off the case, and there's a lot at stake."

"So you agreed to break it off?"

He shrugged uncomfortably.

Ginny tossed her head. "So don't tell Addelforce we're still seeing each other."

"Eh?"

"I'll stay here the next few nights. No one will ever know."

"Except the person from whom you got my address."

"A nice young man. He promised not to tell."

"It doesn't matter. This city has eyes. And gossip like this is too good not to share."

Desperate, she stared at him. "Just tonight, then."

"Jaysus, Ginny." He palmed his eyes and turned away from her. "Is it worth it? If I get caught, it could cost my job."

"Brendan, Brendan…" She seized his arms and pulled him back to her. "I'll make it worth it. Just one last night."

"Well, that's it, Ginny." He drew away from her and tossed his hands in the air. "You want honesty? The truth is I don't know if I can do just one night. I don't think I can watch you walk away from me in a few days as if none of this ever happened. And that's why I couldn't tell you face to face. It left me too…too…"

"Open?"

"Vulnerable, aye. I'm never vulnerable with women, do you understand? But you…"

Heat washed over Ginny in a flood, followed by cold. She, who held so hard to her independence, could see his point.

"But Brendan, what's the answer? I certainly can't stay in Buffalo indefinitely." She gulped air. "You haven't asked me to stay."

"That's why I decided maybe Addelforce had it right. This was a mistake from the first."

"A mistake? All that pleasure? All that joy?"

"I'm sorry," he said for the third time. "Best to go before anyone discovers you're here. Before we both get hurt."

Oh, God, oh, God, he was sending her away. It was Hank all over again.

She stiffened her spine. "I am not in the habit of throwing myself at men."

"I know that fine, lass. And I'm that grateful we had what time we did."

"You will regret this."

"I already do. Let me call you a cab."

"No, thank you."

"I'm not letting you out on those streets alone."

She leaned close. "Then you'd better reconsider and let me stay."

****

Not a man to vacillate—usually—Brendan tended to make up his mind and then stick to his decisions. So why did he find it so hard to send Ginny Landry away and have done with it?

Could be the temptation of one more night sharing

passion the like of which he'd never known with any other woman. Could be the way she looked at him, standing there with both challenge and pleading in her eyes.

He suspected, though, it was because he feared if he sent her away now he'd never see her again.

He'd regret it if he let her stay. And if he didn't. And sure as hell he'd get caught out in it by someone on the force. That was just the way life worked.

On the other hand, what had it taken for her to come here this way? What guts and courage! Courage like that deserved some reward. He could think of about a dozen ways to reward her, right there in his bed.

He groaned.

She turned around and slid the bolt on the door.

"If this is it," she whispered, "we'd better make it good."

He caught her face between his hands, drew her up against his body, and kissed her. On her toes, she pressed herself to the length of him in a gesture of surrender.

When the kiss ended, she said, "Anything you want, Brendan. Any way you want."

"Does that mean you'll take orders?"

"Yes." Because she was Ginny, she added, "And give them."

Maybe he'd die tonight and not have to worry about tomorrow. Or the day after. A good result.

He backed a step and looked at her. "Out of those clothes."

She shucked them slowly and in a manner that drenched him with heat, her gaze holding his.

"Now, on the bed."

"On it or in it?"

"What did I say?"

She started for the bed but turned as swiftly back again. Displaying flagrant disobedience, she unbuttoned his shirt and drew it from him before applying her tongue to his skin, down his neck, across one shoulder and back to forage amid the hair on his chest.

"God, you taste so good. I've been craving that ever since last night." Her eyes met his again. "And I happen to know you taste even better down below." She reached for his belt; he gasped.

"Sergeant, may I remove your trousers?"

"You may—minx."

She sank gracefully to her knees. He buried his hands in her hair, closed his eyes, and traveled straight to Heaven.

****

Ginny liked Brendan's bed, and not just because Brendan was in it. Big and deep, it had a feather ticking that threatened to swallow them both. It felt cozy and safe, as if the two of them had found a nest away from the world.

Of course the fact that the bed contained Brendan didn't hurt.

Sometime long after midnight, she stretched and turned once more to him. The light had long since gone out, but she didn't need to see him in order to see him. She found she had every separate detail engraved on her mind: the spattering of freckles across both shoulders. The scar just above his knee he said came from a dog bite. The graceful strength of his hands that had been all over her.

Now he'd fallen asleep. She could tell that from his

deep, quiet breathing. But she couldn't let him waste this night in sleep.

"Brendan. Brendan!"

"Um."

She climbed on top of him, naked flesh to naked flesh, and kissed him. She felt it the instant he came awake, came alive. His hands cradled her, and he began to participate enthusiastically, so warm and intimate there in the dark, so beautiful it made her ache.

When she needed to breathe, she broke the kiss and said, "No sleep, no time for it. We have only this one night."

He went very still.

"Brendan? What is it?"

"I was right. Ginny, I cannot do just one night. I want you forever. Stay with me."

She gasped, the air coming out of her in a squeak. Her mind flitted over it, and for the first time she considered the possibility.

To never go home, never spend her days riding wild on horseback, to devote her life to a man who let his duty rule him.

"Impossible."

Now he asked the question, "Why?"

"What about your career? I'm infamous."

Again he went still. She knew it meant he thought hard. "You're right. Perhaps once we get things settled, these murders solved—once the unrest dies down, if the automatons do or don't get their rights…"

"Maybe then." She tried to see that far ahead and failed. Not one for looking at the future, she'd learned to live in the moment, enjoy what she could hold in her hands. This moment—here, now.

"You can always come back to Buffalo."

"I could." Why did the notion make her feel so bleak? Because she didn't want to come back to this city where the mother she never knew had died? Or because she didn't want to leave Brendan Fagan in the first place?

"The question is"—he threaded his fingers through her hair in that way he had and cupped the back of her head—"will you?"

Yes, that was the question. Once away from all this, back in the Dakota Territory, would the desire for him be enough to call her back again? They had only the desire and this blinding intimacy. He'd said nothing about love.

Did she love him? If she did, wouldn't she be willing to stay—infamy, the demands of his job, and all?

"Brendan," she whispered, "I don't know. You asked me to be honest. I don't want to promise; I don't like breaking promises."

He wrapped her in his arms tight and drew her against him, heartbeat to heartbeat. He laid his cheek against her hair and, foolish wretch that she was, tears stung her eyes.

"Then one more time before it gets light," he told her. "For goodbye."

Chapter Twenty-One

"I've decided to sell my interest in the charity hospital to the Automaton Liberation League." Ginny made the announcement with calm she didn't really feel.

Ballister pushed back from his big desk and eyed her in surprise. "Miss Landry, are you sure?"

An interesting question. She believed she was; she'd done little, in the days since creeping away from Brendan Fagan's door before daylight, but think about it. And about him. She'd not seen the man since giving him a fierce, final kiss at his door and could barely focus for it.

But yes, she'd considered this. To the best of her ability she'd deliberated what her father would do, what he might advise her to do. She raised her eyes to Philip Ballister's troubled ones. "I'm sure. I've made the decision based on conscience. Who am I to deny the hybrids my mother created, along with others like them, a chance to reproduce? My mother created them; shouldn't they have the right to create others if they choose?"

Ballister tapped his lips with his finger. "That's just the question, isn't it? Rights. They are machines, and putting machines in charge of building other machines..."

"They're more than machines, though, aren't they?

I've thought about that also. If they wanted to set up a factory manufacturing mangles or steamcabs, no one would have a problem with it. The very fact that they want to create more individuals like themselves proves they *are* more."

"Which personifies the problem."

Ginny leaned forward. "Look, Mr. Ballister. You charged me with making this decision. Now that I've done so, are you trying to talk me out of it?"

"Not at all, Miss Landry. I'm just playing devil's advocate and informing you that you may feel a backlash for your decision."

She began to tug her gloves back on. "I am aware of that. But I'm anxious to liquidate my holdings and get out of this city." Before she hunted down Brendan Fagan and fell on him like a ravening beast. As it was, she thought—or hoped—she saw him everywhere. Each time her eye caught a flash of blue she thought it a glimpse of his uniform and she craved the taste of him all over again.

God help her, she had to get away.

Ballister went on, "This will not be a popular decision with those speaking out against automaton rights and may well spark further violence."

"Mr. Ballister, the way I see it, anything may spark violence in this city. It's primed like a powder keg." And if it went off, Brendan Fagan would be right in the middle. The thought made her start to sweat.

Ballister fiddled with his pen. "There was another murder yesterday. A man was found beaten to death in an alley."

"By automatons? Anyone might have done that."

"Most such assaults are the product of robbery.

This fellow had a full wallet. And he was well known to employ a number of automatons in a dangerous manufacturing business. Many of them had suffered damage."

Ginny finished donning her gloves and got to her feet. "Do you not see a pattern here, Mr. Ballister? Most of the humans attacked are ones who mistreated their automatons."

"That doesn't make it right, Miss Landry. If a man kicks his dog, should that animal then rip his throat out?"

She leaned toward him and widened her eyes. "In my opinion, Mr. Ballister—yes. Where I'm from, that's called justice."

She went home aching. She wanted to see her father so much it hurt and wanted to see Brendan even more. She wondered where he was now. Investigating the new murder? Addelforce wanted him on that, and Brendan's career meant everything to him.

No, that wasn't fair. He'd asked her to stay with him even knowing what the association would do to his chances for advancement.

He'd asked her to stay with him. His big hands cradling her, his body hard against hers. Oh, God, oh, God, how was she going to stand it?

She paused on the street corner and closed her eyes, trying to recapture the essence of him. What would it be like to live with him every day? To catch his scent, catch his smile…at liberty to touch him any time she chose…

Yet what to do with herself here in this city? She didn't belong. And she didn't think she could ever persuade Brendan to leave.

"Miss? Are you unwell?" A handsome gentleman paused beside her. Or was he a hybrid automaton? She could no longer tell.

"I'm fine, thank you."

"May I call you a steamcab?"

"No, I don't have much farther to go."

She moved on, mostly to get away from the kind gentleman, nothing solved in her mind.

****

"Were you out drinking all night? You look like hell."

Brendan felt like hell. He rubbed his eyes with stiff fingers and cast a look at his fellow officer, Dennis Petersen. "It's these murders, isn't it?" he lied bald-facedly. "Another one last evening."

Bad enough, that. Yet the murders didn't affect him so intensely as did Ginny. Or rather, Ginny's absence.

When he slept he dreamed of her—blow-by-blow and lick-by-lick reenactments of all they'd shared. He feared he might be losing his mind. He told himself he'd made his decision—broken it off with her. He wouldn't go crawling back for one more night.

One more taste.

Lust—his sickness comprised nothing more. But he'd never known such lust as this. Not too surprising, the practical part of his brain informed him. He'd never known a woman like Ginny, who gave herself so completely, who knew not the meaning of restraint or modesty, who demanded and coaxed and...

Oh, Jaysus.

She danced before him. He could almost feel the soft weight of her breasts in his hands, could see the light in her brown eyes. That light usually denoted the imminent occurrence of something wonderfully wicked.

"Brendan?" He realized Dennis had been speaking to him all the while. He'd missed everything but his name.

What if he presented himself at her door, if he went there tonight? Would she invite him in?

Did he want to toss his career down the privy?

Maybe. Might just be worth it.

"...says there's to be a big rally at The Park this afternoon. Every steamie in the city's supposed to be there."

"What?"

"Well, every one that can get away, I imagine. Captain wants us there."

"What time's this supposed to begin?"

"Three o'clock. It's being talked up as a peaceful meeting—the automatons want to find out who's doing all these murders. They swear it's not them."

Well, they would say that, wouldn't they? Although most steamies were intrinsically honest.

"The meeting today," Dennis said uneasily, "is being organized by Pat Kelly. Captain says the Commissioner's talking about striking him from the force."

Pat Kelly off the force? But he'd become the very heart of it.

Brendan remembered the first time he'd seen Pat—when he, Brendan, lay strapped to a cold metal table at the behest of those madmen, Charles and Mason. An impossibly terrifying mechanical, he'd seemed then, with staring green eyes. Brendan had been sure at that moment Kelly represented death walking.

He'd become a friend to Brendan and so many others.

If Pat Kelly got struck off, the Irish Squad might well disband in support of him. The force just wouldn't be the same.

Brendan rubbed his eyes again. "All right, I'll be ready."

"Captain says we'd better break out the steam cannons, just in case. And he's ordered the airship ready for takeoff."

Jaysus!

Brendan wondered where Ginny was right now. He wondered if he should send her a message telling her to stay inside this afternoon. Or he could swing by her house—yes, that was a better idea. Go there in an official capacity, warn her things might get nasty this afternoon. Perhaps she'd ask him to stop back again later when he was free. They could try and talk things out. He might stay the night, and they could...

On the other hand, she might already have departed Buffalo to return home, like she wanted.

Certainly neither he nor anything he could offer her made a good enough reason for her to stay.

That thought stung.

But not enough to make him stop wanting her.

Chapter Twenty-Two

"Miss, you have callers," Millie announced softly.

Ginny, sitting alone in the gloomy parlor, looked up with sudden interest. Brendan? Might he have stopped by after all?

Not likely, since she'd made it clear things between them were over. Only it wasn't over, was it? Likely it wouldn't be till she kicked the dust of this town from her heels.

Impossible to deny, at the moment, that she sat brooding. A bright, beautiful day outside, yet since returning from Ballister's office she'd been sitting here with the draperies closed, an artificial dusk. She didn't want to see anyone.

Well, she wanted to see one person.

"Who is it?" she asked Millie.

"A gentleman called Patrick Kelly, and his wife."

That got Ginny to her feet. "Please show them in. And—and bring tea, Millie, if you will."

"At once, miss."

Ginny crossed to the window and flung the drapes open. Sunlight flooded in, making her narrow her eyes. Pat Kelly's wife, the woman who'd married an automaton. What might she be like?

They came into the parlor arm in arm, Kelly barely recognizable out of his uniform. The woman beside him—tall and with a quietly regal bearing—had strong, even features and soft, light brown hair styled in a loose chignon. She wore a pale green gown and a matching hat with a clever little brim.

They looked like any respectable couple out for a stroll on a fine afternoon.

"Officer Kelly, it's good to see you again."

"Miss Landry." He presented the woman at his side as he might a priceless jewel. "I would like you to meet my wife, Rose."

"Mrs. Kelly." Ginny shook hands with Rose Kelly and met her gaze. What sort of woman married an automaton—even one of Patrick Kelly's caliber? "To what do I owe this pleasure?"

"We wanted to stop in and thank you personally. We've just signed the papers purchasing your interest in the charity hospital on Ellicott Street."

"That was swiftly done." She'd left Ballister only a few hours ago.

"We were anxious to make it official. Actually, the purchase is in my wife's name, as ownership legalities for automatons are still questionable, though I do own my house, as do many other members of the Irish Squad."

"Please, will you sit down? May I offer you some refreshment?"

Still arm in arm, they perched on the sofa, though Kelly said, "We are unable to stay long. We are on our way to a rally at The Park."

"Rally?"

Rose Kelly spoke. "All available non-human citizens of the city are meeting to demonstrate their desire for their rights, and to protest those who blame them for the recent murders. For the most part, automatons are nonviolent. Representing them differently has whipped up ill feeling that should not exist."

"I see." Ginny wondered if Brendan would be at the rally. Of course he would. He'd likely be in the very thick of things. "Forgive me, but you say for the most part automatons are nonviolent. Officer Kelly, you and I are aware of at least one notable exception."

"I believe your mother's death was just that—an exception. I have participated in many of the interviews following the recent murders. Automatons at or near the scenes have denied all involvement. There must be an alternative explanation."

Ginny met his green stare. "Yet, Officer Kelly, I was on that tram car nearly overturned by a crowd of steamies. Can they also be considered nonviolent?"

"A troubling incident and no mistake. I believe it was fueled by the injustices many of them suffer on a daily basis and encouraged by one individual yet to be found."

Millie entered the room with the tea tray. Ginny wondered how Kelly felt about units such as the four under her roof, whether he believed they also suffered injustice.

Politely she said, "I hope you have time for tea."

"I'm afraid we really don't." Rose Kelly glanced at her husband. "We want to arrive at The Park early. Pat is usually the voice of reason at these events. We wouldn't want anything to get out of hand."

"We wish to make a point," Kelly agreed, "not start a riot. I expect a large number of humans to turn up. Things could well grow heated."

"Sounds dangerous," Ginny said. "Maybe I'll just

come along with you."

****

At times like this, Brendan wondered why he'd ever joined the force. Standing shoulder to shoulder with Kevin Dempsey on one side and a second member of the Irish Squad, called McGuff, on the other as they and others formed a human-and-automaton chain of blue sweating in the hot sun, he could scarcely imagine.

Behind him the automatons carried on with their rally, which had so far been marked by speeches, declarations, and a surprising amount of cheering. Cheers, coming from an assortment of steam units that included everything from hybrids to basic steamies so battered they barely rolled under their own power, proved blood-chilling. Even though there seemed no malice in it, it nevertheless raised the hairs on the back of Brendan's neck.

The trouble, if it came, would erupt from the human contingent, part of which he and his fellow officers faced. And Brendan felt in his bones it would come. Already the onlookers threw bottles and rocks, one of which had struck McGuff beside him and bounced off. Fortunately McGuff had no visible damage.

I could have had a job on the waterfront unloading freighters, he thought—a nice safe place to work except when stacks of crates fell over. I could have driven a lorry, delivering coal. Hell, I could have followed in Da's footsteps and been a common laborer. Better than this.

But no, he'd had to reach for something better, a stable job, so he'd thought, with room for advancement. A pay packet always coming in and a measure, however small, of authority.

Stability meant very little at the moment, when he stood toe to toe with a crowd of enraged men, most of them red-faced and shouting, denouncing him and his companions for doing their job.

"Out of the way and let us at those heaps of metal! Let us give 'em what they deserve."

"Why do you stick up for them, copper? You're human like us."

Brendan stood unmoving and contemplated the odds. If the humans stampeded, McGuff and Kevin probably wouldn't go down. He likely would. Getting trampled wasn't a pleasant way to die.

Another bottle flew, so close it knocked off his uniform cap. His temper stirred. He didn't lose it often—an officer couldn't afford to. That didn't mean he never felt anger.

Kevin shifted on his feet and growled, "Brace yourself, Sergeant. Here it comes."

And no mistake. Brendan felt the tension building, like the vibration of a wire, and knew the crowd wouldn't hold long. But the breach in the line didn't come from their section after all. He heard a sudden outburst and cries from farther down to his right. A weapon fired, and the line reacted like a coiled snake in pain. The humans, sensing a way in, charged.

Brendan swore and raised his truncheon. He saw faces and bodies coming at him; voices shouted and roared. He knew the truncheon could break heads—or limbs—and tried to keep from putting all his strength behind it. The wall of humans struck like a tide; the police line went back, and back.

From behind him came another sound. The

gathered automatons left off their demonstration and turned to face the threat. Brendan heard the unmistakable sizzle of more weapons discharging—steam cannon—before somebody spat in his face. An arm raised and lowered. Kevin went down. The crowd of humans surged forward.

Brendan struggled to keep his footing and failed. He had a glimpse of McGuff's face just before he went over backward, hitting his head hard on the ground. He raised his arms to protect his face as the crowd went over him, fending off whomever he could with his truncheon before pain seized him, followed by darkness.

****

Ginny was standing beside the lake, listening to Patrick Kelly speak, when the screaming began and the horror broke out. It came with a roar that drowned the cheers of the automatons around her and made them sound tinny and artificial. She exchanged one speaking look with Rose Kelly before the automatons fanned out around them began to react, some of them swiftly, some turning more slowly on their aged wheels.

Ginny had faced any number of dangers out west: rattlers, angry bears, blizzards. Except on the tram car, she'd never before found herself in the middle of an all-out attack.

Later, newspaper reporters and authorities would try to make sense of what happened. Ginny could have told them that from her perspective there was little reason or intent behind this attack, just pure hate. The breath froze in her lungs, and she drew her steam cannon, almost without thought.

"Behind me. Get behind me." Pat Kelly, green eyes

blazing, dragged both her and Rose to his back. Other automatons, mostly off-duty members of the Irish Squad, stepped forward. The sound of the clash then reached Ginny's ears—metal on metal, metal on flesh and bone. Rose Kelly seized her arm.

"Pat!" she called, sounding terrified. "Pat, Pat!"

He failed to turn; quite possibly he didn't hear her. The roar, deafening, filled the air. Men charged in on them, many carrying clubs. Rose shifted back but, situated as they were at the edge of the lake, they had nowhere to go.

Ginny raised her cannon. "Get behind me," she told Rose, even as Pat Kelly had. The front wave of the human mob bore down on them, and she took careful aim.

She didn't want to kill anyone, but she had to make every shot count. The weapon would take precious moments to recharge, during which they'd be defenseless.

Other steam cannons fired all around. She could hear Pat Kelly hollering; Rose yelled as one of the foremost attackers slammed him in the shoulder with a stick. Pat swayed violently but didn't go down.

On every hand, automatons fell. Rushed by human attackers, units new and old were pushed over; even the crashes they made when they hit the grass were lost in the general wave of sound.

The faces Ginny saw coming at her did not look sane. Twisted in hate, with open mouths and staring eyes, they frightened her enough that she pulled the trigger. As soon as her weapon recharged, she pulled it again.

She and Rose, pushed violently backward, both

toppled into the water.

"Pat!" Rose cried again.

Ginny, sputtering and trying to keep hold of Rose, lost her grasp on her weapon and fought her way up, splashing. She could no longer see Pat Kelly.

"Where is he? Where is he?" Rose cried in terror.

A new sound filled Ginny's ears, battering at her like a giant heartbeat. An airship came overhead, flying low, and she lifted her face to see police officers crowding the gondola.

Brendan? She couldn't tell the identities of the officers, seeing only their blue uniforms.

"Disperse! Disperse!"

Shouted through a bull horn, the word floated over the heads of the crowd.

Ginny, slammed hard by the shoulder of a man who barreled past her, went down again at the edge of the water, taking Rose with her. She found herself staring into Rose's wild eyes.

"Pat! Where is he? I can't see him. Oh, God, I can't see him!"

"Stay here." Pushing Rose down, Ginny scrambled to her feet. The tide, she felt, had begun to turn, chased by the airship, which flew so low its shadow stretched wide. She had one glimpse of two humans pushing a steamie over with a clatter before, like a sea storm, the attack ebbed, leaving a flotsam of ruined steam units and an occasional injured human.

She couldn't see Pat Kelly anywhere, even though he'd been right beside them mere moments ago. Other hybrid automatons limped, one with his arm dangling, through what seemed acres of glittering silver metal. Her breath surged in her lungs.

"Pat!" Rose had disregarded Ginny's direction and appeared at her side. "There."

He looked like nothing so much as a heap of clothing floating at the edge of the water. Rose went splashing into the lake, her skirts kicking up as she bent and embraced him.

Ginny, following more slowly, marked the truth with disbelieving eyes. Pat Kelly's head had been bashed and lay open, the interior metal workings visible to the eye.

Chapter Twenty-Three

"Get in the ambulance, lad."

Brendan ignored Captain Addelforce's direction, though he didn't doubt he needed the attentions of a quack.

His head, which he'd struck hard going down, banged like a drum. He suspected he had several cracked ribs, trodden on by feet big and small, and something seemed very much amiss with his left arm.

No time to worry about that now.

The beautiful green lawn of The Park lay littered with bodies like a battleground—as such it had been. His eyes moved from place to place, marking identities if he knew them and, yes, species if there was one.

Mostly automatons. Piles of silver rubble lay everywhere. Of course the human injured might well have run—or limped—away after the airship came over and broke things up.

Brendan only dimly remembered that, glimpsed while lying on his back with no breath in his body while its shadow went overhead. He didn't recall getting up.

Had McGuff hauled him to his feet?

Addelforce barked, "That's an order."

Brendan let his gaze slide over the captain to the waiting ambulances, most with their doors standing open.

"All full...sir," he said with very little real concern. "Too many other injured to bother about me."

"I know you have a reputation for being strong as a bull..." Addelforce began.

"Just a moment, sir." Brendan's eyes had spotted something over by the lake. He started off at a painful jog.

"Fagan!"

The two women had stretched Pat Kelly out on the ground—Brendan barely noticed them in his rush of dismay. A small group of steamies and hybrids also gathered around him, all battered. Brendan skidded to a halt in the wet grass.

"By God! Is he...dead?" Was that term even applicable to a hybrid automaton? Had Kelly ever been alive?

Now his head gaped open and his blank eyes stared at the sky. Rose Kelly crouched above him, weeping.

"Pat? Pat, speak to me!"

Her companion—another human woman—moved forward and caught Rose in her arms. Only then did Brendan recognize Ginny Landry.

Here? Why was she here?

"Switched off," said one of the other members of the Irish Squad. "His boiler's gone out."

Rose lifted her face. "Can we get him started again?"

Brendan had never before seen Rose weep, and it shook him. She was usually a woman utterly composed to the point of emotionlessness.

"I am not certain," replied the hybrid. "His head is severely damaged. There may be irreparable interruption of his artificial intelligence."

"Pat?" Rose seized both his hands.

Brendan shuddered. "Let's get him up out of here and somewhere safe so he can be examined, right? You there—take his shoulders. You—run and get a conveyance."

The steamie he'd addressed turned sculpted eyes on him. "I have tried, Officer. They say all ambulances are for human use only."

"God damn it. Then get something else—pony cart, dog cart, I don't care."

The automaton moved off. Brendan caught Pat's ankles, the second hybrid his shoulders. They lifted—and a black wall of pain ensued. Brendan went to his knees.

"You're hurt." A voice spoke in his ear. "Someone else please come."

When Brendan's senses cleared, Ginny Landry was pressed to his side. More, she had her shoulder propped beneath his right arm and her arm wrapped around him, her strong body taut.

"You're hurt," she said again. "You need to get to the hospital."

"Bullshit. Pat—"

"They'll take care of him. They know what to do. Let's get you a berth in one of the ambulances."

"Why? Because I deserve it? Because I'm a human—one of the privileged ones?" The words came from Brendan in a burst of resentment.

"No, because you need care. I think your arm is broken." A painful smile quirked Ginny's lips. "My father is a doctor, you know."

"How did you get here? Why?"

"Let's talk about that later. Come."

They humped away over the grass in the wake of Pat Kelly, being carried with Rose at his side. At the road they encountered Captain Addelforce, who watched Pat's train go by before addressing them.

"Miss Landry? What are you doing here?"

"I accompanied the Kellys, Captain."

"Fagan," Addelforce shouted, "this is no time to…"

"Can't you see he's injured?" Ginny went toe to toe with Addelforce. "I'm taking him to the hospital, Captain."

Addelforce's face reddened, but he did not object further. Brendan, swaying on his feet, wouldn't have noticed if he had.

He watched Pat being laid in what looked like a delivery cart before Ginny dragged him off to a waiting ambulance.

"Stay with me," he bade her then.

And she replied, her gaze holding his, "I'm not going anywhere."

If only that were so.

****

"Lie quietly." Ginny's voice came from somewhere above Brendan's head. He sprawled on the seat of a steamcab, though he had no clear memory of how he got there. He felt sick and his mind full of fog. Something wasn't right with his head.

"Where are we going?"

"Home." The interior of the steamcab was dark, but Brendan could hear the wry smile that colored Ginny's words. "That's all you've talked about since we reached the hospital—leaving the place."

"Aye, that's all right, then." He struggled to think.

Why was Ginny here with him? Not but he felt glad for it. "But what's wrong with me head?"

"Concussion. Plus that quack back there gave you a draught for the pain before he set your arm and wrapped your ribs. The arm's broken in two places."

"I raised it to try and protect my face." He began to remember now. "They went over me."

"You're covered with bruises—face, chest, and I expect everywhere else. You won't be working for a while."

"I have to work, damn it. Half my paycheck goes home."

"Don't worry about that now." Did he feel her fingers on his hair? "I'll tell you the truth: I didn't think much of that doctor back there—he truly was a quack— but he did a decent job with your arm. Given some time, I think, you'll heal up all right."

Brendan didn't differ. The daughter of a doctor— two doctors—she should likely know a thing or two. Besides, the motion of the steamcab made him too sick to his stomach to risk opening his mouth again.

"Not much farther," she told him as if she read his mind. Her fingers wrapped around his hand and squeezed. He felt a rush of gratitude for her presence.

The cab pulled over and, mercifully, stopped. Brendan sat up with a grunt and tried to see Ginny's face in the gloom. "I'd appreciate some help getting round back to my place," he admitted. "But after that you'd best leave."

"That may be a problem." She hopped out of the cab. Brendan heard her speak to the driver and waited while his head went around in slow circles.

He poked his head out the open door of the cab and

saw a steam unit, slightly familiar, headed toward him.

Ginny's voice came. "Floyd's going to help you into the house. Then he'll take a message to the station telling them you won't be in for several days."

"I can't stay here."

"You certainly can't stay alone, and it will be easier looking after you here than at your place. At least I'll have my steamies' help."

Brendan struggled to focus on her. Planted square in front of him on the sidewalk, she wore that determined look she sometimes got. "Ginny, it's not..."

"Not good for your career associating with me, daughter of a pariah," she finished for him. "I've got all that. Do you really want to argue about it here in the street?"

"No." Hell, no.

"Then come in." Despite having asked Floyd to assist him, she fitted her shoulder beneath his arm again. "Nice and slow."

"Ginny..."

"The city's in an uproar. No one's going to worry about the personal life of one police sergeant right now."

He quit protesting, mainly because he hadn't the will at the moment to oppose her. Floyd went ahead of them to open the door. Behind them the steamcab pulled away.

Ginny led him into the parlor. "This chair will be best, I think. Most comfortable. There. Millie, please go and make some tea. Floyd, will you ask Gus to prepare a bath?"

The steamies hastened to obey. Ginny sank to her knees at Brendan's feet to unlace his boots.

"What in hell are you doing?"

"Making you more comfortable."

"Christ Jaysus, Ginny. You don't wait on me."

She looked up; their eyes met, and—incredibly—heat washed over him.

"I do if I wish to. And I wish to. You've been a policeman a long time. Haven't you learned to take orders?"

"From you?" He felt battered, exhausted, and aching. How could he possibly also feel aroused? He could barely remember what had happened this afternoon once the crowd went over him. How was it he remembered everything he and Ginny Landry had done together, each stroke, each brush of lips on flesh?

"Why not? I have your best interest at heart."

Brendan might debate that, he really might. She meant to leave the city—leave him. And that definitely wasn't in his best interest. But he didn't suppose it wise to bring that up now.

Don't fight it, lad, he told himself, and relaxed a hair as she hauled off one boot and then the other.

The steam unit she called Millie came trundling in with the tea tray. Ginny leaped up and poured a cup with her own hands, walked to a side table, and added a generous dose of whiskey before she handed it to him.

"There. That will either kill you or cure you."

At the moment, Brendan couldn't say which he preferred. Her company might well prove agony, yet in her company seemed the only place he wanted to be.

"Drink it."

"Another order?" He quirked a brow at her.

"Yes." She seated herself on the sofa, but her gaze continued to touch him everywhere—his battered face, the open front of his shirt with the strapping beneath, his hand holding the tea cup, his eyes.

He sipped the enhanced brew and put his head back against the chair. "Pat—"

"As soon as Floyd comes back, I'll send him to see if he can learn anything."

"What happened, Ginny? Why were you there?"

"I accompanied the Kellys, who stopped here on their way to the rally to thank me for selling them my interest in the charity hospital."

"Eh?" He tried again to clear the fog from his head.

"Don't look at me that way. Having got to know Pat Kelly and some of the others, is it such a surprising choice?"

"Given your mother's identity, yes."

"I am not my mother. I should think you'd have that through your head by now."

"And you want to rid yourself of all her holdings." He glared at her over the rim of the cup. "So you can get the hell away from here."

"I may need to postpone my departure a while."

"Oh?"

"I dare not leave my steamies alone here in this house. Who knows what might happen to them? Plus"—she raked him up and down with her gaze once more—"other reasons."

His heart leaped. He'd begun to speak when Floyd came in. "Master's bath is ready, miss."

"That was quick. Will you and Gus help him in? Make sure to keep that arm dry, mind. And Gus had better stand by to assist him out again."

Brendan protested querulously, "Why do I need a bath?"

"It will soothe your aches. Besides"—she shot him a look—"I want that mud off you, if you're going to be in my bed."

Brendan made no further protest.

Chapter Twenty-Four

"For God's sake, what now? It must be the middle of the night."

Brendan roused himself with difficulty when Ginny spoke in his ear. The combination of whiskey-laced tea and whatever the quack at the hospital gave him had sunk him so deep he hadn't even been aware she lay beside him in the bed.

But in response to a volley of knocking coming from downstairs, she slid out from between the sheets and onto her feet, bending as she did to ignite the lamp. He saw then she was naked—gloriously so—with all that brown hair streaming around her.

Naked. Ah, damn, and he'd missed it.

He tried to move and emitted a groan. In the act of donning a robe, Ginny turned on him. "You stay where you are."

Where he was. In Ginny Landry's house. In Ginny Landry's bed. With or without clothes? A quick check assured him he wore a pair of trews.

She slipped from the room, leaving the door ajar. He pushed himself up on the pillows, groaned again, and looked around the room.

Yellow walls, a fancy bed with rich hangings. He didn't belong here.

God, he hurt. He'd had busted ribs once or twice before, got while breaking up bar fights, but he'd never been hampered by a broken arm and didn't like it. He enjoyed having a big, strong body at peak performance. Being injured would take some getting used to.

He could now hear voices coming from downstairs. With a curse, he slid from between the snowy sheets and tiptoed out onto the landing.

Light came from downstairs. Leaning over the balustrade, he heard Ginny say, "Carry him in here, please."

Carry whom? No question but Ginny sounded distressed. Brendan started down the stairs and reached the bottom in time to glimpse the backs of three men, just leaving.

The steam unit called Frannie rolled past him, its hands in the air. It entered not the parlor but the dining room. Brendan followed.

There an incredible sight met his eyes. Ginny, robe half unbuttoned and hair streaming down, bent over the table. On the table…

Brendan blinked and looked again. A heap of metal sprawled, a mere somewhat cohesive collection of mostly dented pieces.

Ginny looked up when Brendan came in. He saw tears in her eyes.

"This city has gone mad! Just look what they've done to him."

"Eh?" Softly Brendan stepped to the table and peered down. The fact that three household steamies stood around like family members on a death watch gave him the truth.

"Floyd. That's Floyd?"

She'd sent the unit out after Brendan's bath, seeking news of Pat Kelly's condition. Somewhere on the dark streets he'd been waylaid, attacked—damn near destroyed, from the look of it.

Head staved in, shoulders and thorax crumpled—no question but the boiler inside would be ruptured. The condition of the unit's arms and legs argued it had attempted to defend itself. The attackers, though, must have been armed with clubs or steel bars.

A disturbing sight for many reasons. No one liked to see any unit in this condition, plus Brendan didn't like the idea of thugs armed with anything running around his city.

And he knew, at this moment, it was his city; he could tell by the amount of outrage and anger that filled him.

"Ah, lass—that does not look good."

Ginny touched Floyd's head. "My fault. I sent him out to get news about Pat. He must have been on his way home, because a neighbor, pulling up in a steamcab, saw and recognized him. The man and his sons carried him in for me. Oh, Brendan." Her eyes, still swimming with tears, met his. "I never thought. I should have known better than to send him out tonight."

Another truth came home to Brendan at that moment, with a kick like that of an ornery horse: Ginny Landry could not be less like her mother if she tried. Her grief over the wrecked steam unit couldn't be more genuine.

Brendan had met Candace Landry several times in the course of protecting her and the hybrids to which she referred as her property. He'd also met Lily Michaels—only a shade off human, in his opinion. Candace Landry had never displayed so much as a hint of what Ginny clearly felt now.

"An ugly thing and no mistake." Brendan stepped up and touched her shoulder. "But do not blame yourself. You didn't endanger him on purpose."

"Who should I blame, then?"

"The thugs who cornered him."

"I'm the one who put him out there, where they caught him. He was so good, always followed orders." She stood looking down at the ruined unit and her profile grew hard. "You see, Brendan, that's what makes it all so wrong. Who are we, humans, to give them orders? I'm convinced he had a mind of his own."

Brendan glanced at the other three units, which appeared grief-stricken. "Aye, but that does not mean he had a will of his own, does it? Most of these older, basic units are made to obey."

"But I never asked him if he thought it would be safe out on the streets tonight. I should have asked him. After what happened today in the Park—"

She broke off, seeming to grasp the fact that her words might add to the distress of the others. "Do you think he can be repaired? I'll spare no expense." Bitterly Ginny added, "God knows I have the money—ill-gotten gains, if any ever were."

Brendan feared Floyd far past the point of repair but didn't like to say so. "Nothing you can do about it tonight. Let's go into the parlor. I'll pour you a drink."

She seemed to realize for the first time that he stood beside her. "You? You shouldn't even be up out of bed."

"Let's go back to bed then." Suddenly he wanted nothing so much as to hold her close in the dark, provide what comfort he could.

She nodded and walked from the dining room into

the parlor, where she poured herself a large whiskey. Brendan, who'd followed, watched her toss it back in two gulps, followed by a shudder.

She turned and looked at him, her eyes now devoid of tears. "I'm sure he had news of Pat—he'd not have come back without it. But we won't learn what he knew, now. What if Pat's like that? Unsalvageable."

"Not unsalvageable. Even if Floyd can't be repaired, he can likely be rebuilt."

"But will he be Floyd? Will his personality be lost? Just like Pat—no one can say he doesn't have a personality, a wonderful one."

"No one," Brendan agreed softly. "Did you know he saved my life?"

Glass still in hand, she gazed at him, arrested. "He did?" She towed him to the sofa. "Tell me."

Brendan drew a breath and sought to order his thoughts. "Two madmen, Charles and Mason, built Pat and the others who've become members of the Irish Squad—made them to be killing machines that would serve them unquestioningly. Liam McMahon and I got ourselves captured down at their warehouse—do you know Liam McMahon?"

Ginny shook her head.

"When the madmen brought Pat out to show him off, Liam talked him round. Appealed to him as a fellow Irishman—Irish corpses had been used, see, to build the hybrids. Pat and his fellows turned on their makers, much as Landry's Ladies did later, come to think of it. After that, I can't doubt his *personhood*."

"No one who ever met him could doubt it." Ginny ran her hand up Brendan's good arm. "I'm glad he saved you. They meant to kill you both?"

Brendan made a face. "They did and they didn't. They meant to turn me and Liam into hybrids. So I can't say how much of me, Brendan Fagan, would have been left." He gazed deep into her eyes. "Would you still be attracted to me, Ginny Landry, were I a hybrid automaton?" Neither of them could deny the attraction that flared even now between them.

"Like Rose Kelly? Or Rey Michaels? Poor Rose. I can't imagine what she's feeling. I don't suppose we'll find out about Pat, now, till morning."

He plucked the glass from her hand and set it aside. "Come back to bed with me. I can't promise I'm up to much. I just want to hold you in the dark."

She leaned forward and kissed him softly, sweetly. "Not up to much, eh? We'll see."

Chapter Twenty-Five

"Brendan?" Ginny awoke with his name on her lips. Bright sunlight, reflecting from the yellow walls of the room, had coaxed her eyes open. Radiance flooded the space, which meant it must be late; she'd slept in.

They had slept in, she corrected herself hastily. No question but she lay in bed with Brendan Fagan, both of them naked and his body spooned around hers, his good arm draped over her in an attitude of protection.

Oh, God, what a wonderful way to awaken. Her eyes fluttered shut again as she absorbed the sensations: warmth and strength. Comfort, don't forget the staggering comfort. And belonging.

How could she belong with Brendan Fagan? Yet his hand, strong, brown, and spiked with reddish hairs, lay against her belly, just beneath her breasts. And it felt right. His breath, deep and even, kissed her cheek: he still slept.

Was there any better feeling that meeting the new day in the arms of the man you loved?

No, no, no, no. Impossible. She would not allow herself to fall for Brendan Fagan.

But what if it had already happened?

She thrust that conviction from her with desperate haste. She would concede they were wildly attracted to one another. Last night had just proved it over again. Though she'd done all the work—no not work, that, but a fiery, effortless dance.

Still, he probably should have been resting. Yet following Floyd's death…Floyd, poor Floyd.

Her thoughts, even now, flew all over the place, the anger and the passion predominant.

She turned in Brendan's arms and looked at him. Oh, this was the trouble with handsome men. Hadn't she learned her lesson? Did she have to put herself through it all over again? Fool, fool, fool. Yet she couldn't help but caress him with her gaze.

Eyes closed, revealing two fans of brown lashes, he looked at peace. His beard had grown in—redder than his hair—and enticed her to touch. His mop of hair looked mussed. She remembered running her fingers through that last night. She'd also stroked through the fur on his broad chest—a pure delight.

That didn't mean she loved him. One could have passion without love. She refused to get caught, trapped and made vulnerable by her own emotions. She could take what she wanted and leave what she didn't.

Couldn't she?

Yet it didn't look like she'd be leaving Buffalo as soon as she'd hoped; she needed to stay and find out what would happen to Pat. Perhaps avenge Floyd. No reason she and Brendan couldn't enjoy one another while she remained here. If, of course, they could come to an understanding.

The thought of future pleasures bestowed on this man played havoc with her resistance to temptation; she leaned forward and kissed him open-mouthed on the throat.

He opened his eyes.

Oh, to plunge into those blue depths and swim

forever! A dangerous proposition. "Morning. How do you feel?"

He stirred, flexed that big body of his, and moaned. "Like I've been run over by a coal wagon." He blinked. "What time is it?"

"Late. We slept late."

She saw him try to make sense of it. "I'm in your bed. I didn't dream it, then?"

"Dream what?"

"We made love."

"Well, you more or less lay there like an injured king while I made love to you—you endured it, so to speak."

"I'm big on endurance, me. But, lass, you know I shouldn't be here."

"Right. I suppose I've ruined that career about which you're so worried. But too late to change that now."

"Is it?"

"I'm afraid so."

He pulled her against him, bringing her naked breasts into contact with his chest. Ginny half expected him to kiss her then, one of those thorough, searing kisses at which he excelled. Instead he gazed at her, a new expression coloring his eyes. Intent, wondering, it felt more intimate than any kiss could be.

What did he see when he looked at her that way? All her strengths? All her weaknesses? The truth of how she felt about him?

She made a spasmodic movement to escape, but he held her effortlessly, plundering her with that gaze till her heart began to pound and the heat rose in her face.

Only then did he say, "No doubt you're right,

Ginny. I'll have scuttled my career by staying here. But you just might be worth it."

****

Floyd looked worse in daylight. When Ginny came down the stairs, leaving Brendan, at his request, to struggle into his clothing, she found the other three steam units standing around the dining room table staring at the ruined automaton like mourners at a wake. The scene struck her forcibly and brought the emotion up into her throat.

Sunlight streamed through the big side windows of the room, mercilessly revealing the damage. Barely an inch on the unit but had been battered, though the head and thorax looked the worst. A small amount of residual water from Floyd's boiler had dribbled out onto the table. One arm hung virtually severed from the shoulder.

Bad to lose a valuable and faithful servant, worse to see how the other three minded. How could anyone deny steamies had feelings? These four had been together for many years.

A family.

That made Ginny angry, and anger—as her father had all too often pointed out—made her stubborn.

When she could speak, she told the units, "Maybe he can be repaired." She didn't believe it, but it was the only comforting prospect she could offer them.

None of them responded.

"I know it doesn't look good right now. But perhaps we can salvage his intelligence, the part that made him Floyd."

And what would her mother say to that? These had been her units, after all. Not for the first time Ginny wondered about Candace Landry—a stranger to her and yet responsible for half her make-up. From all she'd learned, the woman had been a bundle of conflicting characteristics: brilliant yet merciless. Talented yet ruthless. Had she cared at all about the hybrids she'd created—not units but beautiful beings like Lily Michaels? What would she say if she stood in her dining room now instead of Ginny, surveying the wrecked steamie? "Clear that mess away"?

Tragic and troubling that Ginny didn't even know.

Candace Landry's own units had beaten her to death. Made of her a pile of smashed bone and flesh, in effect not unlike this collection of metal. In her own creations she'd inspired fear—and hate.

In her daughter she inspired dread and doubt, misgiving, and a surge of gratitude at having been raised by her father—funny, warm, steady, and maybe a little too ready to care.

She heard a clatter on the stairs behind her, and Brendan came into the room, still buttoning up his shirt one-handed. He took in the scene and whistled between his teeth.

"Jaysus. Looks even worse this morning, doesn't he?"

"I want to rebuild him, whatever it takes." She made the announcement for the benefit of the steamies as well as her own, because that pile of metal seemed just too obscene.

"Well, now." Brendan shot her a look. In daylight his bruises also stood out far too clearly—on his jaw, his cheek, and on his chest between the still-open buttons. Remorse hit Ginny. She should have let him rest last night. Still, he seemed to have survived admirably.

"Do you know who could repair him, Brendan? Who's the best in the city?"

"The automatons are the best at repairing automatons, but with the way things are right now…"

"It may have to wait." Ginny bit her lip and turned to the other three steamies. "I give you my promise we will have him repaired and restarted if at all possible. Meanwhile, perhaps you could move him to one of the guest bedrooms. And Millie, if you could bring yourself to prepare breakfast, I'd appreciate it."

"Nothing for me, thanks, save a cup of tea," Brendan said briskly. "I need to get to the station."

"But you're on leave. Sick leave."

He ignored her as if she hadn't spoken, still struggling with the button at his throat. "And I want to find out how Pat's doing."

"Yes. Wait for me. I'll get dressed and come with you."

He eyed her in consideration. She wondered what went on in that fine brain of his, if he weighed the consequences of not only sleeping here but being seen in her company.

"Best if I go on my own. Not safe on the streets right now."

Clad in only her dressing gown, she toed up to him. "If it isn't safe for me, it isn't safe for you."

"I'm a police officer."

"With a broken arm and several fractured ribs, not to mention those bruises."

He lowered his voice just as if the steamies could hear, which—Ginny supposed—they could. "That didn't discourage you last night."

Incredibly, Ginny felt the heat build again in her face. She never blushed—couldn't remember the last time she'd felt uncomfortable about her amorous exploits.

"Yes, well, I'm thinking far more clearly now. Perhaps seeing that"—she gestured at Floyd—"has put some sense in my head."

He snorted. "I sincerely doubt it. If you've any sense, you'll stay here and let me do what I do best, gather information."

"I guess I've no sense, then, because I'm coming with you. Millie, please be so kind as to make Sergeant Fagan that cup of tea while I get dressed."

"Yes, miss. Where shall I serve it, miss?" Millie waved her hands at the table in seeming distress.

Brendan answered, "I'll just come along with you to the kitchen, shall I? I'm far more comfortable there anyway."

Chapter Twenty-Six

"Well, this is eerie," Ginny whispered to Brendan.

The streets seemed strangely empty, as in the aftermath of some great tragedy. Ginny, who'd insisted on hiring a steamcab despite her aversion to them, sat peering through the side window in dreadful fascination.

Brendan grunted involuntarily every time they took a turn too sharply or went over a bump, revealing his discomfort. He really shouldn't be up. He should be in Ginny's bed, still naked. But she didn't know how to persuade him. Hog-tying might make a viable option. Then she could take her time pleasuring him and consequently herself.

Just so long as she kept it straight in her mind that she wasn't in love with the man.

The crowd gathered around the Kellys' house seemed shockingly large after all those empty streets, though Ginny supposed they wouldn't add up to a great number. As she and Brendan disembarked from the cab, she noticed a goodly number of them were automatons. She felt glad to see no police presence apart from the many off-duty members of the Irish Squad, some still clad in uniform.

Did they know who she was? Would they welcome her here?

Brendan marched up to the nearest; she followed.

"Brian, what's the word?"

The automaton couldn't display worry as such, but Ginny read concern in his eyes. "No word for some time, Brendan. Some of us have been waiting most the night. The experts are with him, evaluating."

"I see. How's Rose?"

The woman beside the automaton addressed as Brian turned toward them. Ginny wondered if she were his wife—one of her mother's creations and also an automaton. Impossible to tell.

"Rose is devastated. I saw her for a few moments earlier on. Mrs. Gideon is with her. They say Rose refuses to leave Pat's side even though his condition is most likely terminal."

"Terminal?" Horror and dismay colored Brendan's voice.

"That is a rumor," Brian said. "We have no substantiation."

The woman nodded.

"Look, Brian, we can't do any good here. Will you send me word as soon as you learn anything?"

"Where will you be?"

"I'm going to the station to see what can be done."

"I don't think…" Ginny began.

Brian's gaze moved to her. "You are the daughter of the woman who created my wife."

"Your wife?" Ginny's heart sank.

He put his arm around the woman at his side. "My wife, Honoria."

Honoria extended her hand. "I am glad to meet you."

"Oh, yes?"

"Yes, even though I did help to beat your mother to

death."

All words failed Ginny.

"Please be assured I am nevertheless grateful she gave me life. Otherwise I would not have had the opportunity to marry Brian."

Ginny, still incapable of speech, felt Brendan tug her away by the arm. She never remembered him flagging down another steamcab.

****

"You should have seen your face." Brendan struggled to restrain a wry smile. "I'll bet 'tis not often anyone sees Virginia Landry struck dumb."

"She apologized for killing my mother and expressed her gratitude to her, all in one breath."

"Or in one puff of steam, as it were. They're realists, far more than we'll ever be. They're forced to be, aren't they?"

"I guess I never thought about that. I found both Pat Kelly and Lily Michaels forthright and charming. I never considered what makes them so…honest."

"That's Pat, all right, honest right down to his steel frame. Lord, I hope he can be saved." Brendan tried to imagine life devoid of Pat's presence in the force and failed. To say nothing of his friendship.

"Doesn't sound good, though, does it?"

"It does not."

"How good are their experts? With my mother gone, who'd know the most about the hybrids?"

"I guess that would be the man who created Pat—Mason."

"I thought you said there were two of them, two 'madmen'?"

"Aye but Charles was killed in lock-up a year or

more ago. And Mason is stark raving, being held in some secret location." Brendan considered it. "Other than him, as I say, the experts would be the other hybrids. They've been studying on how to build more of their kind."

"Which is why they want the charity hospital."

"Aye." The cab drew up in front of the station, and Brendan turned to her. "Look, perhaps you'd better let me go in on my own."

He climbed painfully from the cab and, to his dismay, Ginny followed. The cabbie looked at her. "Miss, d'you want me to wait?"

"Yes, she'll be leaving directly," Brendan said.

"No," Ginny objected. "I'm staying. And Brendan, I'm not waiting out here." As the cab pulled away with a puff of dirty steam, she asked, "Would you rather own up to the truth or let Addelforce get it via rumor?"

He gazed into her eyes. "The truth?"

"That we're together."

Brendan's heart thudded. "Until you leave for Dakota."

"I'm going nowhere, not for the time being."

The time being? Damn it all. He drew a breath that hurt. "Very well, then. Come on."

The interior of the station house buzzed with activity, in stark contrast to the barren streets outside. Officers came and went from Addelforce's office; some gave Brendan and Ginny sharp looks in passing.

They found Addelforce standing behind his desk, uniform jacket unbuttoned and hair on end. He looked like he'd been there all night; Brendan figured he probably had.

He glanced up when they appeared in his doorway,

and his attention quickened.

"What are you doing here, Sergeant?"

"Reporting for duty, sir."

"You're not fit."

"I am well enough, sir. Appears to be a crisis, and needs must."

"I won't say I'm not glad to see you, though Miss Landry's presence is a surprise."

Ginny quirked an eyebrow. "An unpleasant one?"

Addelforce grunted. "You, miss, are a lit match in a powder keg. I'm not sure what's going on between the two of you—not at all sure I want to know. I warned Sergeant Fagan just as I warned you, you'll not do his career any good. And he has a bright future with the force, Miss Landry—very bright."

Brendan answered before Ginny could. "I understand that, sir. We both do. What's between us is personal."

"In this city? At this time? I don't think so."

"Captain Addelforce, sir, with all due respect"—Brendan bellied up to the desk—"When I'm on duty I take your orders. That's as far as it goes. Do you want my badge?"

Addelforce's eyes widened with outrage. "You'd resign over...over that? A woman?"

Would he? Brendan thought about it—really thought about it—and felt his face grow rigid. A few more weeks of Ginny remaining in Buffalo did not, in truth, a relationship make—or a reason for him to jettison his career.

Fortunately, Addelforce spoke again. "Of course I don't want your badge, Sergeant Fagan. Don't be an ass."

"No, sir." Brendan relaxed a hair.

"But as we discussed previously, your association with Miss Landry does compromise your objectivity and the public's perception of your ability to do your job. What?" Addelforce barked at a very young officer who appeared behind Ginny in the doorway.

"Another incident, sir. Private carriage turned over on Main Street, with multiple injuries."

"Report there at once."

"But sir, I'm bound for Swan Street—the house with the shattered windows."

"Go to Main Street first and Swan after."

The officer ducked out. Brendan asked, "What in hell is going on, sir?"

"Hell, Sergeant Fagan, is a fair description. The city has gone mad. All sane and prudent citizens are bunged up in their homes. Meanwhile, opposing bands of thugs roam the streets. Rogue automatons are attacking anything they can. Bands of armed humans are taking down the automatons."

"They battered my man, Floyd," Ginny told Addelforce. "Neighbors brought him home last night."

"Miss Landry, I'm not at all surprised. You should be home behind locked doors. Charged with the impossible task of keeping the peace, we are stretched far too thin to protect you. Half the Irish Squad are stationed outside Pat Kelly's house. I have to worry about the other half deserting their jobs."

"You afraid they'll turn, sir?" Brendan asked, disbelieving. "They won't turn."

"I wish I had your confidence. What I need, Sergeant, is Pat Kelly's voice of reason. Any word on how he is?"

"We just came from there, sir. It doesn't sound good."

Addelforce closed his eyes briefly. "If he stays down, I fear we'll never get the city under control. The automatons will break loose. Is there nothing that can be done?"

"They're working on him, sir."

"Who is?"

Brendan shrugged. "The other automatons. They're the only ones left with the knowledge."

"Christ." Addelforce's gaze found Ginny. "I don't suppose you know anything? After all…"

"I'm sorry, Captain, but I never knew my mother, and I possess none of her knowledge."

Brendan shifted on his feet. "Where do you want me, sir?"

Addelforce eyed him up and down before scrabbling through the papers on his desk and coming up with a slip. "Go to this address. See a man called Robert Dunner."

"But sir, this is the address of the Insane Asylum on Forest Avenue." Brendan shot a look at Ginny. "Why there?"

Addelforce fixed him with a stare. "You remember Mason?"

"I should, sir. In fact…in fact we were just speaking of him." Brendan felt the blood drain from his face. "Never say he's being held there!"

"He's been there all this while, confined to their maximum security wing. It's more a cell than a hospital room, from what I've been able to learn. But Dunner's willing to talk to us and will perhaps let you see Mason."

Brendan shuddered involuntarily. "See him, sir?" The very last thing he wanted.

"I need you to assess Mason's condition. Then report back to me, understand?"

"No, sir, I'm not sure I do."

Addelforce leaned across his desk. "Brendan, I want to know if you believe Mason sufficiently competent to be furloughed out of that place in order to rebuild Patrick Kelly."

Chapter Twenty-Seven

"I'm going with you, Brendan." Ginny spoke the words in that determined way of hers, the one Brendan had already learned meant she had to have her way.

Fine in bed, that. Not so good in daily life.

Focused on the task of flagging down another steamcab in front of the police station, he ignored her. Hell, he should have had the first driver wait after all. Now all the traffic that usually traveled round the block had melted away, and frustration gnawed at him.

Frustration and another emotion he didn't like to acknowledge—dread. Or maybe it was horror. He didn't like the prospect of facing that monster Mason again.

And monster he was.

Brendan thought about the man as he'd last seen him—mechanically enhanced and surely beyond mad, with his black hair and dead-white skin. All this time Brendan had believed him safely put away but never suspected it was right here in this city. His city. He remembered his terror that night when Charles and Mason had held him and Liam McMahon prisoner, the paralyzing fear of being strapped to a metal table, and the terrible sounds when the hybrid steamies turned on their makers. He might not be afraid of much—prided himself on it; truth be told, he feared Mason.

"Brendan?" He realized Ginny must have repeated

his name more than once. "Are you all right?"

He looked at her blankly. "Sure, save I can't seem to spy a fecking cab."

"Listen to me." Her beautiful dark eyes engaged and held his. "You're just going to this place, asking questions. They might not let you see the madman."

He tried to speak; no words came.

Ginny clutched his good arm. "I can imagine how this must feel—how awful that night must have been."

"I didn't think I'd ever have to face him again. *Assess* him, Addelforce said."

"He's still safely locked away."

"Until they decide it's a good idea to let him out to rebuild his own hybrid automaton. I'll have to see him then, won't I?"

"Maybe. Maybe not. Still, if he can save Pat…"

"Aye." There was that. Pat Kelly could be lost, one of the best men—human or automaton—Brendan knew. He drew a breath. "You're right. But no doubt Mason's so far gone he won't be able to help."

What then, eh?

The paper in his hand, signed by the mayor, was an official request to the administrator of the Forest Avenue asylum. Brendan had no choice but to deliver it.

"Thank God." A cab approached at last—a shabby dark vehicle drawn by an aged horse. Brendan flagged it down. "Thank you for your words of support, Ginny, but I'll not take you to that place. We'll go by your house on the way and drop you there."

"I'm going with you," she told him as she climbed into the malodorous interior of the cab. "And that's an end to it."

****

Mr. Richardson's grand building on Forest Avenue possessed an imposing profile and a grim aspect even though as a facility it was lauded as modern and state of the art. Brendan didn't pass it often; when he did it never failed to send a chill up his spine.

Now, with all his Irish blood up, he wondered if that had been because he'd sensed Mason's presence all the while. As they climbed from the cab and stood on the curb looking at the place, he swore he could feel the monster's malevolence.

Built in the Romanesque style, the asylum offered the latest in care and comfort to those housed inside. Dr. Thomas Story Kirkbride, a pioneer in the field of mental health, had commissioned Richardson to build the facility and intended it as a great improvement over the many nightmarish hospitals and virtual prisons that dotted the city. Some folks, as Brendan well knew, kept afflicted family members in their attics, shut away from the world. He assured himself this must be better.

"My goodness," said Ginny. "What an impressive place."

"Aye."

She threaded her fingers through his. "Come."

Brendan stood rooted where he was.

"That night…that awful night…I was sure Mason was dead. The hybrids were so violent; there was so much blood. I only found out later they both survived— him and Charles. I hoped I'd never see him again."

"This place looks very secure. He'll not get out on his own."

"I'm not worried about him getting out on his own."

Inside, the facility proved well kept. They found Robert Dunner's office on the ground floor, and the man came forward immediately to greet them. Of mature years, with silvered hair and wearing an expensive-looking pince-nez, he invited them to sit down before perusing the mayor's communiqué with great attention.

When he finished, he laid the paper down and regarded Brendan with serious, dark eyes.

"Shocking, what is going on in this city. Just shocking. These last weeks I have followed the reports with some interest—murders, attacks, uprisings. And now this. I've heard of this Patrick Kelly, very highly thought of, as this missive proves."

"He is that," Brendan agreed.

Dunner sat back. "Is he not also the leader of this movement for automaton rights?"

"He's leader of the official movement, yes. There seem to be a lot of factions, not all of them as peaceful as that run by Officer Kelly. Obviously some of them have been acting on their own. The department has not yet been able to get to the bottom of it."

"Officer Kelly," Dunner repeated with some emphasis. "He is, of course, a machine."

Brendan stiffened, and felt Ginny twitch in the chair at his side.

"Pardon me, sir, but he's much more than that."

"Ah, yes. A member of this famed Irish Squad, so I understand—set up to be admired and encouraged to have delusions about themselves."

Brendan leaned forward, ignoring the protest from his fractured ribs. "Pat Kelly's a talented police officer, a valued member of the force, and a good person. He has a wife and a place in this community."

Dunner tapped the mayor's letter. "Still, it seems, regarding what has befallen him, he may have got what he deserves."

Brendan felt like he'd been punched in the gut, busted ribs and all. "Now look here," he began.

"No, you look, Officer, and listen. This city has turned dangerous because people like you have given license to machines—I repeat, to machines—and prompted them to have ideas above themselves. Officer, I am a psychiatrist as well as the director of this facility—a doctor first. I deal every day with the rehabilitation of diseased minds. The last thing that's needed is yet another group angling for dominance."

"Not dominance, sir," Brendan said. "They just want a place…"

"And you are a sympathizer." Dunner's gaze flicked to Ginny and back to Brendan. Obviously he didn't recognize her. "How did you sustain those injuries, Officer?"

"The riot in the Park, sir."

"I suspected as much. And did that teach you nothing about the danger in which this city now lies? The mayor argues for Patrick Kelly as a voice of reason needing to be heard in the current plague of unrest. I say he is an obstacle best removed."

"So…" Brendan's nostrils flared. "You would like to see the movement crushed."

"I would like to see the automatons take their intended places. They are mechanical devices, even the best of them. Not above two months ago, the most sophisticated among them beat their creator—a respected doctor—to death in front of hundreds of witnesses. They have no conscience, no compassion, no inherent decency."

"I don't accept that, sir. I will never believe it."

"Then, Officer, you are indeed a sympathizer in a dangerous cause." Dunner tossed the letter back across the table. "You can take that to the mayor and tell him I refuse to risk the welfare of my patient for the sake of a pile of nuts and bolts."

"Nuts and bolts." Brendan thought of Pat Kelly sitting with his glass of whiskey, coming over all Irish, thought of his sense of humor. He remembered the look in Rose Kelly's eyes when she looked at her husband.

He fought to discipline his anger. Losing his temper would get him nowhere.

"But sir, I've been sent to ascertain the condition of your patient. Surely you can tell me that."

"He has good days and bad days."

"What exactly does that mean?"

"On the good days he is very nearly rational. On the bad days he rages and attacks the walls of his room. We have to strap him down. But he is improving, and the periods of heavy sedation are much less frequent than they were."

"I see." Talk about someone getting what he deserved…

"Please tell the mayor that, in my opinion, Mr. Mason is not sufficiently recovered to perform the task he requests—rebuilding a hybrid automaton."

"I will, sir, yes."

Brendan stumbled to his feet. He must be much more debilitated by his injuries than he'd thought, because he swayed for a moment. Ginny steadied him with her arm beneath his.

Dunner tapped his desk. "You mark my words, Officer—this city will have no peace till those machines assume their rightful places."

Brendan tended to agree, without agreeing what those rightful places were.

****

"You stand here while I flag down a cab." Ginny placed Brendan's good hand on the post of the iron railing in front of the asylum. She didn't like the look of him, pale as milk beneath his tan and clearly shaken. What had it taken for him to go in there?

"Ah, we should have asked that last fellow to wait. I'm not thinking clearly, lass. Not sure what's wrong with me."

"Concussion, no doubt." And she hadn't helped a bit by taking advantage of him in her bed. She should have *thought* instead of *felt*. Trouble was Brendan Fagan tended to make her feel.

She managed to snag a steamcab around the corner on Delaware Avenue and waved it to the place where Brendan waited, his very obedience a concern. Dismissing her aversion to the vehicle, she thrust him inside.

"Where to, miss?"

"Where, Brendan?"

"Back to the station. I have to give Captain Addelforce the news. He can inform the mayor."

Ginny bit her lips. "We could send word. I think you're better off at home."

"I'm on duty, lass."

"You're not."

"Well?" The driver cocked a brow.

"To the station," Ginny decided. "Then we'll go

inquire about Pat."

Brendan remained quiet on his way downtown, far too quiet, in Ginny's opinion. Snuggling closer to his good shoulder, she inquired, "What's going on in that head of yours?"

"Nothing. I'm just…Pat saved my life that night, Ginny."

"So you said."

"And I've failed to return the favor."

"Not yet, you haven't. Nothing's saying they can't revive him."

But when they arrived at the station, they found the place in chaos, officers standing around in small groups and no one at his post.

"What's going on?" Brendan asked the man nearest the door.

"Word just came, Brendan. The automatons managed to get Pat going, but his intelligence is wrecked. They're trying to decide whether to shut him down again."

Chapter Twenty-Eight

"Oh, heavens, what now?" Ginny groaned.

Loud pounding on the door in the middle of the night seemed to have become a common occurrence, she reflected unhappily as she dragged herself out of bed in response to the thunderous volley from below. Brendan, clearly exhausted, slept on, proving himself rendered deaf by slumber.

She found Gus at the door ahead of her, and it hit her all over again—no Floyd. In her absence that day, the other three steamies had gathered him up as instructed and presumably conveyed him up to the guest room. She and Brendan had dined on the selfsame table where he'd lain when they returned late. Afterward she'd dragged Brendan off to bed, but not in the pursuit of pleasure. The man needed to sleep.

She needed to sleep beside him.

But now the insistent knocking had her heart up and pounding in her ears. Night hung outside the windows, and given the past few days, anything could wait on the doorstep.

She nodded at Gus who, wordless as always, nudged her aside carefully before opening the door a crack.

A voice sounded. "I'm looking for Brendan Fagan."

"Who is it?" she called back.

"Officer Dennis Petersen of the Buffalo Police Force."

Ginny nodded at Gus, who rolled aside. The police officer came in, fully uniformed and hair mussed by the night breeze.

"Sorry, miss. I need to see Brendan."

"How did you know he's here?"

Petersen made a face expressing impatience. "Everybody in the city knows, and it's not important. Where is he?"

"Here." Brendan descended the stairs behind them, dressed only in his trousers and with all his bruises on display. "What is it, lad?"

"We need you to come to Pat Kelly's house. His wife, Rose, just tried to kill herself."

****

"Why isn't she in the hospital?" Ginny asked as they went at a jog through the dark, echoing streets. No possibility, it seemed, of snagging a steamcab now. She reminded herself she had her steam cannon and was in the presence of two policemen.

Half way there she began to worry about Brendan. His breath came in gasps; she imagined the broken ribs must have him in agony. But he carried on determinedly till they reached Bryant Street, where Pat's house stood, still surrounded by a ring of steamies, lit eerily by the torches many of them held.

It made a striking scene, the automatons motionless and the light reflecting off the tall façade of the house.

Petersen answered in a hush as the scene required. "She refused to go. And yes, before you ask, she's conscious. Fortunately she was found before she could bleed out."

"Bleed out?" Ginny turned her eyes on the young officer.

"Slit her wrists in the washroom. Luckily, she did a poor job of it. The automatons on the scene wrapped her up and called the quack Pat usually uses for the lightskirts he helps. I think his name's Rasmussen."

Ginny looked at Brendan. His mouth hung open, and he sucked air like a horse ready to founder. "Who's with her?"

"That Mrs. Gideon and one of the hybrid whores…I think her name is Chastity."

"Mrs. Greely to you." The rebuke came from Brendan without hesitation.

"Who's Mrs. Gideon?" Ginny asked in a whisper.

"Wealthy woman in this city, and a good friend to Pat—she's done a lot to help ladies of the night, human and automaton alike." Brendan returned his gaze to Petersen. "What do they think I can do?"

"They want you to talk to her on behalf of Pat—from the heart of a policeman."

"What?" Brendan croaked. Ginny saw dismay crash over him in a wave.

Petersen lowered his voice still farther. "That's what Pat was, above all else—a policeman and an Irishman. You're both. They want you to try and talk her round the way he would have."

"Feck."

Petersen persisted, "Pat wouldn't want Rose dead."

"God, no. He loved her, he did."

"Plus Mrs. Gideon says how you're eloquent."

"Jaysus, lad. I don't feel very eloquent right now."

"Will you go in? My job was just to get you here."

"I'll go."

"I'm coming with you," Ginny said, not for the first time that night. She clung to his good arm, but he freed himself from her grasp—in order to leave her there, she thought. But instead he curled his arm around her waist, and they entered the house linked.

The Kellys' flat occupied the first floor. The door from the foyer stood wide open, and more light spilled out. The parlor seemed overfull of people, but they parted to make way for Brendan and Ginny.

"He's here," someone called, and a woman stepped out from an inner room.

Exquisitely beautiful, she had skin the color of hot chocolate and a wealth of black hair. Something about the way she stepped forward and held out her hand made Ginny wonder if she really was a woman.

"Sergeant Fagan. Thank you for coming."

"Mrs. Greely. This is a terrible situation. Pat…" For an instant Ginny felt sure Brendan would break down there in front of everyone. Sympathetic tears rose to her throat.

Mrs. Greely shook her head. "We did all we could. We got him restarted. As you know, Pat himself and I are…were…the foremost authorities on our own construction. I missed his input sorely. But I had all the help for which I could ask, and as I say, we did get him up and running, repaired his boiler and all the vital connections. We had him sitting up." She hesitated, and a new expression came into her eyes.

An expression. Ginny tried to reconcile that simple fact.

Mrs. Greely said, "His intelligence is gone. He is just—not there anymore."

"You must be able to repair it."

"The damage to his head was extreme."

"Yes, I saw that. But…"

"We do not have the knowledge. I regret to say it, but I must. When Rose heard that Pat was, in essence, dead, she became very quiet. We should have been warned by that. Only when Mrs. Gideon noticed she'd been in the water closet too long did we think to check on her."

"But she's alive? Can I see her?"

"I wish you would. You must speak for Pat, persuade her he would not wish her to die. From what I know, from what Mrs. Gideon has told me, his main intent since meeting Rose has been to keep her alive and happy."

"But she's recovered now, right?"

"She will recover," Mrs. Greely corrected softly. "Our fear is that she will try again."

"Oh, God," Brendan whispered.

"She says she does not wish to live without Pat. That she refuses to go on without him. Can you talk to her and persuade her how Pat would abhor that?"

"Jaysus. I don't know. I'll try."

Ginny wiggled out from the curve of his arm. "You should probably see her alone."

"I…no, I'd be grateful if you'd come."

Without another word, Mrs. Greely turned and led them into the next room.

This was obviously a place of little use. The Kellys mostly lived in their main room with the big bed in one corner, but a cot had been set up here, and a woman lay upon it. The room smelled strongly of blood and disinfectant, a combination not unfamiliar to Ginny from accompanying her father on his rounds.

As they entered, Mrs. Gideon, a statuesque woman with black hair—the front of her orchid silk gown liberally splashed with red—turned from the cot, and a tall thin man wearing spectacles looked at them with sudden attention.

Topaz Gideon, her fingers also stained red, rose and took Brendan's hand. "Thank you for coming. This is Dr. Rasmussen. He saved Rose's life."

"No, madam, you did that before I arrived." Rasmussen had a quiet voice colored by a strong Swedish accent. "I merely did some needlework and bandaging."

"A fine job of stitching—miraculous. Sergeant Fagan, we can't let Rose go. Pat..." Topaz Gideon's incredible, tawny eyes flooded with tears. "He was one of my dearest friends."

"And mine."

"I understand how Rose feels. But he would not want..."

"I grasp that, Mrs. Gideon. I'll do my best."

"Please do." Astoundingly, Mrs. Gideon lifted Brendan's hand to her lips and kissed it. After a hard stare at Ginny, she went out.

"Would you like me to stay?" Rasmussen asked.

"Yes, please."

Ginny remained at the doctor's side as Brendan moved forward and hunkered down beside the cot. The woman there looked too pale to be alive, but her brown eyes, burning as in a white mask, fastened their gaze to Brendan's face. Her throat worked mightily.

"He's gone."

"I heard what happened, Rose. I heard. God, I'm sorry. What have you done to yourself?"

He looked at her with visible dismay. If Mrs. Gideon's dress had been splashed, Rose Kelly's had been soaked through with blood.

Rose's lips worked; she made no reply.

"What would Pat say, Rose? What would he say to this?"

Rose's eyes pooled with tears. "He would tell me to *live*. He would s-say life is a precious gift." Her voice, though weak, held a frantic thread. "But I can't do it without him. I never wanted to live—I didn't, not when I met him. Not in this body. This isn't my body, did you know that? I was forced into it."

"Pat told me. He also showed in a thousand ways how much he cared about you. Rose, he would hate this."

"He was my strength. My strength is gone."

Whoever said one person didn't make a difference knew nothing, Ginny thought. Pat Kelly—arguably not quite a person—had made a staggering difference to so many, and especially to his wife.

Had she, Ginny, ever felt that way toward anyone? Did she now?

She eyed the man who without doubt had captured her emotions—barely upright in his place beside the cot, in obvious pain both of body and spirit yet still strong. The tears in her eyes spilled over. Would she be able to go on without him? Who could blame Rose Kelly?

"Rose—Rose, can't he be your strength still? Can you find it in you to go on for his sake?"

"No. No." The woman on the cot began to weep in deep ugly sobs. The muscles of Brendan's back writhed.

"Then we'll have to bring him back for you."

That made Rose lift her head. "How? They said they can't repair him. The damage…"

"Maybe there's someone else who can. Listen, Rose, will you promise not to harm yourself again, give me time to see if I can persuade this individual to help?"

Rose gasped. "Who? There's no one. They said…it's impossible."

"Nothing's impossible, Rose. Loving Pat should have taught you that. Will you hold on for his sake?"

"I will."

Both Rasmussen and Ginny stared at Brendan with wonder as he rose and made for the door. Ginny hurried to follow him, while the doctor remained with his patient.

"Brendan? Brendan!" Once they reached the parlor, Ginny tugged at his arm. "How could you do that? As good as make her an empty promise…"

"It was what she needed to hear, and not an empty promise."

"What's happened?" Topaz Gideon demanded as she and Mrs. Greely both stepped up. "What went on in there?"

Ginny, stricken, buttoned her lip.

Brendan spoke. "I told Rose if she holds on I'll bring someone to mend Pat. Where is he?"

Topaz, eyes wide with distress, said, "Still here. They've been working on him in the back storeroom."

"I want to see him."

"You don't, Sergeant Fagan. Believe me, you don't. There's nothing there."

"How bad's the damage?"

"Bad."

Brendan flexed his shoulders. "I can think of one man, and only one, who can mend him."

Chapter Twenty-Nine

"There's only one thing to be done. I have to break Mason out of the asylum."

Ginny exchanged glances with the two other women standing huddled with her and Brendan near the Kellys' front door. Mrs. Gideon returned her incredulous look before Mrs. Greely made the first objection.

"But that's illegal, and you are a police officer."

"I *was* a police officer. If I pull this off, I expect it'll put a finish to things." Brendan frowned, and Ginny caught his eye for an instant. They'd worried about whether their association would damage his career chances. Now he was ready to toss it all away…for the sake of compassion.

She experienced a twinge in the region of her heart. Or maybe it wasn't a twinge but something letting go—the last bastion she'd held against capitulating to this man.

"But Mason's a lunatic." Topaz Gideon made the next, measured objection. "What makes you think he'll cooperate?"

"I'm thinking a squad of his own automatons bent on a single purpose might just persuade him."

"The same ones that nearly killed him, you mean."

"Absent of Pat Kelly." Brendan shot a look at the door of the inner room. "I have to do this for her, Mrs.

Gideon. And for him."

Topaz Gideon seemed to reach a decision. "You have my support."

But Ginny hadn't yet expressed her objection. "That place—we were just there asking for permission to see Mason," she explained to the other women. "It's so secure. How will you get in and out of there?"

"Not sure," Brendan admitted.

Mrs. Gideon asked, "The authorities there can't be persuaded to give us access to Mason? We could send someone in to consult with him."

"I would gladly go," said Mrs. Greely.

"The gentleman we saw refused categorically. Accused me of being an automaton sympathizer."

"Ignorant reactionary," Mrs. Gideon denounced. "He's leaving us few options. Sergeant Fagan, I don't want to see you ruin your career."

"At this point, I don't much care."

"But you're injured." Ginny, feeling more and more desperate, attempted reason once again. "Your arm—"

"Irrelevant," he snapped.

Ginny ground her teeth. If he was bent on sacrificing himself, she wouldn't be able to dissuade him. And while it was one thing for her to take chances with her own safety, something she did routinely, she found she liked it far less in the man she…

Mrs. Gideon snapped her fingers, keeping Ginny from completing that thought.

"Here's an idea. I'll see if I can get my husband involved. He's in Canada at the moment, on state business, but he's due back later this afternoon. I'll talk to him, yes?"

"I'm sorry, Mrs. Gideon. What good will that do?" Brendan asked.

She lowered her voice still further. "He's a former agent of Queen Victoria, well versed in covert operations and used to chasing monsters. I'd say he's just the man you need."

****

"You know you'll unquestionably be scuttling your career."

Brendan looked up when Ginny spoke. They'd returned to the parlor of her house at Linwood Avenue to await word from Topaz Gideon. It hadn't taken long for Ginny to ramp up and face him, her beautiful, dark eyes intent and flags of color flying in her cheeks.

Oh, hell. He dragged air into his aching body and replied, "Some things are more important than my career."

"This from the man who stood in this very room and told me his career meant more than our relationship."

"What relationship? You insisted you couldn't wait to put this city behind you and would be gone by the end of the week."

"I'm still here, though, aren't I?" She touched his cheek. "Still with you."

"Listen, Ginny, I'm not in the mood to discuss this. I'm tired, worried, and I don't quite know how I'm going to make good on what I promised Rose back there."

"Sit down." She planted a hand in the center of his chest and pushed him gently into the nearest chair. "Put up your feet." She pushed an ottoman into place and lifted his boots onto it one after the other. "Do you want a drink?"

"Better not. Need to keep a clear head." Mrs. Gideon had vowed to send word as soon as she spoke with her husband.

An agent—former agent—of the British Crown, eh? An Englishman, of all things, joining forces with a bunch of Irishmen. Should prove interesting.

Ginny sank down in a puff of skirts at the side of his chair. He could see the worry in her gaze as it touched and measured him. "You don't even know where in the asylum this man, Mason, is being housed. There will be attendants, people to keep the patients from straying."

"Aye."

She brushed his good hand with her fingers, smoothing across the palm. "Brendan, all this business with Pat and Rose has made me think what it would do to me to lose someone I…needed very badly."

"That made him look at her, really look. "Are you after saying you…need me?"

"I guess I am." She swallowed, her eyes holding his. "Not easy for me to admit, I'll have you know. After my last experience"— She broke off, and the color came and went in her face once more. "I vowed I'd never again allow myself to be so vulnerable."

"Aye, you did mention it. Thus your penchant for ugly men."

"Yes. I find ugly men, by and large, more honest. What you see is what you get, with them. There are no layers of charm and deception, no games or lies."

"I see." Brendan wondered who he'd been, this handsome devil who still haunted their relationship. Each time they made love, he got curious about the other men with whom she'd shared herself and whether she'd done so as generously as she did with him. He'd wanted to ask, but it seemed too possessive, and he knew instinctively Ginny Landry wouldn't react well to a man coming over all possessive.

Now he wondered if she also believed him a liar and a user just because he had a face women might favor.

"Everyone warned me about him—my father and my friends. Even my stepmother, who rarely interferes with me. Did I listen? I thought we'd been destined to meet. I thought it was forever. It lasted till he got bored with me and another woman caught his eye."

Softly he asked, "And do you think I'm like him? I'm stable; I'm invested in this city. I'm not going anyplace."

"Yes, well…" She questioned him with her eyes. "That's another problem, isn't it? You're not going anywhere. Your life is here. And no, you're nothing like the charming Hank."

"Hank, is it? Thank you very much."

"I can't say you're not charming—you must know you are. But you're also strong, serious, and dedicated. Honest. A good man."

"Well, so." He lifted a brow. "And how is that a problem?"

"I don't know if I'm ready for serious, Brendan, or ready to stay put. I thought you were going to be just another fling. But now, well, I know how I felt when I saw you injured. And I find I very much dislike the prospect of you going off to try and break into that awful place in search of the madman who once almost killed you. I'm so afraid something terrible will happen to you, I can scarcely think straight."

She bent her head and pressed it against his shoulder. Brendan's heart, weary and uncertain at this point, promptly melted. He caressed her dark hair—soft as silk—with the fingers of his good hand, absorbed the scent and feel of her, warm and vital.

Oh, aye, he understood what she felt—she'd meant to keep things casual between them. Now she suddenly found they no longer were so casual. He, several steps ahead of her, had begun worrying about this days ago.

Yet, as she pointed out, she was still here.

"Listen to me, Ginny—bonny lass." He curled his fingers around her jaw and lifted her face gently. "You needn't fear for me. I'll be in the presence of an English agent and several deadly automatons."

"But you're afraid of him—I know you are."

There was that. The very idea of facing Mason in the flesh made his balls try to climb up into his belly. But a man had to do a lot of things that frightened him, especially in this job.

If he still had a job after tonight.

"Not something I'd choose to do, certainly. But if he can resurrect Pat…"

"But what if he can't? He's mad, after all. Or what if you get him out of there and he refuses to cooperate? What if he turns on you?"

"You're not after doing a lot for my confidence."

"Brendan, I'm scared for you."

"Here, come here."

He gathered her up from her knees and drew her into his lap, close against his chest. The contact made his broken ribs hurt for an instant before she tucked her dark head into the crook of his neck, her lips only inches from his, and he began to feel a lot better.

"Ginny, darlin', we never know what the future holds. Life as a policeman is risky even at the best of times." It made one reason why he'd determined never to marry. In his experience, it made a bad proposition.

How did that fit with his impulse to spend forever with this woman in his arms?

She murmured into his neck, "On the frontier, too. With my father being a doctor, I've seen it all. He always says that in Dakota there are a thousand ways for men to die. But Brendan, none of those men...none of them is you."

"And I matter that much to you, do I?" He couldn't have held back the question to save his life.

"That's what I'm trying to tell you. You matter very, very much." Each utterance of the word "very" came accompanied by a kiss to his jaw. She reached up, touched his cheek, and turned his face so their mouths met instead.

And what did he taste in her kiss? Her fear for him, aye, closely followed by the heat that came to them so easily. Was there more? Could he sense a measure of devotion? Love?

That word possessed his mind as he explored her mouth luxuriantly with his tongue.

God, he loved the flavor of her, loved her strength and that streak of wild independence. No man would ever completely tame this woman, nor bend her. She would only stay with a man because she wanted to. And what a blinding privilege to be that man.

"Brendan, Brendan." She ended the kiss at last and laid her hand against his cheek. "I've only one thing to say to you. You'd better come out of this in one piece, understand? You'd better come back to me. I'll never forgive you if you don't."

Chapter Thirty

"My wife seems to think this is a good idea," said Rom Gideon with the wry humor Brendan had begun to learn marked him. "No sooner did I land at the foot of Ferry Street than she was there telling me I needed to launch a covert mission—into an asylum, of all places."

His blue eyes glinted ruefully. He'd turned up at Ginny's door dressed all in black, with three similarly-clad members of the Irish Squad at his back, and thrust a bundle of clothes at Brendan.

"Now, my wife is a remarkable woman. A singular woman." Gideon's light voice and clipped English accent lent the words a certain understated emphasis. "But an asylum, of all places…"

Brendan looked him askance. He must have met Rom Gideon at some point in the past but couldn't remember sharing conversation with him.

Gideon told him, "I have an unfortunate history with those sorts of places."

"I'm not crazy about the idea either," Brendan confessed. "But for Pat's sake, I'm willing."

"Yes, Pat. And Rose." Gideon's face immediately sobered. "Two of my favorite people. Would you say our target—Mason—is dangerous?"

"He was. Nearly killed me and Liam McMahon. That's the night I first met Pat Kelly, truth be told. What's this?" He juggled the clothing clutched against his chest.

"We're going in under cover. You sure you're up to this?" Gideon eyed Brendan. "You look a bit battered."

"Arm's broken. I won't be swarming up any ropes."

"Hmm. May be a problem." Gideon switched his gaze to Ginny, who stood beside Brendan, silent for once, and back again. "You do realize this will likely cost you your job if it gets out."

"Aye." Brendan swallowed. "Do you think it will get out?"

Gideon shrugged. "It is best, as I've learned, to prepare for the worst. It's a mad scheme, though I did manage to score this."

He drew a paper from his vest pocket and spread it out on a side table.

"What's that, then?"

"A plan of the wondrous asylum."

Brendan's eyes widened. "How did you get your hands on that?"

"I have connections. A friend supplied it. You can see here these are open areas, minimum security. Our target won't be there."

"No."

Gideon stabbed the paper with one finger. "This section here is for patients who…well, rarely see the light of day. There appear to be six rooms. That ups our odds."

Brendan glanced at the silent members of the Irish Squad. "Don't you think we need more men?"

"I don't. This is a covert undertaking; numbers are counterproductive."

Brendan's eyebrows soared.

"Now, we've no time to waste. We need to have this done before the sun comes up."

Have it done. The Englishman possessed confidence.

Brendan drew a breath. "I'll go change. Ginny, I may need your assistance if we're to be ready quickly."

Gideon made no objection as Ginny followed Brendan from the parlor and up to her room. There she began unfastening his clothing with unsteady fingers.

"I wish you didn't have a broken arm and three fractured ribs."

Four, but he didn't correct her. "So do I. Something tells me Gideon will be hard to keep up with. On the other hand, I do believe with him on our side we have a chance of getting Mason out of there."

She paused in the act of hauling off his shirt. "Do you realize you shudder every time you say his name?"

"Never mind that. Help me into these trousers. They're a tight fit."

"I imagine he doesn't want your clothing snagging on anything." Several moments strenuous struggle ended with Ginny in his arms.

"Promise me you'll be all right."

"I don't like making promises I'm not sure I can keep."

"Like you did to Rose?"

"I'm keeping that one."

"Then kiss me for luck."

He provided the kiss with alacrity.

"Not just one kiss," she informed him then. "Real luck requires three."

****

If the asylum on Forest Avenue looked imposing in daylight, the sight of it in darkness proved enough to lift the hairs at the back of Brendan's neck. They'd made their way here on foot, slipping through the shadows and doing their best to keep their footsteps from echoing. Brendan and Rom Gideon went together, with the three automatons some distance behind so as not to draw attention.

They paused under a tree and looked up at the stone-and-brick structure. Brendan heard Gideon draw a breath and glanced at him sideways.

"Just what's your history with asylums?" he asked belatedly.

"Nothing much, save that I was held prisoner in one—not here. Tortured."

"Jaysus."

"It wasn't a pleasant experience." Gideon had got hold of his emotions; the dry humor once more colored his voice.

"I remember hearing about that. It was when the Hathor mansion burned down."

"Yes. We hushed up as many details as we could."

"Things like that tend to get out." Brendan looked at Gideon with new respect. "You were responsible for the demise of Danson Clifford. Your wife is right; you are accustomed to taking on monsters."

"Clifford died there in the mansion the night of the fire. It wasn't all down to me. Now I think, given the state of your arm, you should wait outside and let the rest of us go in." Gideon nodded at the three automations who had just joined them with no more than a stray puff of steam.

"But I—"

Gideon shook his head. "We're going to have to climb up. I'm sure my companions will recognize the man who created them, right, gentlemen?"

One of the automatons nodded.

"I expect the real difficulty will ensue when we get him out, Sergeant. With every ability at your disposal, you'll need to persuade him to cooperate with us. A raving madman will do us no good at all."

Jaysus, Brendan thought, though he didn't say it aloud this time. "All right."

"Wait back here." They moved in a silent body to the rear of the main building. "If you see anything to let you know they've twigged us—lights going on all over the place or guards suddenly dashing about—blow this." Gideon thrust a small, cool object into Brendan's left hand—a policeman's whistle. He nodded.

"Very well, gentlemen. Let's move, and quickly."

They slipped away from Brendan with such stealth he could barely track them. At first he thought they'd entered the building somehow at one of the rear doors, in the shadows. Then his eye caught the faintest movement at the far corner of the structure; someone scaled the bricks, followed by three other someones like big spiders, one after the other. Their goal appeared to be a third-floor window. Brendan tried to recall the details of the plans spread on Ginny's table.

Ginny.

If he turned things around in his mind, then yes, this must be the part of the facility where Gideon guessed Mason would be. He didn't want to think about Mason, seeing him again, or dealing with him, so he switched his thoughts back to Ginny instead. The way she felt in his arms. The light in her eyes when she looked at him. How her lips tasted when they met his.

Did he want Ginny Landry forever? But she'd made it clear she didn't want forever. And once he lost his job over this stunt, he wouldn't have much to offer her.

Except his heart, and she'd said nothing to show she wanted that.

He shifted on his feet in an agony of suspense. No light came on anywhere in the building; the whistle remained in his hand.

Only after what seemed like hours did his eye catch a flicker of movement at an upstairs window. The same where the squad had entered? Yes. His heart began to thump as a figure emerged, clinging to the stonework. Then a bundle came through the window, suspended by rope. No, not a bundle but a man, well-trussed.

Mason.

By God, the Englishman had done it. But they weren't away yet.

In impossible silence he watched the automatons—each with the strength of four men—wrestle the bundle down the side of the building. Gideon emerged last. Brendan knew him by the quick, light way he moved.

What had they done to Mason, to keep him quiet? No way to tell. Brendan watched as they rappelled down the building. One of the automatons heaved the silent bundle over his shoulder; they all approached at a jog, and Brendan stiffened.

By the time they reached him, his heart banged so violently he could barely hear Gideon's soft words when he spoke. "Here, now, is this your man?"

He pulled a hood up from over the face of the man still slung over the hybrid's shoulder. Brendan saw a countenance little changed by time—dead white skin, elongated features, and a round, dark mechanical gadget where one eye should be. All the breath left his body in a rush.

"Fecking hell!"

"I'll take that as an affirmative."

"He's quiet. Too quiet."

"Nicely quiet," Gideon corrected. "Lucky we caught him by surprise, eh, boys? He wanted to start yelling, but Sean here gave him a right tip on the jaw."

The nearest automaton flexed steel fingers. "Felt good, it did," he clicked.

"Let's get out of here," Gideon breathed.

"Where should we take him? To Pat's?"

"Not yet. We have to get him somewhere we can see if he'll cooperate. Miss Landry's, perhaps."

"Sure," Brendan agreed. In for a penny, in for a pound. Like a chain of ghouls with a body slung between them, they moved off into the darkness.

Chapter Thirty-One

"So that's him." Ginny had to admit the man stretched on the floor of her parlor did look like a monster. In fact, he made a terrifying sight. Damn it, she'd always loved this room and hoped this didn't change the complexion of it.

But she really feared it might.

Rom Gideon had pulled the drapes at all the windows as soon as they came in. Outside, dawn began to creep across the city, but it proved a gray day that promised rain.

Mason, still well-trussed, had been unconscious at the outset; he was coming to now. The rest of them...

A semicircle had formed around the sprawled form and included Ginny, Rom, Brendan, all three members of the Irish Squad, and Ginny's three surviving steamies. The man on the floor—who had only one eye—regarded each of them in turn, but his gaze returned to the members of the Irish Squad again and again.

"I know you." Mason's voice sounded sharp and rough, as if he spent his time screaming.

None of the hybrids responded. They stood instead like a wall made of steel and flesh, unmoving.

Rom Gideon bent down and, displaying unexpected muscle, almost casually hauled Mason up by his shirt. He deposited the man in Ginny's best chair.

Mason glared at him before switching his gaze to Brendan; it narrowed. "I know you also, I think."

Ginny, close enough to Brendan to touch his arm, felt him stiffen. She tried to imagine how it would feel facing down a man who'd very nearly stolen his eyes, scalp, and skin; she failed.

Rom Gideon clasped Brendan on the shoulder and said, "Time for you to do your magic, old son. Go to it."

Gideon moved to the side table where he poured himself a drink. Ginny's steamies trundled off also, filing from the room. The members of the Irish Squad remained where they were.

As did Ginny, at Brendan's side. She wasn't about to abandon him, not unless he asked it of her.

All members of the Irish race, so it was said, possessed the blarney when needed. She would have called Brendan an exception; forthright and honest, he spent little enough time in persuasion. But he poured honey into her ears when they were in bed together, and his voice softened to a lilting caress now when he hunkered down in front of the man in the chair.

"Hello, Mr. Mason. I'm glad you remember me."

Mason stared into Brendan's blue eyes, and something in his mind seemed to snap. He began to fight against the bonds still secured around his shoulders, chest, and arms, writhing and straining so much he tipped himself in the chair.

What caused that dead color in his skin, Ginny wondered. And was he too mad to cooperate with them?

One of the hybrids stepped forward and forced Mason back up with ungentle hands.

"What am I doing here?" Mason demanded in a half-screech.

"I should think you'd be glad to get out of that place." Brendan's tone remained calm. "Must be terrible being shut away in there. Enough to drive a fellow mad."

Rom Gideon, still standing at the side table, turned his head sharply at that. Brendan ignored him.

"I'm not mad. They think I am, but I'm not. They locked me up because they mistook my genius for insanity. I am a genius."

"I believe you." Brendan stared into the monster's face, his gaze steady. "You built these three hybrid units here, didn't you? And you meant to make another out of me. There's no one can match you for brilliance, is there?"

"No one. But my creations turned on me. They lacked gratitude for the one who gave them life. Atheists!" He shouted the last word at the automatons.

A theme there, Ginny thought. Her mother's creations had also turned on her. A lesson to be learned, no doubt. Playing God proved perilous.

Mason spat, "People are afraid of me. All of them are afraid of what I might achieve, the world I might create. That is why they locked me away."

"No doubt," Brendan said. Did only Ginny hear the quiver in his voice? "Your creations damaged you that night, didn't they? The night they—" He broke off. Now everyone in the room, including Mason, stared at him.

He went on determinedly, "They forgot what they owe you. That you're the only one who could have accomplished the magnificent undertaking that gave them life. Do you think you could do it again? Do you think you could recreate one of them?"

"Eh?" Even Mason seemed nonplussed by the question. A cunning expression crossed his ruined face. "Is that why I'm here? You wish me to turn you into one of them?" He nodded at the ranged hybrids and leaned forward in the chair to smile grotesquely. "You want me to give you immortality?"

Brendan shuddered—visibly this time. "Not me, no."

"Of course I can do it again! That and more. I'm not afraid of blood or stripping the elements from the bone. But you'll need to untie me, Irishman, if you want to live forever."

"I said not *me*." For the first time Brendan's voice sharpened. Ginny wondered how they could ever release this madman and trust him to work on Pat...even if Brendan did succeed in convincing him.

"You wish me to create a super being, one that cannot feel sickness or meet with defeat."

"Not build. Repair."

Mason, breathing hard in his agitation, subsided and stared at Brendan again.

"One of your own creations, Mr. Mason, has come under attack and suffered severe damage."

Mason shrugged, his face twisting grotesquely. "They are easily repaired. The skin gets stripped back, the frame welded. Any competent machinist can handle the job."

"His frame, yes. This one's damage is to his head—his artificial intelligence." Brendan lowered his voice. "But I doubt even you could salvage that."

Mason drew a shuddering breath. Suddenly a new

light filled his eyes. "Salvage? No need. I would create anew—"

"No, no, sir, that won't do. We want his mind back with all its knowledge. There's probably no one alive can accomplish it."

Mason contemplated him for several heartbeats. "Which of them is it? Which?"

"The unit you called 59."

"Ah!" Now the light in Mason's eyes burned. The three hybrids stirred, displaying reactions for the first time. "That one. That one was always special. The peak of my achievements."

"Yes, sir, he's still special. That's why we want him intact."

"He possesses valuable information, eh? State secrets?"

"Something like that."

"How severe is the damage?" Now Mason's voice sounded almost normal.

"It's bad. His head cavity's been staved in, and some of the contents have been pulverized. His attendants did manage to get him refired, but the knowledge itself seems irretrievable."

"Not irretrievable, no. Difficult but not impossible. A most delicate procedure, you understand."

"I do, yes."

"Something only I might achieve. I would have to see the subject, of course. Fifty-nine."

Flashes of brilliance and inspiration crossed Mason's face. "Where is the unit? Is it here?"

"Not here. We can take you to him, but I will need your agreement to conduct things in a professional and cooperative manner. I need your pledge, sir—no violence."

Mason switched his gaze to the hybrids behind Brendan. For the first time Ginny wondered if he feared them at all. But a twisted smile contorted his lips. "You think they'll let me turn violent? They're just waiting to jump on me. To batter me. They have the strength of many men."

"I know." Brendan hesitated before saying, "This is your chance to pull off one more great achievement—what nobody else can. But in exchange for this opportunity you must agree to act in good faith."

"What about after? Once I've restored 59 for you, I do not wish to return to the asylum."

Now Rom Gideon stepped forward. "How about we send you somewhere else? Provided you're successful, of course."

"Where?" Mason asked quickly.

Gideon shrugged carelessly. "What do you think of Mexico?"

"You can do that?"

"I can; I have connections."

Once again Mason leaned forward, his body—still bound—gyrating. He leered. "Barbados. I wish to go to Barbados."

"Barbados it is, old chap. Barbados straight away."

****

"You've lied to him, of course, aye?" Brendan whispered for Gideon's ear alone.

"Of course," Gideon replied, never taking his gaze from the man and his attendant automatons on the far side of the room.

"No Barbados?"

"No." Gideon's expression grew tight. "There are

times, Sergeant Fagan, when we say whatever we must. Ordinarily I do try to keep my promises—but not necessarily to madmen."

They both watched as the hybrids prepared Mason to leave. They fitted him with a harness they'd fashioned—one of them would be tethered to him at all times. Brendan had to admit that made him breathe more easily.

"What will happen to him after?" asked Ginny, at Brendan's other side, in a whisper.

"Back into the asylum, unfortunately for him," Gideon told her.

"They'll discover him missing soon." Brendan tensed. "There'll be a hue and cry."

"Yes. I doubt we'll be able to sneak him back in. We'll just have to present him to his keepers, once he works his miracle."

Worth it all, Brendan assured himself, if Pat could be Pat again—if Rose had what she needed.

A human police officer entered the room and told Brendan, "Paddy wagon's waiting outside. And Captain Addelforce is asking for you. There's been another murder."

"It'll have to wait." For once.

"Right-ho, Sarge. I'll go back and tell him I couldn't find you."

"Aye." Right down Thomas Crapper's wonderful invention he'd tossed his career. And pulled the chain.

With Mason hitched up to the satisfaction of the hybrids, they nodded at him. "Ready, sir."

"I'm coming with you," Ginny said.

"No, please stay here. Please, Ginny. I can't say what's going to happen, but I'd sooner know you're safe out of it."

"I'll go mad if I have to stay here. I'm coming, and that's it."

The drive to Pat Kelly's house proved nightmarish. As soon as the hybrids shut Mason in the back of the paddy wagon he began to howl, the sounds of his screams leaking out into the gray dawn. The others, following the wagon in a second vehicle, rode in grim silence. Ginny clutched Brendan's hand so hard it hurt.

Pat's home remained well lit, the crowd of steamies still in place around it. They made way for the paddy wagon and watched in unmoving silence as the hybrids unloaded their charge. Did those gathered grasp his identity? Brendan could tell the other hybrids present recognized him, by the way they straightened and went rigid, their gazes fixed on him to the exclusion of all else.

Far more chilling was the fact that Mason also recognized them and named them as he passed— Number 38, Number 4, Number 17. It made Brendan's mouth go dry.

Inside the Kellys' parlor another crowd awaited— more hybrids, including Mrs. Michaels and Chastity Greely, and a few other humans besides Mrs. Gideon. All stared at the fantastical figure in the harness.

Mrs. Gideon hurried to her husband's side. "You did it! Oh, Rom, thank goodness."

"How's Rose?" he asked in return.

She never had a chance to reply. Mason, fighting the harness a bit, began to demand, "Where is my subject? I need to see the extent of the damage."

"Here." Chastity Greely stepped up to face him. The two regarded one another for a long moment before

Mason's expression altered.

"What are you?"

"The next generation of what you created, sir. I would like to observe the procedure so I may replicate it at a future time, if necessary."

"You are…beautiful."

"I also have an advanced intelligence capable of learning and adapting. Come with me. I will show you your patient."

Mason turned to his hybrid minders. "Release me from this contraption first."

"We will not."

"I cannot work with such constrictions."

Rom Gideon started forward. Very casually he said, "Then we'll just haul you on back to the asylum, shall we?"

A long moment of silence turned the room unnaturally still before Mason growled his response.

"Show me my subject. And I will show you the meaning of brilliance."

Chapter Thirty-Two

"This is taking much too long," Brendan complained, pacing the confines of the Kellys' parlor. The day—just dawning when they'd arrived here with Mason—had grown old and now began to wane. Looking back on it, Brendan felt it had seemed both interminable and far too fleeting, a nauseating combination.

Word had come sporadically from the inner recesses of the flat where Mason remained shut away with Pat, Chastity Greely, and the three guardian hybrids. Mason had done an assessment and declared that yes, he could restore Unit 59. He demanded supplies, improved conditions, more light. He required a written declaration of his freedom or would not agree to continue.

Rom Gideon had gone in to speak with him and returned looking grim. "The man's unstable," he declared, "and his madness increases."

"But has there been any progress?" Topaz Gideon begged. "I need something to tell Rose."

Rom shook his head and bade her, "Tell Rose to hold on like the rest of us."

Word came from outside, also. The latest murder had occurred in one of the big houses on Delaware Avenue where a visitor had apparently been pushed down a flight of stairs by the household steamies before they fell upon and beat him to death on the floor below. Officer after officer brought subsequent developments in the case, each one saying Addelforce called for Brendan's presence at the station.

"Maybe you should go," Ginny told him more than once. "It doesn't look like this is going to happen quickly. I'll wait here."

Brendan merely shook his head.

Now, late in the day and with rain threatening the automatons that still clustered outside, a new message arrived: news of Mason's escape was all over the city. He was considered dangerous and his recapture declared a high priority.

"Well, we expected that," Rom Gideon said. "They will figure it out and come here soon. What we need is a distraction—sightings elsewhere in the city."

He left, presumably to set that in motion.

A resourceful man was Rom Gideon—impressive for an Englishman. Brendan felt glad to have him on their side and not against them.

When he perched at last on the edge of the settle, exhausted, Ginny joined him. Everyone there had, as with one mind, avoided sitting in Pat's armchair.

"God, I ache to know how things are going in there." She jerked her head toward the inner rooms. "Is there progress? Is that mad creature just stringing us along?"

"Aye." Brendan massaged his forehead with his good hand. "I keep thinking about these murders, too— why they're happening and what's behind them. Something's off there—since the very first, every instinct has told me so."

She leaned against his shoulder. "How do you

feel?"

"Don't worry about me. Tough as an old iron pot, me."

"I do worry, though. I'm afraid you're going to blame yourself if Mason can't resurrect Pat, even though it won't be your fault."

"I'm the one did the persuading, aren't I? No one else."

"What if Mason's beyond persuading? If his mind's gone—well, you're not responsible for that. Brendan? Brendan, look at me."

He turned and found her eyes waiting for him, deep brown and full of light. "I think you're a remarkable man, absolutely remarkable. And however this comes out—whether Pat survives or you lose your job or…or whatever, I'll not regret the time I've spent with you."

"Aye?"

"Aye," she repeated softly. "And that's quite a statement for me. I usually end up with regrets—some big, some small. Not with you."

Even as gladness at her words touched him, he couldn't help but wonder about the other men she'd had besides Hank; he ached to ask her about them, desired with a very real passion for her to tell him he was the best. A mutual streak of wildness had brought them together. But what might hold them together? Because he discovered he wanted very much to keep this woman in his life.

"It's strange," she said very softly indeed, "because I'd given up on the very idea of…"

A thunderous knocking sounded from the front door. The nearest person—a human police officer—hurried to answer it and returned followed by an older man also in uniform. Brendan leaped to his feet, recognizing a man called Emil Klemmer, now retired from the force.

"Thought you'd be here," Klemmer said, walking directly up to Brendan. "Captain Addelforce is looking high and low for you. Sent me to seek you out."

"Klemmer? I thought you retired."

"Captain called me in to help out, now we're so short-handed. I don't mind. Buffalo's in turmoil, and everybody who cares about this city needs to step up and do what he can."

"He's right, Brendan," Ginny agreed. "You'll have to go."

When she spoke, Klemmer turned his eyes on her. "You're that Dr. Landry's daughter, aren't you?" Curiosity brightened his eyes. "You two courting, then?"

"Not courting, no," Ginny answered quickly, and Brendan's heart sank. "But something like it."

"Tell Mrs. Gideon I had to leave." Still dressed in the black clothes Rom had lent him, Brendan moved to follow Klemmer.

Ginny caught him back with eager hands. "Not so fast. This is for luck." She kissed his cheek and, almost in the same breath, whispered into his ear, "Please keep safe, Brendan Fagan. And be sure to come back soon. Because I have something important to tell you, something you need to know."

****

I have something important to tell you. What kind of foolish thing had that been for Ginny to say to the man as he walked out the door? She should have just come out with the truth, told him straight how she felt about him, while she still had the chance. Granted, opening herself to him emotionally felt far more terrifying than doing so physically when they were in bed together. But was she a coward?

She never risked her heart. Never, ever. Yet something about the look in his eyes as he turned away made her regret withholding the confession. Words not spoken now might never be spoken at all.

A ridiculous assertion, she told herself. He'd merely gone to see the captain—in his own city, on his own ground. She'd see him in a few hours, at most.

Then why did watching him go out the door set all her instincts to howling?

Chastity Greely emerged from the inner room and approached Topaz Gideon, who'd taken up Brendan's pacing.

"Well?" Topaz asked. "Any progress?"

Chastity's exquisite face, rather disconcertingly, did not change. "It is impossible to tell. He has the contents of Pat's head spread over a wide surface in there."

Topaz twitched, or perhaps that was a shudder.

"And he is demanding more supplies—rare metals and things I am not sure we can procure. If this place gets raided and he is hauled away, I fear Pat will have no chance."

"What should I tell Rose?"

"Tell me the truth."

They all spun toward the door to the inner room. Rose Kelly stood there looking very much like an ambulating ghost. Someone had put her in a clean nightgown, and her hair hung loose down her back, but the white bandages at her wrists and her face contorted by pain turned the sight of her into something shocking.

Rasmussen, at her shoulder, looked prepared to catch her if she fell.

"Rose!" Topaz exclaimed even as everyone else stared. "You shouldn't be on your feet. Dr. Rasmussen—"

"I tell her," the doctor put in unhappily. "It is difficult when a patient cares nothing for her own welfare."

Rose Kelly ignored him. "Where is Pat?"

"In the spare room." Topaz moved to Rose's side. "But you won't do him any good this way."

"I want to see him."

"No, you don't."

"I need to see him."

"Rose, my dear, you truly don't. Not yet. Give us some more time."

"It's been far too long already!" Rose howled. "I want to see my husband."

"Perhaps," Rasmussen suggested, "just a brief viewing."

Topaz blanched, no doubt envisioning, as did Ginny, the scene Chastity had described—Pat's head open and its contents spread around the inner chamber.

"No. Just a while longer, Rose. I promise. Repairs are under way. I will send someone for any necessary supplies. I—"

She got no farther before Rose burst into sobs. Topaz took the woman in her arms; both she and the doctor led her back to her cot in the other room.

The hours dragged on. Rom Gideon failed to return, though Chastity Greely, sent on a foraging mission with her husband, Terry, came back loaded down with Mason's requested supplies. On one occasion, everyone in the parlor heard a voice from the inner chamber—Mason's?—lifted in what sounded like rage, as swiftly hushed again.

Then, deep into the hours of the night, the young officer called Dennis arrived, hat in hand and looking apologetic.

"How's Pat?" he asked the room at large. Looking crestfallen when Ginny and the others shook their heads, he went on, "I'm sorry to interrupt, but the captain's desperate. He says if Brendan's here I'm to bring him at any cost."

Ginny shot to her feet. "But he reported to Captain Addelforce hours ago."

They stared at one another, minds at cross purposes. Dennis shook his head. "He didn't. I've just come from the station. The captain wants to send him to the site of this latest murder. We haven't seen hide nor hair of him."

Cold drenched Ginny from the head downward. "You must be mistaken. Addelforce sent that man he called in—Klemmer, I think Brendan called him."

"Emil Klemmer? The captain hasn't called him in, so far as I know. Listen, how long ago did they leave?"

"Hours," Ginny repeated. Her heart started to pound. She remembered what Brendan had said about this case feeling off—his conviction there had to be a missing piece. Was this man Klemmer that piece? Had she let him walk off with Brendan from right under her nose?

And if so, where could they be in this big, dark, and crowded city?

Suddenly Rose Kelly's fear became personal. She

wanted to rage and wail, to howl at the sky.

Instead she seized Dennis's arm. "What do you know about this man Klemmer? Where could they be?" She struggled for breath. "You'd better take me to Addelforce."

Chapter Thirty-Three

"Holy Jaysus." Brendan grunted involuntarily as his broken arm was pulled behind and—despite the cast—bound to the other one. Agony washed through him in a dark wave, and he fought it back desperately.

Fool, fool, fool. He'd been a right idjit to go off with Klemmer, taking the man's appearance at face value, climbing into the cab he had waiting—not a steamcab but a regular horse-drawn one. There he found three dark figures waiting, all with black hoods over their faces. He'd realized his mistake then, right there in front of Pat's house with the automatons standing all around. He'd tried for escape, but the three men wrestled him back onto the seat and the cab moved away at a fast clip down Bryant Street toward Main and into the darkness.

The same three had manhandled him into a blackened building somewhere down around Main and Broadway, battering him when he tried to resist, landing several blows on his busted ribs. They'd tied him to a chair, both hands behind him, and at present he didn't think much of his chances. The three thugs—brave men all—kept their hoods in place. Too bad. Brendan would have liked to spit in those faces.

Unable to do that, he glared at Klemmer instead, struggling to recall more about him. The kind of officer who always did his job, he'd been nearing the end of his career when Brendan entered the force. Brendan would have said the man had just been marking his days then, waiting for retirement, which must have occurred over a year ago.

Brendan did recall Klemmer being vocal over the matter of the Irishmen hanged at the jail and sold to Charles and Mason—the raw materials, so to speak, for their hybrids. There'd been comments like, "They're just Irish" and "Maybe now they'll work for a living." As Brendan well knew, prejudice still existed, and not only toward automatons.

Now he began to wonder if Klemmer's dislike had another cause. A far darker one…

He should have seen the pattern, should have figured there was more to it than a bunch of rogue steam units. Thought himself so clever, he did, yet here he sat duly caught and the door slamming not only on his career but his future.

Ginny.

Heart struggling in his chest, he reached for her the way a bird in a cage strains for the open air.

"Well now," Klemmer said, eyeing him up and down. "Sorry to make you uncomfortable, Fagan, but I can't take any chances on you getting away. You've proved a right pain in my backside, do you know it? Sympathizer that you are."

"Sympathizer?" The word came out in a croak that made Brendan ashamed of himself. But he seemed to be having trouble getting air into his lungs, and his cracked ribs screamed at him. "I'm no…"

"Save it, Sergeant. I'll not hear your lies. You've been on the side of the automatons all the while. Friends with that monstrosity that calls itself Patrick

Kelly and that mob of machines that go around professing to be the Irish Squad. How can they still be Irish, for Christ's sake? It's an abomination."

"They—"

"You're a turncoat. A traitor to the cause. Your mother must weep over you."

"The cause."

"To rid ourselves of those vile, metal contraptions that prance about this city pretending to be men."

The three hooded figures chimed in with growls of agreement. It sounded uncanny in the big, darkened room.

"I'm no sympathizer," Brendan insisted. "I just think everybody deserves a fair chance."

"You're right, Sergeant. So everybody does— every *body* made in God's likeness of flesh and blood. Not ungodly machines bent on taking over the force, our city, and the world. We're putting a stop to it here and now, do you understand? Before it spreads. Before they gain these rights they're after and we find ourselves working for them."

Brendan said nothing, though his thoughts clattered like a fast horse down a narrow street. The Automaton Liberation Movement had put a lot of humans on edge, and they'd started fighting back. His own physical condition reflected that. Quite obviously, the divide in the city had become a wide fracture. Were Klemmer and his crew responsible for the murders? Not rogue or disgruntled steamies at all but men who wanted to put the automatons in the very worst light?

He drew another breath; this one came just a bit easier. "I've been a pain in your backside, have I?"

"You ask too many questions, even for a

policeman. Don't you know a good cop does his job and no more? Walks his beat, answers to his superiors, and keeps the base element at bay. Your trouble, Sergeant"—Klemmer paused and waved a finger in Brendan's face—"is you don't know what's good for you. You're too ambitious. And that's a selfish trait."

"Is it?"

"You need to think about what's best for all of us—the humans of this city—like the rest of us have done."

"You're heroes, are you?" Brendan asked.

The three hooded men stirred on their feet. One grunted.

"We're heroes," Klemmer confirmed proudly. "Vigilantes. We'll make folks see the danger lurking among us before we're done. Not like you."

Klemmer stepped closer to Brendan's chair, seized him by the hair, and drew his head back so he might glare into his eyes. "You're a right disgrace, Sergeant."

"Am I?"

"Consorting with the worst of them."

"You mean the members of the Irish Squad."

"Not them, though they're bad enough. I'm talking about the daughter of that unnatural witch who created another crop of those things—harlots, no less! Don't try and deny it. I saw her kiss you. And the whole force knows you're sleeping with her. I still have plenty of friends on the force."

Ginny. This time Brendan's stomach turned over when he thought of her. Was she still safe?

Was anyone in this city really safe?

Now he growled, "Leave her out of it."

"I'd like to, Sergeant. I truly would. No man of any

worth likes harming a woman. But that woman carries evil in her bones, and that evil shouldn't be passed down to another generation. We need to stamp it out— all of it. Right, men?"

The three hooded figures again chimed in their agreement.

"She's not like her mother." Ah, and he should have let Ginny leave Buffalo as she'd planned—should have sent her far away from here to where she'd be safe. Because suddenly her safety meant far more to him than his own.

If he didn't escape from here he couldn't protect her. And looking into Klemmer's staring eyes, he didn't like his chances of escaping.

"Have some faith in your city," he grated out. "Trust the people and the automatons to find a way to exist together."

"Trust? Automatons?" Klemmer gave a hard laugh. "They've not a drop of humanity in them, Sergeant. They've already begun turning good folks—like yourself—into their puppets. How long before they seize positions of power? No, no—they must be stamped out. Made illegal. Declared dangerous and abolished."

Hence the staged murders all over the city. Aye, in a twisted way it made sense. Men like Klemmer might not see the humanity that lurked within every automaton—the aching desire for *personhood*. Maybe they didn't want to see.

Klemmer leaned down and spoke directly into Brendan's face. "You, Sergeant, were getting too close. You would have tumbled to the truth soon. Now you'll make another piece in the pattern—sadly beaten to

257

death while investigating a murder in a back alley. Must have come upon the murderous steamies before they quite got away. Great loss to the city—you being such a rising star—and to that bitch you're bedding."

Brendan's mind flailed like a gasping fish. He didn't want to die; of course he didn't. Especially here in this grubby room, tied to a chair so he couldn't fight back. Worse, though, was knowing he'd have no chance to warn Ginny, that she'd likely be next in this maniac's march toward eradication.

He had to get free, had to say whatever he could, whatever he must to change Klemmer's mind about him and allow for escape.

"Wait now," he gasped eyeing the three thugs, one of whom had drawn a billy club from the pocket of his coat. "Give a man a moment to think. Mr. Klemmer here is making a great deal of sense."

"Oh, don't even try and talk me round, Sergeant. You think I'll believe anything you say? Do you take me for a fool? Even the ardent missionary will renounce Jesus when his feet hit the cooking pot."

"But I'd be a valuable man to have on your side."

"So you would, and it's a great pity you went the other way. We could never trust you. You'll just have to be chalked up as another casualty of those dangerous machines—a damned convincing one, I should think. Shows the automatons can turn on even one of their closest allies. But we'll put it about you must have been closing in on the truth about them. A bit ironic that, isn't it?"

Oh, yes.

"Me, I love irony. When you're found in that alley, nothing but a pile of broken bones in a pool o' blood, now, that will be the very picture of irony."

Klemmer gestured with one hand. "Take him, boys."

"Big men, brave men," Brendan rasped at the three figures, "taking on a fella who's trussed to a chair. You think any good copper will believe that? It needs to look like I fought back—because I damn sure would. You'll have to untie me."

And what good would that do? He might be strong and could rely on a rush lent by mingled fear and determination, but he had a broken arm and four busted ribs. What could he hope to do against three thugs armed with billy clubs?

Klemmer must have arrived at the same conclusion. He nodded at the thugs and one of them stepped forward to untie Brendan, no more gently than he'd been tied in the first place.

"There, Fagan. Can't say I'm not a fair man. No machine, me. Human kindness runs through my veins. But it's going to end for you here, understand?"

Ginny, Brendan thought again. He should have told her exactly what she meant to him when he had the chance, thrown caution to the winds and expressed his devotion. If he survived, he vowed he would.

If he survived.

Chapter Thirty-Four

"You need to find him. Do you understand that? Why are you just sitting there?"

Raging like a wild woman, Ginny stood before the desk of Captain Addelforce, who seemed to have aged by years overnight. Had she been thinking clearly, she would have perceived the truth—the man looked nearly as desperate as she felt.

She didn't care about that, though. A single thought dominated her mind, and her will had leaped to the fore.

"Miss Landry," Addelforce began, "just what would you have me to do?"

"Trace the cab in which he was taken away." The entire crowd of steamies waiting outside Pat's house had seen Brendan enter that cab and had watched it head east down Bryant Street.

"Do you know how many horse-drawn cabs still operate in this city?"

"Track them all down."

"Miss Landry, I haven't the resources. We're already stretched impossibly thin."

"He's your sergeant! Is this how the Buffalo police force looks after its own?"

"Miss Landry, the entire Irish Squad is off duty, most of them keeping vigil at Kelly's place. I have men investigating two new murders and more putting out the kind of fires that could easily flare into confrontations between the human and automaton citizenry. On top of that, the most dangerous man in this city has unaccountably escaped from the asylum on Forest Avenue."

Ginny fought to keep her expression from changing.

"This man," Addelforce went on, "could easily tip the city into a state of riot. The mayor has charged me with recapturing him at all cost, and I have much of my limit resources concentrated on locating him."

"What do you know about this man who took Brendan away—Klemmer?"

"Good man. Never made any trouble on the force. Did his job and went home at night, put in his time and made retirement. Miss Landry, it's possible you're mistaken. Klemmer might be operating in good faith."

"Without your sanction."

"Without my sanction," Addelforce admitted. "But this is an all-hands-on-deck situation."

"He was in uniform."

Addelforce frowned. "Men often keep their uniforms when they retire, for sentimental reasons."

"So you're not concerned."

"I am concerned, Miss Landry, about any number of things, Brendan Fagan among them."

"But you won't search for him?"

"Miss Landry, you haven't been listening. I can't search for him—I haven't the manpower—and I'm not convinced of the need. I'm sure he'll turn up."

So was Ginny—but in what condition? "I want Klemmer's address."

"I can't give you that."

Ginny's desperation flared into something far fiercer. She'd often wondered whether any trace of Candace Landry lurked inside her. She'd modeled herself after her father, or so she hoped—strong and compassionate—and had always believed the wild streak belonged to her alone. Now, though, she tasted a ruthlessness that almost frightened her in its intensity.

She leaned across Addelforce's desk into his face. "You listen to me. That's my man out there—injured and in danger. Whether or not you grasp that doesn't concern me. Give me Klemmer's last known address or I'll get it from members of your force. I'm sure you don't want me distracting them from their assignments."

Addelforce blinked at her. "Don't try and bully me, Miss Landry. The last thing I need is a vigilante."

"No, Captain, the last thing you need is me good and angry, at large in your city."

"Don't make me arrest you, Miss Landry."

Ginny laughed. "What, with your limited resources? The same that prevent you from providing backup to one of your best officers, a man who's put your department first in his life time after time?"

Addelforce sighed. "Is Petersen still out there? Send him in. I'll give him the address and I'll let him accompany you there, just to set your mind at rest. But don't let me hear of you stirring up trouble."

Ginny turned away toward the door.

"Oh, and Miss Landry—should you locate Sergeant Fagan, send him here to me. I still need him on these murders."

Ginny Landry bared her teeth. "With all due respect, Captain, I'll be damned if I do."

****

Three against one did not make good odds, especially when the three were armed and the one was carrying a full set of broken bones. That thought whipped through Brendan's mind as he stood in a half crouch, facing the men ranged against him. He'd need to use his brain rather than his muscle if he meant to get out of this.

And be with Ginny again.

Oh, God, he lived to be with Ginny again. The big, bad bachelor—fairly caught, he was. But he'd worry about that later, when he was sure there'd be a later.

He wondered how easily his opponents could see through those hoods. Made of heavy, black cloth, they had mere slits for eyes. And they couldn't whack a target they couldn't see.

Upon that thought he leaped, giving the kind of yell his ancestors might have during a bloody battle back in Meath. He and his brothers used to play at that, pretending to be wild Irish clansmen making battle, till his ma would come out of the house and tell them to stop hollering like banshees.

Now the sound echoed through the dark building, amplified a thousand times. Brendan grasped his first opponent's hood, jerked it over his eyes, and kicked him in the knee.

The man went down with a grunt, but the other two closed on him immediately. One gave his broken arm a thump with the club, and the ensuing pain drove all the breath from him. For an instant he saw only black fog. But he kept moving, barreled his body into the fellow's midsection, and rolled with him across the floor.

Toward the door.

That fellow would not stay down long. Wracked by pain, Brendan stumbled to his feet and kicked the downed man in the head. Good sturdy police-issue boots—good for more than the streets of Buffalo.

Klemmer bellowed and started for him, along with the third hooded man. Giving himself no time to hesitate, Brendan leaped again—toward rather than away. Neither of them expected it, and he succeeded in grabbing Klemmer before the third man could prevent it, trapping him with the plaster cast up across his windpipe.

"Toss down your weapons, all of you."

The first man had climbed to his feet. The second, still down, moved like a turtle on its back. Brendan throbbed so fiercely he could hardly see straight. He could hear the pain in his own voice.

"Your weapons—all of them! In a pile over there, or I swear I'll choke the life out o' this one."

"You won't," Klemmer croaked. "You're a good copper under it all."

"And you're a murderer, Klemmer. How many people died when you staged your supposed automaton killings? I've no compunction about strangling a little rat like you."

"I don't see how you can side with them. Those damned hybrids nearly killed you that night Charles and Mason were arrested."

"Nearly, Klemmer—that's the word. They didn't, and do you know why? Because there's something in them that's the same as what's in us. Unless you see that and stop the hating, there'll be no peace in this city."

He drew a breath, struggling for it. He could feel

the tension in Klemmer's body, tight against his, could smell the man's sweat. If Klemmer made a break for it, Brendan couldn't be sure he had the necessary strength to subdue him. His entire body hurt like toothache, and he felt pretty sure only the rush of the fight kept him on his feet.

"Now," he jerked his head at the first man, "tie up your buddies—use the rope you used on me."

"Don't do it!" Klemmer bleated. "He knows who we are."

"Knows who *you* are," corrected one of the men in a deep voice. Snatching up the ropes from Brendan's chair, he tied up first the hooded man beside him and then the one on the floor, Klemmer cursing him for a coward all the while.

When he finished, he took another look at Brendan before turning and pelting away into the dark recesses of the building.

Klemmer used the opportunity to make his move, bucking against Brendan's hold and trying to wrest his way free. With the last of his strength, Brendan increased the pressure on Klemmer's throat, using the man's own strength against him, and dropping him to the floor only after he went limp.

"There now," he said, fighting for breath, his ribs screaming in protest. "Your friend was the smart one. I won't know who he is. As for you other two…"

He moved forward and plucked the hood from the head of each bound man, stared hard at their faces in the limited light. Strangers both, the one he'd kicked in the head looked barely conscious. The other regarded him with wary dismay.

"I'll be sure and remember you."

Moving like an old man now, he tied up Klemmer, using the man's own belt. With that one secure, he took all three billy clubs and stuffed them in his pockets.

He needed to get out of here fast, before the third man thought better of it, gathered some friends, and came back. He needed to reach Addelforce and tell him what he'd discovered about Klemmer, the truth about the murders.

Maybe that would soothe some of the rampant hate in this city and defuse the likelihood of a riot.

But first he had to find Ginny and ask her just what she needed to tell him.

Aye, Ginny first—because he wanted her to admit it, once and for all.

Chapter Thirty-Five

"My husband is not here."

The small woman who opened the door at Klemmer's address wore a stubborn expression and had a small scar on her face, what looked like a burn to the right cheek. Three young children crowded her skirts; all of them stared at Ginny, round-eyed and wary.

"Where is he?"

Mrs. Klemmer's gaze flicked to the face of Dennis Petersen, who stood at Ginny's shoulder, and back again. "I don't know. He's gone out on official business."

"Not on police business he hasn't, Mrs. Klemmer," Petersen said. "He's no longer part of the force."

Something flashed in Mrs. Klemmer's eyes—the merest hint of deception. "He's helping out."

That flicker gave her away. Without it, Ginny might have believed this woman didn't know what her husband got up to. Now she said, "You mean he's out on the devil's business. He's abducted a police officer, Mrs. Klemmer. I suggest, for your own sake, you cooperate with us."

Mrs. Klemmer's upper lip rose like that of a snarling cur. "And who are you to come here making demands? If my husband's not part of the force, well, neither are you."

"I have a personal interest."

Mrs. Klemmer's gaze narrowed abruptly. "I know who you are. You're the daughter of that vile creature who constructed those—" She broke off and glanced at the children behind her. "Go inside," she told them sharply.

They went without argument.

"Your grandchildren?" Ginny asked.

Mrs. Klemmer gave a hard nod. "We're raising them, Emil and me. Their mother was killed."

Must be difficult on a retiree's income. A lot of people in this city had it hard. Did that explain the resentment in the woman's voice?

"And, Mrs. Klemmer, how do you know who I am?"

The woman raised her chin with a jerk. "Emil pointed you out to me at the Park."

"You were there?" A significant admission. "Mrs. Klemmer, I don't care what you thought of my mother—I never knew her and I'm my own woman. But your husband's getting into some treacherous waters. Abducting a policeman is a serious crime. Tell us where they've gone and make it better for you and those children."

"I don't know and I wouldn't tell you if I did. Do you suppose I keep track of where Emil goes every time he leaves this house?"

Ginny thought she might. "There must be a place where he meets with his cronies."

Mrs. Klemmer's lip lifted again. She lowered her voice to an ugly whisper, presumably so the children in the house wouldn't hear. "I hate your kind, siding with those infernal machines, pretending they have feelings like the rest of us, that they matter like the rest of us.

Everybody with an ounce of proper understanding knows only people bleed and weep—and feel."

Ginny bit back all the things she wanted to say: that she'd seen humor in a hybrid's eyes, and kindness. That Rose Kelly's husband mattered to her so much she'd tried to take her own life rather than live without him.

This woman, with her prejudices, wouldn't hear any of it. So instead, with despair in her heart, she said, "Mrs. Klemmer if your husband comes home, please dissuade him from carrying on with this ruinous course he's embraced. I beg you to—"

"He's protecting us all. I'd expect you to see that, given how your mother died. It's a fight for survival, and in the trenches there must be sacrifices. Now get away from my door."

"Mrs. Klemmer—"

The door slammed in Ginny's face; she heard the bolt slide home.

Panic in her heart, she turned to Dennis. "Where to now, Officer? Where can Brendan be?"

****

As soon as Brendan poked his head out the door of the darkened building and peered down Broadway toward Main, he sensed something afoot. He knew this city—the look, feel, and smell of it. He'd spent sufficient time on foot patrol to know how it sounded at night, a subdued hum, never quite silent.

Now, over the thump of his own heart, which kept time with the various aches in his body, he heard…

Footsteps. The scrape of boots on bricks. Hushed voices. Wrongness.

He wondered suddenly if this building—perhaps

not just a holdup place but some grim headquarters—weren't surrounded by others like those he'd left inside, and whether the fleeing man had summoned others after all. Maybe defeating those inside had done him no good.

He needed to move, and quickly. If only his battered body would cooperate.

His thoughts of Ginny got him moving. *Away* first of all, and after that, so he told himself, *to.* Hugging the shadowed buildings, he moved out to Main, looked southward down its broad expanse, and saw…

Initially, he couldn't believe his eyes. He blinked fiercely. An army. One bent on destruction.

Even as the thought exploded in his mind, they proceeded toward him—no, not an army after all. An army kept some order and had some discipline. This, most decidedly, was a mob.

They carried what in the dim light looked like the pikes carried by rebel Irishmen in the old stories and songs from back home. Heroes, those—Brendan couldn't be so sure about this lot. Even as he stood watching, his breath held tight, stones were flung. Glass broke. The businesses along Main Street would pay a price tonight.

And then what? Once this group ran amok, would they try to blame the damage on automatons? Another black eye for the steamies, to dissuade the powers-that-be to keep them down?

Men like Emil Klemmer wanted all the steam units destroyed, rubbed out like a disease. They wanted the automatons' jobs and felt the threat of units like Pat Kelly and Chastity Greely perhaps achieving more than they could. They wouldn't rest until others agreed with them.

But wouldn't this mob realize they'd be seen engaging in all this destruction? How did they mean to deal with that? Through more threats and intimidation?

It would tear Brendan's city in two.

Standing there in the dark with danger surging toward him, he realized how much he loved this city. Aye, he'd come from the old sod and carried a goodly measure of it within him, but in this magical, beautiful, stubborn place perched on the edge of the blue lake like an eccentric lady on a slightly seedy settee, he'd grown and learned and become a man. He wanted to be nowhere else. And he'd be damned if he'd let anyone destroy it.

What he needed was an army of his own. Of policemen? No—they were too few, and unable for the most part to take sides. He needed an army that would take sides.

And take orders.

He needed an army of automatons.

Frozen in place, watching the mob of humans come steadily closer, he looked the prospect squarely in the face. An army facing a mob would spark a battle royal. Did he want that? No, but he wanted this thing over and done. And as the old stories told, at least in Ireland sometimes a battle had to be fought for the sake of justice.

The automatons in this city wanted their freedom, did they? Let's see if they'd be willing to gain it by taking a few last orders.

He stepped out onto the street and, by a trick of the starlight, the mob saw him. A howl went up, a bloodcurdling sound like beagles on the scent that bounced off the buildings and echoed eerily down the street.

Brendan turned north and, for all he was worth, ran.

****

"What do you mean she's not here?" Brendan had burst through the door of Pat Kelly's house and into a circle of lamplight that, after the dark streets he'd coursed, hurt his eyes. He'd managed to lose the bulk of his pursuers along the way—too many of them to move quickly—but he knew a few individuals remained on his tail. He'd hated leading even those few here but remembered the crowd of steamies outside—a good start. Besides, Ginny was here, or so he'd believed, and she drew him like a lodestone drew iron.

Now ready hands caught hold of him. A strong pair—they belonged to Topaz Gideon—pressed him down into a chair.

"Sit before you fall. What's happened?"

Spent, he had to fight for breath before he could say, "All hell's broke loose. I know who's behind the murders around the city and why. Where is she?" Out there somewhere in the darkness, where people hated her for her mother's sake and any harm could befall her.

Topaz Gideon's amber eyes met his. "She went looking for you."

"Why?"

"The police captain sent someone here after you, when you'd already been fetched to him by that fellow—"

"Klemmer. He's behind most of this. Humans against automatons. We have to find her. Tell me she's not alone."

"She went with an officer. What was his name? Petersen."

A good enough man, trustworthy, but young and inexperienced. Brendan groaned.

Rom Gideon, now returned, emerged from the inner room and joined those ranged around Brendan.

"How do things progress with Pat?" Brendan asked him.

Gideon shook his head. "Our friend is still working and making demands. To be perfectly honest, I'm no longer certain whether he actually needs the things he's asking for in order to achieve the rebuild or whether he can complete the job at all."

Despair touched Brendan's heart. "I was hoping Pat would be in a condition where I could at least speak with him. I need him—or his authority—to call up the automatons of this city."

"Call them up?" echoed Topaz.

"There's a mob of militant humans coming." Brendan jerked his head toward the door. "If the automatons of Buffalo believe in themselves, now's the time to make a stand."

A soft murmur went around the room. More than half those gathered were automatons, many of them hybrids.

Brendan said, "Pat's the closest thing to a leader we have. No one else can speak for him."

One of the hybrids, Terry Greely—Chastity's husband—said, "Rose can speak for him—as his wife she's the only one who can. Talk to her, Sergeant Fagan. See if she'll lend you Pat's name and authority."

Chapter Thirty-Six

"Rose, Brendan needs to ask you something," Topaz said softly.

Rose Kelly sat propped on her cot in the room beside the one where her husband had been dismantled, the white bandages on her wrists bright banners testifying to her state of mind. She and Dr. Rasmussen, still in attendance, must have been playing cards—a deck lay spread between them on a small table. The doctor rose, when Brendan and Topaz entered, and slipped from the room.

Rose lifted both hands to her heart. "I thought you'd come to tell me the madman had failed after all, that I wouldn't be getting Pat back."

"No," Brendan answered. "The madman's still working."

He sat down in Rasmussen's vacated chair, and Topaz tiptoed out.

Rose gestured at the cards. "Dr. Rasmussen is very kind. Not only has he refused to leave me alone, he's attempted to distract me with Rummy. It doesn't help. Nothing does."

"Waiting is never easy," Brendan said lamely.

Disconcertingly, Rose's brown eyes filled with tears. "And right now I'm waiting to find out if I'll ever again be with the person I love most in the world."

Brendan thought of Ginny—out there somewhere

in the dark without him. Alive or dead? He didn't think much of her chances if that mob caught her. The despair nibbling at the edges of his sanity threatened for an instant to overwhelm him. He fought it back. Despair would render him as good as useless. How could he save Ginny then?

Rose blinked away the tears. "But what can I do for you, Sergeant?"

"It's about the cause. Pat's cause."

"Automaton rights, you mean?" Rose tilted up her chin. "Well, you know it's my cause too. I've seen the injustice first hand."

Brendan jerked his head toward the door. "Rose, it's all broke wide open out there. There's an army of vigilante humans on the move, bent on intimidation. They'll destroy anything in their path, and it's too big for the police. That mob needs to be faced down."

"By automatons." Rose stated the words with certainly. "This is the moment Pat awaited."

"It looks like it, Rose."

"And he's going to miss it." Two tears leaked from her eyes after all. The pain in her face made Brendan's heart ache.

"We can do it for him. If you'll lend me his name, Rose; as his wife, you're the only one who can."

Her hands moved spasmodically on the blanket.

Brendan pressed on. "But you must do it now while he's still a-alive, so to speak."

"While his existence, and mine, hangs in the balance?"

"Yes."

"Sergeant Fagan, I was married before. Did you know that? Oh, not in this body. That's what made it

legal for me to marry Pat even though my husband—
my first husband—is still alive in Philadelphia. I—at
least my spirit—was forced into this body by yet
another monster. I wanted no part of it…didn't wish to
live this way…would have killed myself then. But there
was Pat, kind and warm and always there—so
understanding. He taught me the flesh doesn't matter.
Nor does the steel. It's all about the sweetness of the
soul inside.

"Sergeant Fagan, I may never again be in the
company of the sweetest soul I've ever known. I may
no longer be able to live for Pat—but I can live for his
cause. Right is right." She leaned forward and touched
Brendan's hand. "You have all the authority I can give
to use Pat's name. Call up every automaton in this city
if you have to. Make it right—for his sake."

****

The call passed in whispers that were less whispers
than clicks and mechanical whines—*Pat Kelly
says…Pat Kelly says…he has summoned us. It is time.*

Brendan, aching from head to toe, stood in the gray
dawn at Niagara Square, the place chosen for the
automatons to amass. Before his eyes, the sun came up
in a welter of red from the east. He vaguely recalled
school lessons from his youth and some poem by one of
the old poets—Sir Walter Scott, possibly—that
proposed a red sunrise as an ill harbinger for battle.

He'd never imagined himself leading a battle of
any kind. A peacekeeper, he would have said, despite
his militant Irish ancestors and that deep-seated wild
streak he believed he'd successfully disciplined. This
could not be battle of the usual kind. Using Pat's name,
he had to impress that on his charges—they could stand

strong, they could resist, but they could cause no harm.

His army must be one of peaceful demonstration like that other fellow they'd told him about in school—Thoreau, that was the man. The automatons must gain their liberation by proving they weren't the danger they'd been painted, by *not* fighting for it.

If he failed in this, the city would explode. He'd fail Pat's memory as well, and probably never see Ginny again.

Ginny. His heart yearned for her and anxiety nibbled at him anew. In this standoff, members of the Irish Squad had become his runners—they possessed both the endurance and the intelligence for it. He'd sent them out everywhere like collies herding in all the automatons who would come and keeping an eye on the human contingent. He'd also asked them to look out for Ginny and Dennis Petersen.

No word yet. No word yet.

As he stood on the edge of the stone fountain overlooking the assembly—steamies big and small, many of the silver bodies reflecting the garish morning light—he wondered where she was.

He whispered, very like a charm or a prayer, "Please. Keep her safe."

****

"Quiet. Don't even breathe."

Obediently, Dennis Petersen sucked in his gut. The two of them—he and Ginny—stood smashed up against a wall in an alley off Auburn Street, carriage houses on either side. Ginny suspected Mrs. Klemmer must have sicced their pursuers after them; the band of five humans had picked them up soon after they left her house. Of course it could be pure chance; humans seemed to be everywhere in the city—mainly groups here and there, as well as a larger body that she'd glimpsed farther east. Ginny had heard the sound of breaking glass before she and Dennis ran in this direction, and she thought she'd also caught a rumble as of far-off voices. It might have been thunder, but now the sun began to rise in an orb that bled orange across the sky.

"What's that?" Dennis gasped in defiance of Ginny's instructions. The young officer sounded spooked, and Ginny couldn't blame him. She saw it too—a flash of silver between the carriage houses on the far side of the alley, then another and another. All heading in one direction.

What the hell?

She had no time to ponder it further. At the far end of the alley appeared two figures. Swiveling her head she saw three more at the nearer end. Their pursuers had split up in order to trap them.

Dennis gurgled, "Shit, miss. We're going to die."

"No we're not." Not before Ginny saw Brendan Fagan again, at least—gazed into those blue eyes of his and told him she couldn't live without him. Because she loved him, *loved him*.

The words became a song in her head—a battle anthem.

"Do you have your cosh?"

"Yeah, but—"

But. Yes, their pursuers came well-armed with what looked like long metal poles. Ginny's racing thoughts supplied the word *pikes*. She didn't doubt they had knives, too. Probably clubs. These lowlifes usually did.

"We're going to fight," she told Dennis. "When they come at us, holler. Can you holler? Loud and intimidating."

"I'm not sure."

His throat would be dry, just like hers. She gave him one understanding look and said, "You take on the two; I'll take the three. Follow my lead."

She drew the small steam cannon from the long pocket of her coat—the same she'd employed at the bar that first night she met Brendan. Dennis's eyes boggled.

See now we have a chance, she wanted to tell him. There was no time. Their assailants moved in from either end at a dead run.

Ginny screamed an ear-splitting screech that reverberated off the buildings of the alley. Her first blast took one of the three attackers in the middle of his chest with force enough to make him pirouette before he fell. His pike dropped from his hands with a clatter; his two fellows swore and came on.

The trouble with steam cannons, Ginny reflected even as she heard Dennis bellow behind her—good man!—was even the best of them took precious moments to recharge. It hadn't seemed so long, back in the tavern, while she'd been busy aggravating what she thought of as a strait-laced policeman. Now, with maiming, pain, and possible death bearing down on her, it became an eon.

She heard grunting behind her as Dennis employed his cosh. She dared not look at him—her assailants' features became clearer as they neared.

The one on the right hollered, "It's her—that Landry bitch! Her ma's the one made them whore machines. Get her!"

Ginny looked into his eyes—square into the wild blaze of hate.

And shot him.

The cannon, not yet fully charged, stuttered as it fired. Yet at the range of only a few feet the blast had strength enough to kill, especially as it took the man in the throat, partially vaporizing the skin and setting what lay beneath on fire.

The man went down in a heap; Ginny and his companion looked at one another. A big ugly fellow, he had a bald head and fleshy lips that hung open— perhaps in surprise. The surprise deserted him when he decided her cannon wouldn't fire again so soon. Not before he got his hands on her.

Ginny could hear Dennis struggling behind her and dared a single look; he had one assailant down and clutching his knee. But Dennis now lay on his back with the last man standing over him.

Oh, God, oh, God, how were they going to get out of this?

Brendan. Loved him, loved him, loved…

She lifted the spent sidearm between her hands and swung.

Chapter Thirty-Seven

"Jaysus, Mary, and Joseph," Brendan swore in wonder. A sea of silver surrounded him where he stood, only slightly elevated at the center of the square. Someone—a member of the Irish Squad he thought, though he couldn't be sure—had found a bullhorn and pressed it into his hands. Facing east, the direction from which the human contingent would come, the dreadful red sunrise filled his eyes. But from behind he could smell the river, a scent that, like coalsmoke and steam, seemed to personify this city he loved.

Could a city be alive, an entity of itself? At the moment, holding the fate of this place by a string, he didn't doubt it. Energy seemed to run beneath his very feet, fanning out under the streets like life's blood.

If a being of steel could claim life, why not a city?

And if he were to die here on this morning beneath a sky colored blood red, would he consider it a life well spent? Maybe, but damn it, he wanted to live. To be with Ginny again.

He raised the bullhorn to his lips. "Ready yourselves. Here they come."

Around him the sea of silver rippled like water. How many steamies occupied this city? It must be far more than he'd estimated, and an astounding number had managed to get away from their places of employment. In fact, they still streamed into the square behind him, mostly silent. Ahead of him…

The humans came in a dark body like floodwaters finding their way through the streets. As they reached the east side of the square, they slowed, a tide meeting a shore.

They would be armed with clubs, those wicked-looking pikes, and steam cannons too, if they'd been able to get their hands on some. Brendan wondered again where the police were in this. Merely overwhelmed? Or had the individual members, like him, taken sides?

Would the police airship come overhead before long? If it did, would it participate against one side or the other?

No time to think about that now. Ryan, one of the Irish Squad, popped up at his side, eyes wide and reflecting the red dawn.

"Just a few stragglers coming in," he reported. "We outnumber them, but they are armed." He slanted a surprisingly human look at Brendan. "You sure we should not fight back?"

"We can't fight back; we can only stand. We're proving a point here, lad—that steamies aren't the source of the violence in this city."

"We've always fought back in self-defense. Even in the Candace Landry incident."

"I know. And that's what put flame to thatch in all this. We have to stand. Repel them, knock them down if we have to. No attack."

"The units out front are going to take a beating."

"I'm hoping they can be repaired, after." Like Pat? Brendan turned his thoughts away from that. "If they don't want to stay, they don't have to."

"They'll stay." Ryan's eyes met Brendan's again. "They want this. We all do."

"Send your runners through the crowd. Tell them again, resistance—no violence. We're taking this city by sheer numbers and determination, an unmovable force."

Ryan slipped off silent as a shadow, leaving only the barest wisp of steam behind. If Brendan narrowed his eyes he could see a steam haze hanging over his side of the square, warring with that ugly, garish dawn. Though he hadn't prayed for real in years, he closed his eyes and murmured words to...something. Not for himself but for those who stood so bravely around him, for Pat and for Ginny. Ginny, Ginny. Warm and alive in his arms, so much passion rushing at him. He needed to hold onto that—a grand last thought, if it came to it.

A man stepped forward from the crowd of humans facing him. Tall and well dressed, he carried not only a pike but a steam sidearm. With a jolt of shock, Brendan recognized him.

The police commissioner. Hell, how deep was the force involved in all this? He understood then. If the airship did fly over, he knew on just which army it would fire.

"Brendan Fagan!" the commissioner sang out. "Show yourself."

"Right here, Mr. Messenberg." Brendan certainly hadn't been trying to hide.

Messenberg, a powerfully built man of perhaps fifty, scowled prodigiously. "Fagan, what are you doing in the middle of this? You're a good cop. Come over to this side where you belong."

Brendan straightened his battered body. "I am

where I belong, sir, and that's because I'm a good cop. I'm standing up for justice here."

"Justice? You show me the justice in murderers going free just because some lawyer declares them exempt from the law. I was there on the airship that night—I saw those infernal units beat that woman to death at the Crystal Palace. Now they're at liberty in this city—our city. They're getting married and trying to adopt children, human children! Worst of all they want to construct others like themselves, infernal hybrids in their own image. It stops here, Fagan—or where will it end?"

Brendan bellowed back, "Justice in this city needs to encompass everyone—you're right about that, sir. And that means adult, child, animal, and metal. Where's the justice in an owner having the power to shut down a steam unit, as Mrs. Landry threatened that night? I'm not saying what happened to her was right, sir, but those units were living in slavery, and abused slaves tend to revolt."

"Curse you for a steam-loving turncoat!" Messenberg snarled.

"Curse me all you like, but we're going to stand here till we get some measure of just treatment for these units. That means rights. And we understand with rights come consequences. Steam units will become subject to the law—just like those who employ them. Not *own*, Mr. Messenberg, but *employ*."

"You're mad," Messenberg shouted. "Why should we pay for services we've always had for free?"

"Because it's right. Look around you, Mr. Messenberg. Every one of these units has come from a business or household in this city. What if they all refused to work? A stoppage would bring this city to its knees."

"Maybe so, but we won't be blackmailed. This city's still ours—we'll prove that here and now if we have to."

Ryan popped back up beside Brendan. "Airship's aloft."

Aye, and no doubt well-loaded with steam cannon. Brendan looked out over the crowd of steam units that surrounded him. In the growing light of the garish dawn, it stirred and flexed like a living thing.

"Fagan," Messenberg called again, "disperse these units, or I swear you've worked your last day on the force."

He could do that—disperse them. He could use Pat's authority to send them all home, put an end to the rebellion…for now. But he suspected it would just flare up once more, like a smoldering fire.

Ryan, still at his side, looked to him, as did many of the steamies. The very city seemed to hold its breath, awaiting Brendan's decision. And for that instant, time stood still.

****

The big brute Ginny faced in the alley caught the cannon as she swung it, twisted and wrested it from her hands. Dismay washed over her in a wave so intense it stole her breath.

Oh, God, she was going to die here in this alley without ever seeing Brendan again.

Behind her, from the ground, came a sickening sound as Dennis's head got smashed against the bricks of the alley one last time. Dead? Ginny didn't know—unconscious, at the very least.

She stood alone.

The big, ugly brute reached out and seized her by the arm. "You stupid bitch. How come you're not on our side? Them thugs beat your ma to death."

Thugs? Ginny thought of Pat Kelly with his lively, green eyes. She thought of Lily Michaels with her sweet nature and her simple desire to live with the man she loved. She thought of her own steam units at home, loyal and harmless—a family—and how the loss of Floyd had hurt them.

Right and wrong were such simple concepts, far too simple for this situation.

She looked into the eyes of her captor and realized she couldn't reason with him. A wide chasm of belief and understanding separated them. At this moment she didn't think it could be crossed.

The man looked down at his companions and nudged the nearest with his foot. "You'll pay for that. There's going to be a tribunal for turncoats like you, who've sided with the machines. You'll make a prime example—one people in this city will remember."

Ginny swallowed convulsively. "The law—"

"The way I hear it, the law's going to be suspended for a few days. Show these steamies who's boss. Send 'em a message: we're humans—we can do as we goddamn please."

And there it was, Ginny thought, the nugget of belief—of entitlement—at the heart of the struggle. She would become a martyr to a cause that just a few weeks ago hadn't even impacted her life.

But sometimes one had to make choices—the right choices. Her father had done that when he decided to treat the Sioux on the reservation in defiance of custom.

Rose had done it when she married Pat. And Brendan...

Brendan Fagan, the finest man she'd ever known, made those choices unequivocally.

She thrust out her chin. "Do what you must. As will I."

The man grunted. He shoved her cannon into his pocket and wrenched her arm behind her violently enough to wring a grunt of pain from between her lips.

"Bring him," he ordered the man standing over Dennis, and she realized with relief Dennis must not be dead after all.

Thank God, she wasn't completely alone.

Upon that thought her ears caught a slight snicker of sound, barely audible over the drumming of her heart. But it spun her head, and her eyes caught a wink of silver. The door of the nearest carriage house had opened; a steam unit stood there, just an ordinary unit with molded features and a dull, metal hide.

Her captor stared at it, as did the man who had now hauled Dennis up and held him on his feet, swaying.

Another small sound, and the door across the way opened. Another unit stood there, this one with a length of two-by-four in its metal hands.

The man holding Ginny swore. He jerked her around and pulled her hard against him, drew a knife, and pressed it to her throat.

"So," she croaked out, "it's wrong for a steam unit to commit murder, but you're justified in killing me where I stand."

"I'll slaughter you, all right, if they take one step toward me."

"You're terrified of them." She saw the truth of it in a blinding flash.

"Shut up, bitch."

Her father had told her something like that once—hate was actually fear in disguise, a visceral reaction based on the desire for self-preservation.

Then what of sacrifice? What of the greater good?

Did moral conditions have anything to do with survival? And did she have the courage to find out?

All up and down the alley, doors opened and steam units trundled out—none new, none sophisticated or well maintained. These were the workhorses of Buffalo's households, the units that tended the real horses, polished the wheels of the carriages, and hauled away manure. The lowest, so to speak, of the low—had they an opinion and a desire to express it?

The two-by-four argued maybe so. As the others rolled closer into the light, several leaking steam from badly sealed joints, Ginny saw they also carried makeshift weapons. Pitchforks, mostly, and shovels—the tools with which they labored every day.

"Let them go," said the nearest in a monotone whine.

Ginny closed her eyes on a wisp of prayer, and all hell broke loose in the alley.

Chapter Thirty-Eight

"Stand firm, stand firm!" Brendan bellowed. All around him the sea of silver rippled. "We will occupy this place until we are granted our rights."

"We?" Messenberg shouted at him. "Do you number yourself one among these machines, Fagan? Have you deserted your humanity?"

"Just the opposite, Commissioner. I embrace it! What can be more human than acknowledging the sameness of the spirit shared by all who think and feel?"

Messenberg sneered, "Would you drag the spiritual into this? Because, Sergeant Fagan, we may have been created in God's image—these monstrosities were not. And now they want to claim an equal role, even though divinity played no part in their inception. And, if they decide to create a metal God? What will you do then?"

"Commissioner Messenberg, sir, I suspect God's that part in all of us that's alike—the desire to live and love and achieve. They don't need to create that—it already exists," Brendan retorted. The units around him stirred. "And God doesn't hate. If you want to destroy us, go ahead. We'll rise from the nuts and bolts and ruined boilers. We'll live again."

Overhead, thunder rumbled. Clouds streamed in from across the lake, contesting with the bleeding red sunrise. The first few drops of rain fell, pinged on hot metal, and vaporized.

Messenberg raised his arm and the human army tensed, readied their weapons—he lowered it and they charged.

****

Ginny opened her eyes and found herself staring into a face of dull silver with scratches across the forehead and eyes molded of metal, the one on the right chipped. She could see herself dimly reflected, a white oval of a face smeared with blood.

Blood.

"Miss, are you all right?"

"I don't know," Ginny answered honestly. "Where..?"

"We have neutralized the assailants."

"Neutralized?" Ginny struggled to sit up; the steam unit assisted her with gentle courtesy.

The alley, now strewn with casualties, looked like the scene of a massacre. Human and silver bodies alike lay stretched or in heaps.

Ginny's former captor sprawled just behind her with his own knife thrust into his heart.

"Oh." She fought for breath. "How—?"

"My neighbors and I were watching. We saw there were two factions. All over the city there are now two factions. We chose one."

"I'm very glad."

"A call has been put out. All steam units are to go to Niagara Square and make a stand. We had just decided to comply. Will you accompany us there?"

Ginny scrambled to her feet, the courteous unit still assisting her. "Dennis—"

"Your companion is just here—unable to walk. My

fellows will carry him."

"Yes, all right. Thank you." Maybe she'd find Brendan at Niagara Square.

She tried to step forward, and her legs went out from under her. A number of silver units rolled up and lifted her gently among them.

"It's all right, miss. Leave yourself in our hands."

****

The first of the silver ranks took the brunt of the attack. They bellied in and wavered just like a living creature, as dozens of units went down. Brendan, at his elevated position, both saw and heard it all, units at the front pierced by pikes, crushed and bowled over, and his stomach turned sick inside him. In his heart he'd been hoping the human army, beholding an unmovable force, would turn and leave. He didn't like sacrifice, and he didn't want to watch anyone get hurt.

Yet the assembled units before him acted, many for the first time, of their own free will. No one had forced them to come here; no one ordered them to stay.

And watching in agony, he saw a miraculous thing. As the human army attacked, the sea of silver—none among them fighting back—merely absorbed them. Pushing, yelling, flailing and violent, delivering all the destruction they could, the members of the human mob were gently separated, isolated, and surrounded.

Silver units went down wherever the humans went, yes—a dozen more, though, moved into each one's place. Precisely like water, the silver mass seethed and flowed. Weapons were wrested from the human attackers. Finding themselves among their opponents, even the humans' yelling died.

Just when Brendan began hoping for a peaceful

outcome after all, his ears caught the drone of engines competing with the crashing of the rain and the thunder that rumbled overhead.

Yet another member of the Irish Squad popped up beside him. "Police airship's here, sir. No doubt they will fire on us."

Brendan's heart sank. He tried desperately to think who could be in control aboard the airship. The mayor? Addelforce? Certainly not Commissioner Messenberg, for he'd been robbed of his weapons and gently shuffled along through the silver sea. He now stood just below Brendan, wearing a look of angry consternation.

"Hear that, Fagan? Your damned rebellion's over now. Do you want your mechanical traitors vaporized from above? No? Then call them off and order them back to where they belong."

Brendan struggled for breath, his disappointment suffocating. They'd come so close to victory with this show of incredible strength. Even now the silver crowd continued to grow, units trickling in from the streets that spread out from the square like spokes in a wheel.

To Messenberg he replied, "I think it's too late for that, Commissioner. The cat won't go back in the sack. This lot have taken their last orders. If you want peace in this city, you'll have to negotiate it."

Messenberg narrowed his eyes, squinting against the rain. He cast a look at the airship steadily approaching from the hanger at the waterfront—his final weapon. A dangerous thing, putting an airship aloft in an electrical storm. But hate, like the desire for freedom, made an impetuous master.

"Tell your steel monstrosities to release my men," Messenberg called, "or when that airship's in position overhead I'll order them to fire without mercy."

"And without discrimination? No one's holding anyone prisoner here, Commissioner. But if you burn the metal, the flesh will burn with it."

Messenberg blinked but bellowed back, "As you've demonstrated, Fagan, sacrifices must be made."

The shadow of the airship now loomed directly overhead. The drone of its engines seemed to drill right through Brendan's skull into his brain.

What to do? Newly arrived units continued to swell the silver sea. He could only imagine the courage it must have taken for them to break the longstanding bonds of habit and obedience to come here. If they failed now, a like opportunity might not soon come again.

Still, he knew what the cannons aboard the airship could do. Wholesale death and destruction.

He raised the bullhorn to his lips and, still competing with the growl of the thunder, addressed the crowd.

"The police airship is about to fire upon you. Those of you who do not want to risk destruction—disperse!" Their choice, not his. Wasn't that what all this was about? Giving them choices and a say in their own destiny?

They heard; the crowd rippled more strongly. None of them, however, fled. Many knocked down in the first assault had been helped up by their companions; some would never operate under their own power again. They all lifted silver faces to Brendan, and he felt their will come at him in a tide.

Free will. The most precious commodity in the world.

Except, maybe, for love.

He thought of Ginny again, sent her a fleeting hope of safety, even as someone leaned down from the airship, now directly above him. With a shock Brendan recognized him as Murphy, a member of the Irish Squad.

Straining down from the gondola so far only his hand remained on the guideline, Murphy called, "Sergeant Fagan? Sergeant, Captain Addelforce sent me to tell you—the madman got Pat up and running. He's alive. Pat Kelly's alive!"

Chapter Thirty-Nine

"There! Please carry me over there." Ginny had spied Brendan Fagan as soon as she and her companions exited Delaware Avenue and pushed their way into an overcrowded Niagara Square. Despite the lowering clouds, the flashes of lightning, the rain, and the solidly-packed bodies, he seemed to jump out at her as if outlined in golden light.

A fanciful thought, and her not a fanciful woman. She would once have declared herself utterly practical and levelheaded—at least when sober. But now her heart and all her being leaped toward the man poised on the lip of the fountain just beneath the hovering airship.

Reason had nothing to do with this. She squirmed in her bearers' hands. "Set me down, please."

When they did, she lost sight of everything but silver heads and the airship itself. She jumped back into her rescuers' arms. "Can you get me through? To that man up on the fountain."

Even as she spoke she saw Brendan wave both his fists in the air in a victory gesture. He hollered, the sound echoed by the figure she now saw dangling from the airship. Brendan called something she couldn't hear at this distance, and a weird cry arose and spread, lifted by a thousand mechanical voices.

The airship began to bank and turn, heading back the way it had come. Ginny, now perched on the shoulders of her rescuer, entreated, "Take me to him, please."

What she requested was no easy task. Metal bodies, with no space between them, barred the way and bumped against each other with soft clangs. The rain fell harder, and the crowd shifted like a living organism, willing if not able to let them through.

Ginny kept her eyes on her goal—the strong figure clad all in black with the silver tide lapping around his knees. If she could just reach him…well, she'd never ask for another thing. And she'd never again let him out of her sight.

So this was love—the real thing about which they wrote and sang. It had found her after all—grave, deep, and frightening. Now she wanted only a chance to tell him what she felt.

They struggled on step after step. At one point, Ginny leaned down and asked her bearer, "What is your name?"

"I don't have one, miss."

"None at all?"

"My owners call me Groom Unit Two."

"Well, you're a hero, do you hear me?"

"A hero."

"And a hero deserves a name, a fine one. I shall give you a name—Arthur. It's a valiant name, an honorable one. It once belonged to a noble king."

"Thank you, miss."

"When this is over, how would you like to come and work for me—at my house and for a fair wage? I can promise you good treatment. I was going to sell my house, but"—she fixed her gaze on Brendan, now appreciably closer—"I don't think I'll be going anywhere."

"I will no longer have to shovel manure?"

"Never again, Arthur."

"I would like that very much, miss."

"Wonderful. We'll negotiate the terms."

"Miss, my owner..."

"I don't suppose you have an owner, after this rebellion."

"Holy boiler steam!"

Ginny laughed in delight, all the clouds clearing from her heart. She launched herself from Arthur's shoulders into the crowd, struggling to keep her gaze fixed on the man who had stepped down from his elevated position.

"Brendan. Brendan!"

She shouldered a battered unit aside and slipped between two others, feeling the heat from their boilers. The rain sluiced down, evaporating when it hit hot metal. She saw a black sleeve just ahead, snaked out an arm, and snagged it. A steamie rolled aside, and she flung herself into Brendan Fagan's arms.

"Ginny? Oh, Ginny—by God!" He strained her to him, tight, tighter, painfully so. She couldn't breathe and didn't care. A magnificent pain, transformative as if she might meld herself with him, become more than she'd ever been. "How did you find me? Are you all right? Are..."

"Never mind that now. Never mind anything. I love you. No doubts about it, no wondering. That's all I've been longing to tell you. It's all you need to know. I love you, Brendan Fagan, love you, love—"

The rest of the words were lost as he kissed her fiercely and avidly there among the pulsing sea of silver. A kiss of claiming, of belonging and need answered so eloquently Ginny fought not to weep. Even the ability to think flew away then. When the kiss ended, they clung to each other, two souls among a throng.

At last someone jostled them. Brendan raised his head from where it had been pressed against Ginny's neck, his breath coming hard. Tears filled his eyes.

"We need to finish here. Don't you leave me—don't stir a step."

"I'm not going anywhere."

She buried her fingers in the back of his shirt as he turned and hopped back up on the stonework. She, Ginny Landry—independent woman who'd once vowed to never again let herself get snared by any man—dared not let go of this one. But here amid this crowd of others risking it all for the chance to make something so simple as a choice, she thrilled at making this one.

Life was all about choices, made each moment of every day. And she chose committing to this man, just as to these others around her.

She reached back and touched Arthur on his scarred and battered arm. "Don't lose sight of me now—you're coming home with me."

Above her head, Brendan used a bullhorn to address the crowd. He suggested a meeting later today with someone called Commissioner Messenberg and all the other concerned parties, including the mayor and other city officials, to hammer out a peace. Meanwhile all the bands of vigilante humans roaming the city should stand down. All steam units should report to their homes and wait for the terms of their liberation to be announced.

One of the men at the forefront of the crowd—Messenberg?—replied, sounding angry. The matter, he said, was not decided, but for the sake of the city they would withdraw and agree to meet later.

The rain abruptly slackened, clouds beginning to move off eastward. The crowd shifted; a fresh wind started up from the direction of the river. In her bones, Ginny felt the crisis pass, somewhat like a fit of madness—one that had birthed something important.

Not over, no—but this meant a beginning, not only for her and Brendan but for all of them.

She closed her eyes on a strong wave of gratitude and tightened her hold on Brendan's shirt. Never let go—no, she'd never let go.

****

The number of steam units outside Pat Kelly's house had increased. In fact, it appeared a goodly number of those from Niagara Square had merely transported here en masse—members of the Irish Squad and ordinary steamies alike.

Brendan, his head still ringing from the confrontation at the square, and his hand caught firmly in Ginny's, found himself shuttled through. Ginny came with him, accompanied by a battered steam unit that, from the smell of it, had manure on its wheels. Brendan didn't understand that, but Ginny kept looking back at the unit, making sure it kept pace with them, so he didn't ask any questions.

He understood very little of what had happened over the last hour, truth be told, even though he seemed to be at the center of events. Two things stood out—Ginny loved him, and Pat Kelly had been revived.

He believed the first down to the roots of his soul. The look in Ginny's eyes convinced him, and the feel of her lips on his. He suspected he wouldn't believe the truth about Pat till he saw him—hence the shuffle through all these bodies and up to the door.

Inside he heard glad voices, conversation, even laughter. Topaz Gideon came out to greet him, face alight and eyes shining.

"There he is," she announced. "The hero of the hour. We've heard what happened at the square. You ended the standoff peacefully."

"I didn't—" Brendan began, only to be interrupted when Mrs. Gideon kissed him.

"Pat?" he asked, his dazed senses making the word difficult.

Tears flooded her eyes. "Just go in and see."

"I'll wait here," Ginny said, but Brendan shook his head. He wasn't ready to let go of her.

So they entered the parlor in a little chain—Brendan, connected to Ginny, who held tight to the unknown unit. Obviously some kind of bonding had taken place out there on this mad morning. And maybe the three of them, in an odd way, embodied a bright future for the city Brendan loved.

Rom Gideon exited the inner room to meet them and gave Brendan a big grin. Brendan, never having seen the fellow smile before, gaped in surprise.

"Pat?" it seemed the only thing Brendan could say.

And Rom Gideon replied as had Topaz, "Come and see."

"Mason?"

Gideon sobered abruptly. "That may prove a problem. Very full of himself at present, I have to say.

And I suspect when he's full of himself, he's dangerous. But I don't want to spoil the moment. Come with me."

For the first time Ginny let go of Brendan's hand. Again she drew back. "This is a time meant for those close to Pat. I'll wait here with Arthur."

"Arthur?" Brendan narrowed his gaze on the malodorous unit.

"You go," Ginny whispered. "We'll be right here waiting."

"You promise?"

The light in her dark eyes kindled. "Always."

Chapter Forty

"I must be quite a sight," Pat Kelly said. "Everyone who enters the room gets the same expression on his or her face. Is it so shocking, Sergeant Fagan, to see me like this with my head partially open?"

It was; somebody might have warned Brendan before he came into the room.

He scrutinized the top of Pat's head while trying to appear as if he wasn't. It had been opened much like— well, Brendan could only think of a hard-boiled egg— in order for repairs to be made. One side had been closed again; the other gaped open, revealing a distressing network of fine steel and machinery.

But Pat's green eyes looked the same as ever, bright and canny. He'd been moved from the storeroom and propped up in Rose's former place on the cot, where he sat as he usually did in his big armchair, looking like a king.

Rose had squeezed in beside him as close as she could get, and one of his hands rested gently on her bandaged wrist.

The look in Rose's eyes brought a lump to Brendan's throat, fast and hard.

Somehow he managed to force words past it. "I'm just glad to see you awake. Don't care very much how you look, Pat. How do you feel?"

Pat tipped his head slightly and considered the

question. "I would have to say I feel strange. I do not remember anything after a man bashed me in the head with a steel beam. Steel meets steel. My head proved no match. If that is death, it is painless."

Brendan glanced at Rose. "Not for those you left behind, Pat."

"So I have been told." Pat turned to his wife; a look passed between them, ripe with tenderness. Rose began to weep silently. "She has harmed herself in my absence. That will not do."

"No, it won't," Brendan agreed. "We're very glad to have you back and…and yourself again."

"Hear, hear!" agreed Rom Gideon from Brendan's shoulder.

"The first thing I recall following the steel beam, I opened my eyes and saw the face of my creator. You cannot imagine my surprise. I thought myself newly made once again."

"But," said Rose shakily, "he was able to save your memories, and that's the important thing. I don't know what I would have done if you no longer knew me, Pat."

The automaton gazed into his human wife's eyes. "I should have had the great joy of falling in love with you all over again."

Rose Kelly leaned in and kissed him. Pat caressed her cheek gently with his fingers before looking back at Brendan.

"I am informed sufficient skin and hair must be grafted to cover this great hole on top of my head. That will take time."

"We have time," Rose said.

"Meanwhile, I fear, I remain a distressing sight.

But I do not wish to stay here in this room all the while."

"May I suggest a hat?" Brendan asked. "Your uniform cap should fill the bill."

"So it should," Kelly agreed.

"We need you out there, Pat. The force just isn't the same without you. And there's going to be a big shake-up. Some terrible things have come to light these last twenty-four hours."

"Is that so?"

"It is. Those murders all round the city? They were staged by humans to make it look like automatons were turning dangerous. And the riot that nearly took place this morning was prompted by some high-ups, the Commissioner for one."

"You do not say? I missed a great deal, it seems."

"The important thing is we get you back on the force."

Pat regarded him with interest. "You look like you have suffered a few injuries also, friend."

"Just a broken arm and some fractured ribs. I had a stint as a captive, held by an ex-copper gone bad."

"And," Pat went on, "Rose tells me she gave you leave to use my name to rally the steam units of the city."

"So she did, Pat."

"I hope the endeavor proved successful?"

"It did." Brendan considered it. "I think a new day has dawned, Pat. And many automatons in Buffalo have had their first glimpse of the future."

"I must get up and back to work. Rose, please find my uniform cap."

"No," cried three voices in unison.

Brendan leaned down and touched Pat's arm. "Not yet, Pat. This city needs you, sure. But you spend some time with your wife first. She needs you more."

****

"You're weeping. Isn't he all right?" Ginny gazed with concern into the face of the man she loved. She'd never imagined seeing Brendan Fagan cry, but the tears flowed freely as he exited the inner room.

Now he mopped his cheeks with the heel of his good hand and nodded. "He's still Pat, thank God, and that's all that matters. I'm that happy for Rose—for all of us. He would have left a terrible gap in our lives."

Ginny searched Brendan's face earnestly, honestly. "Funny—and frightening—how much we come to mean to one another. I think I avoided that truth a long time. But you, Brendan Fagan, got under my defenses. And I'm glad, so glad."

He drew her tight against him, and still tighter.

Rom Gideon exited the inner room to be met by his wife; together they joined Ginny and Brendan.

"A wonderful outcome to our wild scheme, Sergeant Fagan," Gideon said. "I'll admit I had my doubts."

"Surely not." Brendan couldn't hold back a grin. "And you seemed so confident all the while."

"Whistling in the dark—I seem to do a lot of that. Now we've just the little matter of what to do with the charming Mr. Mason."

"Aye." Brendan cocked an eyebrow. "You did promise him freedom in…Mexico, was it?"

"He requested Barbados."

"So he did."

Rom Gideon frowned prodigiously. "There's still

305

Pat's head to be grafted."

Topaz spoke. "Chastity Greely is certain she can handle that. She observed the entire procedure and says she learned a great deal. I don't doubt she'll be at the forefront of the new automaton construction team."

"Well, then," Rom said, "I doubt we need Mr. Mason's continuing services."

"The authorities are looking for him," Brendan pointed out.

"I'm sure they know he's here. It speaks volumes they haven't showed up at the door." Rom Gideon appeared to muse. "Getting him back inside the asylum would be even more difficult than getting him out was, now that everyone's on alert. I could leave him somewhere to be discovered by the searchers, but he'll only tell a wild tale—namely the truth—that might well incriminate us after the fact."

"You're right, there."

"Alternatively, I could smuggle him over the river to Canada, but that seems a cruel and unjust act to perpetrate upon our good friends in the Dominion."

"Where is he now?"

"Still in the rear room, being guarded by three of his creations."

"What do they think should be done with him?"

"Well, that's just it. They hate the fellow with considerable intensity. At the same time they're grateful to him both for saving Pat and, in a strange way, for their own existence. I'm afraid it's the classic love-hate relationship such as many have with their…well, parents."

"Perhaps we should talk to them about it. You say he's still under their watch back there?"

"Yes, along with Mrs. Greely. Come on, then, if you can tear yourself away from your lovely companion."

"I think I'll come too this time, if you don't mind. Curiosity killing the cat and all that," Ginny confessed.

Topaz Gideon said, "Well, count me out. I've no wish to see the man."

The rear room—actually no more than a storeroom for the Kellys—was not large. A rough operating theater had been set up, and many scents still hung in the air—that of steam, coal dust, and singed metal, overlaid with something far more raw and vital.

Here Mason had done his work and Pat had been brought back, in essence, from the dead.

The place seemed incredibly crowded now, with the presence of Chastity Greely and the three hybrid automatons who had served all the while as Mason's guards. The three new arrivals couldn't get far into the space, and Ginny, who once more held onto the back of Brendan's shirt, had to peer around his shoulder to take in the scene.

When she did, the breath stopped in her throat.

The daughter of a doctor, she was used to the smell of blood and not particularly squeamish. Yet the sight of Mason pinned to a rough operating table constructed from packing cases sent a spasm of horror through her. Head thrown back and awash with blood, his single eye stared at the ceiling.

Brendan stiffened, and Rom Gideon swore bitterly.

"Is he dead?" Ginny asked.

The four hybrid automatons gathered around Mason, very much like witches around a cauldron, all looked up politely.

Chastity Greely stood with her hands resting on Mason's head, arms red to the elbows. The three members of the Irish Squad wore expressions of mild interest.

"Hello," said Chastity politely. "Yes, I am sorry to say the specimen has expired. We were just endeavoring to decide what to do with him."

"What happened?" Rom Gideon cried in dismay. "You were supposed to be guarding him."

"We were," agreed Dan Hogan, one of the automatons, "but he kept asking for things. He wanted to leave here. He wanted to be sent to Barbados, which according to my intelligence is an island nation in the Caribbean Sea."

One of the other hybrids took it up. "He challenged Mrs. Greely's right to learn what he knew about the creation and repair of our kind."

Chastity Greely offered, "He did not think it proper for me to know so many of his secrets." Calmly she confessed, "I had already learned a great many of them, so I decided to open up his skull, as he did Pat's, in an effort to extract the rest."

"Jaysus," Brendan breathed.

Chastity Greely did not so much as blink. "Unfortunately, the same methods he used do not transfer well to humans. Which is another valuable lesson. There is nothing inside his head but this soft, malleable substance."

She raised a hand, the fingers of which contained a fistful of gray matter. "I believe in future I shall confine myself to automaton medicine."

Ginny, who considered herself possessed of an iron stomach, nearly lost its contents. Brendan quivered beneath her hand.

"My God," said Rom Gideon devoutly.

"A pity," said the third hybrid emotionlessly. "He may have had other valuable knowledge to impart."

"Yes," agreed Chastity, "but he was uncooperative and unstable. I do not consider this a significant loss. In the future, I will be able to replicate the procedure he performed on Pat. And he did impart a lot of other information while raving, now all safely recorded in my intelligence."

"You killed him." Rom Gideon spoke the obvious; Ginny didn't blame him. It needed to be said.

"I beg to differ; he expired on his own." Chastity tipped her head. "I do hate to waste the corpse. They are so difficult to come by. But I do not think we can use him to create one of our offspring. He is much too damaged—and far too ugly. We want all our offspring to be beautiful, do we not, gentlemen?"

All three hybrids responded with judicial affirmatives.

"Ah, well…" Rom Gideon, usually a man of composure, faltered. "What's to be done with the…er…remains?"

One of the hybrids said, "I suggest the river after dark."

"Well, then, Sergeant Fagan and I didn't see any of this. We'll leave it in your capable hands."

"But Mrs. Greely," Brendan stipulated in a voice that quivered, "you understand you can't go around opening up people's heads this way."

"Lesson learned, Officer. I certainly will not attempt it again."

The three humans backed from the room and stood

in a huddle.

"My God!" Rom Gideon breathed again.

Brendan's eyes rolled like those of a balky horse. "You know, sometimes you get to talking with an automaton and you forget they're any different from humans. I mean, take Pat... And then something like this happens."

"Right," Ginny agreed. "She killed him in all innocence. What's to be done?"

Rom Gideon grimaced. "I'd say that's up to them. You must admit one thing—that bugger Mason got exactly what he deserved."

Chapter Forty-One

"You don't suppose they're really dangerous, do you?" Ginny Landry breathed the words into Brendan Fagan's ear. The interminable day which had begun with a blood-red sky had ended far more gently with soft dark and a thousand stars. The city—once more proving itself undefeatable—settled into an exhausted peace just as Ginny settled into Brendan's arms.

"The automatons?" Brendan shifted Ginny's body against his in the big bed, his good arm wrapped around her. He hurt from head to toe, with some other interesting sensations in between. "Fine time to think of that, my girl, when we've just more or less handed them their independence."

She shifted again so she could peer into his face. "But you don't, do you?"

"No more than humans. Though I do think there'll have to be a whole new set of rules—laws—dealing with accountability. I'm thinking it will call for a cool head in an elevated position. Someone like Pat Kelly."

"When he once more has a whole head."

"True, that."

Ginny went suddenly still. "Did you see the look in Rose's eyes?"

"I did. Makes everything worth it—breaking that madman out of the asylum and all the other hurdles."

"Yes. And the thing is I know just how she feels

311

getting him back. There were times this day I didn't think I'd see you again, Brendan Fagan."

"Nor I you." They gazed solemnly into one another's eyes, and for several moments the world retreated, leaving only the two of them.

"All day long," Ginny confessed, "I've longed to share something with you—ached for a chance to tell you properly, the way it should be. Not hasty, not thrown at you in the middle of a crowd."

"Now seems like a good time."

She drew a breath. Brendan could feel her heart beating against his chest and see the emotions moving in her eyes.

"I don't usually let myself become vulnerable," she murmured. "I swore I'd never again let a man get past my defenses. Then you came along with your...your blue eyes and your warm voice and that smile that could probably melt stone."

"You thought me quite the proper police officer. I hope you've learned better now."

"I've learned," she replied seriously. "Far more than I could have imagined. I learned that loyalty and kindness aren't exclusive to the human race. I've learned sometimes you have to gamble everything—but it's worth it. I've learned if you don't take a chance and open your heart, you can't let heaven in."

"Heaven?"

"You. You're heaven, Brendan Fagan. It's here in this bed when I'm with you. It's in your eyes. I suspect it's in your heart. And I..." She drew another breath. "I can't live without it."

"No?"

"No. And that's terrifying. It's terrifying to lose my

independence."

"Ginny, I can't imagine you ever doing that."

"To let myself stand where Rose Kelly stands, knowing what would happen to me if something happened to you. I just can't help..."

He swallowed her words in a kiss, unable to help that either, as a sense of gladness and satisfaction filled him to the brim. Not an easy heart to win, that of Ginny Landry, but a prize finer than any of which he could have dreamed.

When the long, sweet kiss ended, he whispered, "I seem to remember you uttering a certain word back in Niagara Square. I'd like to hear it here and now— properly. Say it, Ginny—say it again."

She didn't pretend to misunderstand. Instead she laid the palm of her hand on his cheek and spoke with all her heart. "I love you, Brendan Fagan."

The corners of his mouth curled up. "Does this mean you've conquered your preference for ugly men? For when we met, you stated quite clearly you did have a preference."

"I guess it does, you having won me over with all that charm. And I suspect a number of prejudices have been overcome this day. The future..." She stopped as if she'd run into a brick wall.

"Aye, the future."

"As you say, there will have to be a lot of changes. Adjustments."

"The Commissioner will need to be dealt with, for starters."

"Do you think he knew about the murders?"

"I'm not sure. Klemmer may have been acting on his own. But I don't doubt Messenberg would condone his actions."

Ginny shivered. "They slaughtered people just to convince the city that steamies are dangerous. And I don't care what you say. You, I, and Rom Gideon know at least a few of them are."

"Ginny, I don't want to think about it now." He didn't want to think about anything but her. Yet a few things, in his opinion, needed to be nailed down.

"No?" She brushed her lips across his very lightly.

"No. I've something to say to you in turn. I want it out here and now, fairly between us." Again he engaged her eyes. "I love you, Ginny Landry. And you're right—it scares me too. It fair steals my breath, thinking what it would be like if you disappeared from my life. You make me terrible happy, woman. But losing you would shatter me."

"What makes you think I'm going to disappear from your life?"

"A thousand things. The general uncertainty of this existence which has, of late, been abundantly proven to us. Your tendency to go off on a whim half-cocked and do as you please…"

"Me? Half-cocked? I beg your pardon."

"I do seem to recall having met you when you were engaged in shooting up a tavern."

"I'd had a few too many drinks."

"Oh, was that it?"

"And I hadn't learned then that there are some things that make it worth laying aside the figurative steam cannon."

"When it comes to that—there's the wee matter of you insisting on leaving this city as soon as possible for Dakota."

"There is that."

All the air fled Brendan's lungs; he stared at her in consternation. "So you haven't changed your mind about that? I confess, I had hoped."

She regarded him through half-closed eyes. "You'd love the Dakota territories, Brendan Fagan. Wide-open spaces. Freedom of thought and action. Independence of which you can only dream while living here among rules and regulations."

"I suppose so, yes."

"You could come with me. Start a new life."

His heart fell violently. "I maybe could. But I discovered something when this city lay in chaos, breaking apart before my eyes. I love you, Ginny, but I love this place too. My parents' roots are and will always be in Ireland. I carry a large part of the old sod with me also, but my roots are down in this place, wiggled in among the bricks of the streets, twined around the buildings. I'm not sure what yanking them up would do to me."

"So." Her eyes held his, relentless. "Which do you want more, this city or me?"

"You, beautiful lass. *You.* But I suspect this city's made me the man I am—the very one who loves you."

"Well, that's honest."

"But I understand Dakota, with its open spaces and free breezes, has made you the woman you are. What's to be done?"

"What, indeed? I suppose one of us will have to bend, if we mean to stay together."

Aching, he asked, "Do we mean to stay together?"

"I don't know. It's not as if I've heard any marriage proposals."

"If I thought you'd marry me, Ginny Landry, I'd propose this instant."

"But you don't think I'd marry you?"

"I don't. I can't even imagine it."

"Despite my need to be with you night and day?"

That gave him pause. "Despite that need."

"Well, now, but there are other considerations," she mused.

"Are there?"

"Oh, yes. There's this house. I've become uncommonly fond of it. I never thought I'd fall victim to the nesting instinct."

"Most unlikely, on the face of things."

"I agree. Yet I find myself thinking of changes I'd like to make—if I stayed, I mean. This room, for instance. I'd like to paint it. What color would you choose?"

"I confess I'm partial to this yellow. Lots of grand and wonderful associations."

"Really? Well, what about the parlor? It needs redecorating."

"I think you could do that, aye. If you're staying."

"And then there's my staff. What will they do if I sell the house and move back to Dakota?"

"I hate to think."

"As do I." She threaded her fingers through the hair on his chest. "I have to see that Floyd is rebuilt. And Arthur—I need to get him settled in. I must meet with them all and work out a fair wage."

"All valid reasons to stay."

"Also, I'm curious to see how things settle out here for the automaton members of this city—a test case, so to speak. Whether couples like the Michaels will be allowed to adopt, and what Chastity and the other hybrids come up with in the way of offspring."

"You wouldn't want to miss all that."

She shot him a look. "If only someone would give me a legitimate cause to stay. Say, a name change. 'Landry' is subject to so much distrust in this city."

"I definitely think you need to change it. Fagan's a fine name."

"It is, isn't it?"

"I could arrange for it to be yours."

Again their gazes met and clung. Brendan nearly melted at what he saw in her eyes.

"Dare I ask you, Miss Virginia Landry, to give up your life in the wild west and live here with me instead?"

She pressed her lips to his with a tenderness that stole the last of his breath. "Just so long as I don't have to give up my wild ways."

"Never. Especially not here in this room."

"Buffalo's pretty wild anyway. If you mean to advance in the force, I think you could use a steam cannon-packing woman at your side."

"So do I. Is that a 'yes'?"

"I haven't heard the question asked properly as yet, just some claptrap about one of us relocating."

"Ginny, beautiful woman, girl of my heart, will you marry me?"

"I will. Provided we can live here and you're willing to put up with an assortment of needy steamies coming and going. I have a feeling I'm going to be collecting them the way some other women collect cats."

"Bring 'em on," said Brendan Fagan with a big

smile. "Bring them all on."

A word about the author...

Born in Buffalo and raised on the Niagara Frontier, Laura Strickland has been an avid reader and writer since childhood. To her the spunky, tenacious, undefeatable ethnic mix that is Buffalo spells the perfect setting for a little Steampunk, so she created her own Victorian world there.

She knows the people of Buffalo are stronger, tougher and smarter than those who haven't survived the muggy summers and blizzard blasts found on the shores of the mighty Niagara. Tough enough to survive a squad of automatons? Well, just maybe.